DEADLY GAMES

KYLIE HATFIELD SERIES: BOOK THREE

MARY STONE

BELLA CROSS

DESCRIPTION

Digging up the past can be deadly...

Adam Hatfield disappeared from Kylie and her mother's lives when she was only four days old. Had he only been playing games when he made a family? Or was there something more sinister at play?

Kylie Hatfield, assistant private investigator extraordinaire, has it made. Mostly. But something is missing. A born digger, Kylie isn't one to let a mystery stay a mystery, and her father's disappearance is quickly becoming the most important case she's ever tried to solve.

She needs closure before she can fully commit to Linc Coulter, the former Army MP and search and rescue hero whose new mission is to protect Kylie from herself. But you can't protect what you can't find. And Kylie has, once again, chased a mystery into dangerous territory.

When she finds her father, Adam Hatfield may seem like a successful billionaire on the surface, but something lurks beneath. Something dangerous and deadly that soon makes Kylie wish she hadn't learned the awful truth.

Turns out, digging up the past is not a game at all.

If you like quirky characters and faithful dogs along with your goose bumps, Deadly Games, the third book in the Kylie Hatfield Series, will pull you in and make you rethink ever opening your closet doors.

1

Kylie Hatfield sat back in her office chair and stretched her aching back. She felt like she was eighty instead of twenty-four. It wasn't even six o'clock yet, but the light outside was waning as the shorter days of October took their toll on downtown Asheville. She still had an hour of official daylight, but the dimness made her yawn. She'd driven into work when the sun was just popping up over the mountains, skipped lunch, and now, it felt like she'd been huddled over her computer for a thousand years.

Such was the life of a private investigator.

Sure, she'd had her exciting moments out in the field. But the cheating lover's attempted murder by rattlesnake, the run-in with the serial killer, and the brush with the embezzling murdering art thief notwithstanding, most of her time was spent butt-in-chair, trying to slog through a bunch of dull-as-dishwater research.

Actually, this was better than what she'd been hired for back in the spring. Filing. That was a fate worse than death. Luckily, she'd managed to add other things to her resume, but since it was a two-person office, it was still part of her job description.

She leaned forward and typed some more search terms into the keyboard. At least Greg, her boss, had finally gotten into the century by outfitting the office with two new computers. Actually, Kylie wasn't sure that they were *new*, exactly. Her boss was notoriously thrifty when it came to provisioning the office the two of them shared. These particular computers ran on Windows 98 and had probably been rescued from a dumpster somewhere, but she wasn't going to bite the hand that fed her. She was happy to have something with a screen, and not that infernal typewriter that she'd grown to detest during her first months at Starr Investigations.

After about five minutes of chugging, grinding, and buffering, the computer finally spat out the results of her search. Kylie lifted her notepad and took some notes. The little mystery she'd been hired to conquer was slowly inching its way toward a solution.

Her client, Barbara Davidson, had found out late in her fifties that she'd been adopted by using one of those at-home ancestry kits that were all the rage these days. She'd wanted Kylie to see if she could compile any data that could help her to track down her real parents.

Easy-peasy. But not exactly exciting, or even compelling.

Not exactly the kind of stuff that made Kylie love being an almost private investigator. She didn't even have to look back at her own broken home. She'd seen enough illegitimate births and jilted lovers to make her question whether love really existed, oh, about a thousand times in the past year.

Kylie had been working as Greg's right-hand-girl but was quickly rising in the ranks from his filing clerk to assistant private investigator. In between almost getting herself killed a couple of times, she'd handled plenty of cases that involved a lot of research, and at least five that involved tracking down parents like Barbara's, so this was old hat. There was always a cheating, two-timing lowlife at the bottom of things like this.

Barbara's dad likely had an affair, and she was the product of it. He'd been married, unable or unwilling to part with his wife, and the other woman was shut out and hadn't been able to raise the baby on her own.

Kylie yawned. That was probably the thing she'd come to hate most about her job. All the cheating scumbags out there. It made her wonder if it was possible for anyone to be honestly in love with anyone else, or if lust, desire, greed, or simple boredom always got in the way. These cases were seriously a dime a dozen.

It was the things that happened rarely…the serial killers, the murderers, the bad guys who put her heart in her throat that she loved. She loved *different*.

Not that any of *those* things helped restore her tarnished faith in humanity. No, Kylie sometimes went home and understood very well why Greg, her boss, was the biggest grouch on earth. Even Kylie the Optimist had seen her outlook made slightly stormier by the job.

And *different* hardly ever happened, at least that was what Greg told her repeatedly, although he also told her that she appeared to be a magnet for trouble. That the murdering embezzler slash art thief of Kylie's last *different* case was a one-off, he'd said. As was the serial killer she'd dealt with previously. And the snakebite couple. According to Greg, Kylie had seen more action in the past few months than he'd seen over his entire PI career.

Now, in the past few days since she'd returned to work after almost dying…again…the most exciting thing that could even possibly qualify as *different* was when an old lady had come in and wanted her to find her dentures, which she'd lost somewhere in her house.

Different, yes. Not exactly something that would get her heart racing again.

She was embarrassed to admit that she'd been so bored she'd actually accepted that case. But the old lady was so distraught and looked like she needed an understanding ear, so Kylie had walked her home, taken her inside, and found the dentures two minutes later in her medicine cabinet. She hadn't accepted any payment except a freshly baked lemon cake. Greg still wouldn't let her live that one down.

Once, when she brought down the Spotlight Killer, a case that had gotten her national attention and her own special on *Dateline*, she'd thought she was on her way up.

She sighed, wondering if those last few cases were just dumb luck. After all, very little ever happened in Asheville, North Carolina, the quiet little city nestled in the Appalachians. Even Linc, her boyfriend, hadn't been called out on a search and rescue in at least a week, and his best friend and local detective, Jacob, had remarked that the place had lost whatever pulse it'd had over the summer.

They weren't complaining, though. Only Kylie minded. The men liked boredom, liked tooling around and going out for coffee and donuts and twiddling their thumbs, shooting the shit even as Kylie felt like a noose was tightening around her neck. Too much sitting made her antsy. Was it too much to ask for a little excitement every now and then?

As she prowled around online, running a search of birth announcements around the time Barbara Davidson was born, or any criminal activity that might have been reported around the date of her birth, she yawned even louder. Kylie understood the need to know where a person was from. She did. Sometimes, she wondered it about her own self.

Actually, more than sometimes. Especially in her line of work.

Kylie's mother, Rhonda, was the only parent that she'd known from a very young age. And as she'd convinced herself, time and time again, all that she needed. Rhonda had been the age Kylie was now, with a new baby, when her husband simply decided not to come home. Kylie remembered her mother shedding many a tear when she was younger, and she'd always attributed those tears to her father, who was nothing but an image on a faded photograph.

The bastard had probably traded her mom in for a better model. At least that's what Rhonda Hatfield said on the few times Adam Hatfield was brought up.

The *very* few times.

Rhonda Hatfield had managed quite well without him, so why ruin things by talking about the past?

But truth be told, whenever Kylie got into an investigation like this, her fingers itched. It'd be so easy to simply pop the name Adam Hatfield into the search database and see what came up, especially since another Hatfield had been recently making the news.

It seemed that anytime she saw a man with the last name of Hatfield, she automatically wondered if he was her father. And when she realized he wasn't, she was let down.

Not just let down. Profoundly disappointed.

She was a curious person by nature, which had gotten her into more than enough trouble. But what good could come of digging up the life of a man who clearly didn't want to know her? None. Absolutely none. So, she'd always resisted.

Until now.

The more she thought about it, the more that little itching became a full-on rash, one that she needed to scratch.

"Don't," she said aloud, balling her hands into fists so her fingers wouldn't work the keyboard and type in his name. "Bad idea."

She looked down at Vader, the giant Newfoundland mix she'd rescued from the side of the road. Vader whimpered as if to echo her sentiments. They were the only two left in the office, since Greg had gone off on "surveillance," which he seemed to do more often on nice days like this.

Kylie often found herself talking to her dog. Of course, she often found herself talking aloud to no one in particular. Kylie was just chatty. Sometimes she couldn't keep her mouth shut. She knew it drove a lot of people—her boyfriend especially—nuts, but she still couldn't manage to stop herself.

Impulsive. That's what people called her.

A fact that was so evident now as her hands shook in front of her.

She studied the screen, the search bar, waiting for her to input whatever she wished to know more about. The cursor blinked, taunting her. *Go ahead. Do it. It's not a big deal.*

"Oh, yes, it is," she muttered, clicking the X to get out of the program. She looked at Vader, who wagged his tail at the attention. "What does it matter what he's up to? Really! He doesn't care about me. Why should I give a rat's ass what he's up to these days?"

Vader gave her a *hey, I never knew my dad either* look in return.

"Right. Not knowing your dad doesn't make you any less worthwhile," she said to him, slipping her foot out of her shoe and running it through his thick fur. "You're still my favorite little drooly morsel."

She linked her fingers behind her head, thinking. It was true. A lot of people lived perfectly happy lives not knowing one or both of their parents. And there were people like Linc, who knew his dad, but barely got along with him.

She'd gotten along better with Jonathan Coulter the last time they'd met, but she still thought Linc's father was a grade A douche, nothing like his yummy son. Linc still dreaded going to family dinners at his parents', and she wasn't much better. Knowing how rare a perfect family was, Kylie knew she had nothing to complain about.

Still, that itch was there.

Growing stronger by the minute.

She clenched her teeth together so hard, willing her fingers to be good, until she could stand it no more. She let out a loud, "GAAAAAAH!" before throwing herself over the keyboard. She needed a nap.

Just then, the bell over the door jangled. She peered up to see Linc through the veil of her hair. He looked worried. "Your day's going that good? Wow."

Linc Coulter, dog trainer extraordinaire. Right in the nick of time, as usual.

Still, she stiffened. It wasn't that she didn't love him. But he'd been acting weird around her lately, covering up his phone whenever she came into the room. She didn't think he'd be the type to two-time her, but she wasn't sure. After all, as her father and line of work had shown, it was all too common.

There was another possibility too. Maybe he'd been thinking about getting her a ring? They never talked about marriage, but he'd told her he wanted a family, and he was thirty, and he'd been semi-pressuring her to move in with him. Every time he showed up out of the blue, she wondered if he was going to drop to one knee and propose.

She wasn't sure what would make her more nervous— two-timing or proposing. Because both of them were scary, scary stuff.

She sighed with relief when she saw that he held a couple

of Panera bags in his hands. Not a velvet-lined case. And he didn't have lipstick on his collar or anything, either.

So, neither. Neither was good.

His German Shepherd, Storm, obediently trailed in behind him and greeted Vader with a nonchalant sniff. Vader's tail went wild, but he'd gotten much more controlled lately. Just a couple months ago, he'd have knocked down a brick wall at the chance to sniff another dog.

Kylie jumped out of her chair and ran for Linc, grabbing the bags and giving him a peck on the cheek. "My day's definitely getting better...you brought me lunch?" She looked inside the bag and pumped her fist. He knew her so well. "Yes! Bacon Turkey Bravo! To what do I owe such a surprise?"

He gave her an odd look and followed her into the office that was a converted vacuum showroom. "Can't I just surprise you without a reason?"

I suppose you could, she thought. *But I've been spending all my time thinking about two-timing scumbags, so I'm suspicious that you did it because you feel guilty about something.*

"I guess." She pushed her computer keyboard aside and pulled the cartons out. "That's very nice. Thank you."

He shrugged, but still seemed to watch her closely. "I was in town, picking up the stuff I needed at the hardware store. And you were..." He scratched at his chin. "Exactly what were you doing that got you so frustrated?"

The last time she'd mentioned the possibility of looking up her dad to Linc, he'd told her that if she wanted to, she should. She knew that's what he'd say again, and then she'd do it. His warm, chocolate brown eyes always convinced her to take that extra step. And as much as she really wanted to . . .

She really *didn't* want to, either.

It was just too scary to think of, what might come up the second she punched in his name.

She gave him a sheepish look. "Oh, nothing. Same old work woes."

He nodded. That, he wouldn't question. After dozens of false career starts, Kylie finally felt like working as a PI was her dream job, but it still had its problems, and Kylie wasn't one to keep things in. She complained about the boredom almost every chance she got. He had to have seen her getting antsy for a real case—for the past few days, she'd been practically exuding frustration out of every pore and bouncing around the house like a jumping bean.

He sat down across from her and dug into his salad. "Well, relax. Something'll come along."

Not that you want it to, Kylie thought, putting a straw in her iced tea. If Linc had gotten his way, he'd have wrapped her in numerous layers of bubble wrap by now. He was constantly worrying about her. Of course, he had his reasons.

He'd seen enough terrible things during his time in the war and had been struggling for the past few months with PTSD. He always gave her her freedom, but not without a hell of a lot of overthinking and what ifs. Whenever he got overprotective, she always tried to remind herself that his caution was good for her. She did have a tendency to go off without thinking, again and again, and it *did* get her in trouble.

"I guess."

He looked over at her computer. "What are you working on now?"

"Oh, same old, same old. An adoptee looking for her bio parents."

"Sounds good." That was just the type of assignment she

knew he wished she'd handle all the time. Easy. Safe. Boring as hell.

"Not really."

"I know, I know," he said, reaching over and touching her hand. "But it's important work."

She shrugged. "I don't know. Is it? Knowing who your parents are might bring more bad than good. There are so many cheaters and liars and scumbags on the earth. I sometimes feel like no one is honest."

"That's not true. I'm honest. You're honest." He cocked an eyebrow at her. "Right?"

She gave him a doubtful look.

Alarm flashed on his face. "*Right?*"

She waved whatever he was insinuating away. "Oh, of course. But what I mean is, there are a lot of losers out there, and when parents go out of their kids' lives, it's usually for a good reason. Even present parents can be more trouble than they're worth. You'd probably rather you *didn't* know your parents, considering how much trouble they cause you."

He gave her a surprised look. "No. Yeah, my dad can be challenging. But hell…is that what you think?"

She shrugged.

He studied her face and understanding dawned. "Wait. You're thinking about your dad again, aren't you?"

She didn't answer.

"If it means that much to you, just look him up," he said too breezily for her liking. God, he was so good-looking, almost super-hero gorgeous, but sometimes, he could be so dense. Sometimes she felt like he didn't know her at all.

"Because! It's like I said. It could be a lot more trouble than not knowing him. He obviously had problems and a life that I couldn't be a part of. He left for a reason, and it's nothing good. Do I want to open that can of worms?" She sighed and dropped her sandwich down on the paper. She no longer had an appetite. "He obviously made it clear that he doesn't want to get in touch with me. I might just be opening myself up to rejection again."

"Well...maybe he would like to get back in your life, but he's just worried you'll turn him away," he said, saying the thing that made the wall of resolve she'd carefully constructed start to crumble. "You'll never know unless you try, right?"

Yeah. That was true. Maybe he was out there, thinking about her, wanting to open the lines of communication and apologize. Maybe he'd thought about her just as much as she'd thought about him.

Maybe he was dead. She just didn't know.

She wrinkled her nose. "How can a man just leave a cute, adorable, bouncing baby? I was four days old, for god's sake. His flesh and blood. What the hell is wrong with him?"

What was wrong with me?

Linc studied her. "Maybe he had a good reason."

Kylie shot him a hard look. He was just supposed to agree with her on this, not play devil's advocate. What kind of boyfriend was he?

"Like?"

Linc shrugged. "Can't really think of anything, but you could find out. Track him down. Give him a call. Get his side of the story."

She took a deep breath, and exhaled slowly, just as Linc's phone buzzed in his pocket. He pulled it out and lifted it to his ear. "Hello?"

Kylie licked melted gouda off her fingers, thinking. Her mother hadn't said anything negative about her father before, other than that he'd possibly traded her in for another model. She hadn't said anything positive, either. From the speed with which Rhonda Hatfield changed the subject whenever Kylie had brought up her dad, she could tell her mother didn't want to touch it with a very long pole. But why? Maybe she just needed to attack her mother and demand answers, as painful as that discussion would be.

She was so deep in thought, imagining herself cornering her poor mother and firing questions at her until the woman who'd nurtured her all these years broke down and shouted, "YOU CAN'T HANDLE THE TRUTH!" that she didn't notice Linc had hung up.

"Got a SAR case," he said, fixing the cover onto his sandwich and standing. "Wow. First one in a week."

Kylie pouted. Why did he get to have all the fun? "Lucky. What is it this time?"

"A kid wandered away from an elementary school playground," he said, patting his side. Storm rose immediately, ever the faithful and ready soldier. "Shouldn't be hard. Weather's been good."

Kylie swallowed. Sure, the weather was good. And most likely, the little kid had just gotten turned around, and they'd find him, shaken but unhurt. Nine times out of ten, that's what happened. But those other times, the times when the victim was hurt, or worse…Kylie worried.

And not just for the child.

Linc's PTSD issues had come to the forefront a few weeks ago, when he'd had a panic attack working on a garage collapse. He'd assured her again and again that he was fine, but she still worried that one day he'd run into a situation that undid all of the months of therapy he'd been excelling at.

"Are you sure you'll be okay?" she said, her eyes drifting to the computer. Linc had been a welcome distraction. Left alone, who knew what stupid and borderline masochistic things she could be tempted to do?

He nodded and kissed her on the top of the head. "Yeah. Of course. You worry about yourself. All right?"

She nodded and watched him and Storm leave through

the storefront window. He'd parked right in front of the little brick building, so her eyes lingered on him as he climbed into his big truck with the German Shepherd and pulled away. Again, she found herself grinning goofily after him.

Linc was a person of few words, so he never really said it, but she knew he loved her. And she loved him.

But that was the thing. She'd seen precisely one picture of her parents together, and in it, there was no doubting the love they shared. Her mother loved her father, once. And maybe, once upon a time, he'd loved her mother.

And he'd left.

Sometimes even people you knew well could completely let you down. She didn't know what kind of reassurance Linc could give her, but all she knew was that she still had doubts, and she wasn't sure if anything could ever erase them.

And they were all put there by one person. Her father.

She looked at Vader and shrugged. "I know, boy. I'm an idiot to have my father mean this much when he wasn't around to shape my life at all. But I guess Linc's right. If I'm ever going to get past this, I need to find him."

She picked up her cell phone and dialed her mother.

2

After closing up Starr Investigations, Kylie arrived at her mother's home in downtown Asheville a little bit after six that night. She and her mother were close. Not a day went by that they didn't call each other up to chat, which, because both of them were expert chatters, usually lasted an hour or more. They'd planned to have dinner together tonight, as they did once a week, which gave Rhonda Hatfield the opportunity to fawn over Kylie's boyfriend and hint about grandchildren.

Rhonda clearly adored Linc, and sometimes, Kylie thought the adoration was so fanatical that she may have liked him more than her own daughter. There was no telling what tidbit of Kylie's past Rhonda might pull out to embarrass her only child. Last time, it was a video of her camp talent show, where she'd been all of twelve and had deluded herself into thinking she was destined to be the next American Idol. As much as Kylie loved her mom, she'd shown up every single time with a clenched jaw, just waiting for the other shoe to drop.

Parents. They could sometimes be so insane.

And she wanted to know her father…why, again?

As much as she loved being with Linc, she was glad that the search and rescue he'd been called out on was running late. Linc had texted her to tell her that they hadn't been able to locate the boy, a third grader. He and the other rescuers were preparing for a long night.

Great. That meant her mother would have to save the videos of her dancing naked in the sprinkler for another day.

She parallel parked outside Rhonda's house, clipped a leash onto Vader's collar, and led him up the stairs. She opened the door and brought Vader in.

Bringing Vader into her mother's house had only been a recent thing. Her mother hated animals, dogs especially. But it'd been so rainy lately that Rhonda had let Kylie bring Vader into the mudroom, where he could have water and enjoy the dry.

"Mom!" she called, letting Vader into the mudroom and filling a Tupperware container of water for him. She scratched his ears and closed the door behind her as she heard her mother's footsteps on the stairs.

When her mother came into view, she searched over her daughter's shoulder, as if she'd forgotten something, then pouted. "No Linc?"

Kylie shook her head. "He had a rescue."

"Oh no!" Rhonda was visibly stricken. "I hope whoever is missing is found safe, and I made Linc his favorite. Lasagna."

Kylie rolled her eyes. Rhonda Hatfield held the "way to the heart was through the stomach" mentality. "Sorry. You're stuck with just me."

Rhonda linked her arm in her daughter's and dragged her into the kitchen. The wine bottle was waiting on the center island, already open. She poured a glass for her daughter, and an even bigger one for herself.

"Don't be silly. I'm never stuck with you, my only child

and my biggest accomplishment. Besides, this'll give us some time for one-on-one girl chat."

Kylie took a sip of her wine, her fingers shaking a little. This was destined to be more than just "girl chat." She'd spent the whole afternoon gathering up the courage to broach the subject. Now, she was ready.

Or…as ready as she was going to get.

She took a deep breath and turned to the fridge, where she opened the freezer and pulled out the ice cube her mother always insisted on putting in her wine to mellow it out. After plopping it into her glass, she slipped from the kitchen and went to the cabinet where all the books of photos were held.

Most of them were of Kylie, of course, but one day, when she'd been about ten years old, she'd been looking through her mother's family Bible and found the only picture of her father she'd ever seen. Her fingers trembled as she opened the cabinet's door and pulled the Bible out again. The picture was still hidden between the pages.

It had been taken in a hospital room on the day she was born. She was just a tiny burrito in her mother's arms, and her mother was beaming with happiness. Next to her was a man in profile, smiling broadly under a dark moustache, his mullet unable to detract from his handsome face. They appeared to be the very definition of a happy family.

And so very much in love. Kylie knew this because the parents weren't looking at the camera, or at the baby. They were looking at each other.

The exposure was grainy, and a bit out of focus. But one thing that she read loud and clear? The love. The warmth was practically radiating from the photo paper. If Kylie knew nothing about that couple, she would've thought they were meant to be together forever.

But he'd left...what? Less than a week after that picture was taken.

What had happened to make things change? Why had he decided to trade her mother in for a different model? That was her mother's belief, at least...but Kylie knew there was always two sides to every story.

She was only getting half of it. And she was a private investigator. Almost, anyway. In her line of work, half a story was as good as nothing.

Kylie smoothed her finger down the photo. It was faded and a bit creased, not from age but from Kylie handling it often after that initial discovery. She couldn't count how many times she'd taken that photo out and stared at it, thinking to herself, *Who are you, Adam Hatfield? How could you be so happy with my mother in this picture, and then leave her only a few days later?*

Those and a thousand other questions had simmered in her head for so long, now it felt like a pot about to overflow.

With a sigh, Kylie placed the picture back on the Bible page and was about to put it away, when she stopped and picked it up again. It was time to take it out of the dark.

Tucking it in the pocket of her sweater, she put the Bible away and closed the door before wandering back to the kitchen. Rhonda Hatfield smiled at her, but the look was edged in concern. "How was your day? You look tired."

"Oh, it was okay," Kylie said innocently, leaning against the center island. Did she look tired? No, she probably just looked bored. The inactivity had the same effect on her as a sleepless night. Not to mention, the talk about her father had her rattled. "Same old, same old."

"Don't tell me you're getting restless with that job too," Rhonda said, fanning her face. Kylie might have been cut from the same cloth as her mother, but Rhonda was much less daring. Kylie had to think she must have gotten her impulsive, risk-taking side from her father, but she never knew that for sure. "You always said how much you liked it. I thought it was your dream job."

"It is, it is. It's fine. I'm not thinking of quitting. It's just a little slow right now."

"Slow? You should appreciate slow. That time that serial killer almost killed you still gives me nightmares." She fanned her face even more vigorously.

Kylie gritted her teeth. Like she could forget convalescing in her mother's house for weeks after that injury. She had wanted to keep the most dangerous cases from her mom, but she'd needed to stay with Rhonda while she recuperated from a bullet to the shoulder, and when news of her thwarting the serial killer ended up in the daily paper, there was no shielding Rhonda Hatfield from all the gory details. No matter how hard Kylie tried to make it seem like all she did was file papers all day, she'd clearly never live her near-death experience down.

"Don't worry, Mom. It's fine."

"Or what about that lunatic who ran you off the road?"

Kylie winced. She'd mostly secreted the worst parts of that case from her mother, like the fact that that lunatic who trashed her car had nearly almost killed her too. But she'd had to explain some of it when she suddenly showed up with a new Jeep Wrangler. "I know, I know."

"Well, is everything all right with Linc? You two didn't have a fight, did you?"

Kylie shook her head. "No. He's perfect."

Rhonda Hatfield leaned forward, her eyes sparkling. She took her daughter's hand. "So...tell me..." Kylie stiffened, anticipating her next words. "Do you think he's going to pop the question?"

Kylie gulped down half the wine. "Mom. I don't know. We never talk about—"

"Never talk about it? You've been practically living together. You don't want to wait too long, until you're an old maid."

Kylie drained her glass. "Mom, we don't live together. I just…stay there a lot. And I'm not even twenty-five yet. I'm not old."

"Yes, but he's older than you. He has to be thirty, at least. Doesn't he want kids?"

"I have no idea. Besides, this isn't about him wanting kids. It's about you wanting grandkids, right? Admit it."

Rhonda gave her an innocent bat of the eyelashes before conceding with a nod. "Okay, maybe. I want to be able to enjoy my precious grandbabies before I become an old, crippled lady."

Kylie poured herself another glass and looked her mom straight in the eye. "Mom. You're not even fifty."

She put her hands on her hips. "Stop saying the word 'fifty.' I only just turned forty-seven, thank you very much. And I want to be the cool, hip grandma. And to be a cool, hip grandma, you have to have grandkids when you're young. So, help me out a little."

Vader scratched at the mudroom door. "Vader can be your grandchild. He's willing to have a cool, hip person taking him on walks."

Rhonda sighed and shook her head. "I don't know what your reluctance is. Linc is the total package. I've been saying that since you first met him. He's kind, sweet, treats you like gold…not to mention he's a hunk." Kylie gritted her teeth again at that word. "Most women would kill for that."

Kylie took a deep breath. "Maybe I'm afraid of commitment, like my dad."

Her mother's eyes flashed to hers. It was the first time Kylie had mentioned the D-word in years. "Your father wasn't afraid of commitment," Rhonda said, turning away to check the lasagna in the oven. She dug her hands into oven mitts, opened the oven door, and stooped to pull out the pan. "In fact, he embraced it. At least at first. He was ready to take the plunge even before *I* was ready. He just decided, I guess, after a little while, that he wanted something different."

That was the most Rhonda Hatfield had ever said about her husband. Kylie pounced on it. "You've said that before. So, he didn't beat around the bush when it came to proposing to you?"

Rhonda poked the center of the steaming pan of lasagna with a fork. "I think it's done."

She was purposely evading the question. Kylie sighed. "He *did* propose to you, right? He didn't just say, 'Yo! Marriage!' and you two got hitched?" She used what was probably an awful Brooklyn accent, but she couldn't help it. She knew that she'd been born at St. Mary's in Brooklyn. It said so on her birth certificate, so she'd always known that her father must've been a New Yorker. In her mind, he sounded a lot like Ralph Macchio in *The Karate Kid*. Even kind of resembled him, with his dark, boyish features.

Rhonda Hatfield looked like she'd sucked on a lemon as she lifted the pan. "Let's eat. Bring the wine." She carried the dinner out to the dining room table and set it down on a trivet. Then she shrugged her hand out of a mitt, grabbed the wine from her daughter, and drained her glass. "Why do you want to know all this now?"

Kylie sat beside her mother's place, who'd always positioned herself at the head of the table. "Why have you always avoided it?"

"Because," her mother said, sitting down in her chair and lacing her fingers in front of her, "I don't dwell on things that don't matter. And I told myself twenty-four years ago that your father doesn't matter."

Kylie threw up her hands. "But don't you understand? It

does matter to me! I'm the one who has his blood in my veins, and I barely even know what he looks like. The only picture I've ever seen of him is the one you keep hidden in the Bible, and that one's so old you can't even see it."

Rhonda leaned over and patted her daughter's hand. "You are much more than your father. A much warmer, more caring, more compassionate person."

"Great. Fantastic. I inherited those things from you. But what about the things I inherited from him? Shouldn't I know what those are?"

Rhonda wrinkled her nose, like she'd smelled something bad. "Believe me. You inherited nothing from him."

"I had to have inherited some things. Like…I don't know. I'm impulsive, and you never are. Maybe that's him?"

Rhonda sighed. "I—"

Kylie barreled on. "I mean, he walked out on you, right? Kind of impulsively, without giving you any indication that anything was wrong? So…" She lifted her eyebrows, waiting for her mother to acknowledge the conversation.

But she didn't. She looked down at her lap, as if she'd fallen asleep at the table.

After a full ten seconds, she pressed her lips together, then reached over with the spatula and started to plate their dinner.

That went well, Kylie thought, assuming her mother would just do what she always did whenever Kylie got up the courage to ask about her dad—change the subject.

It was only after a full two minutes, and they each had a square of lasagna and her mother had picked up her fork, that Rhonda finally spoke again. "I was only trying to protect you. I didn't see what good could come of you knowing him. He didn't just desert *me*, you know. You were part of the equation too. He left both of us."

Kylie swallowed. It took a special kind of jerk to walk out

on a baby when she was less than a week old. "I know. But did he give you a good reason, at least?"

"Oh, he gave me a reason. Not a good one."

The lasagna was too hot to eat, but Kylie didn't have much of an appetite anymore. She sucked in a breath and said, "Linc wants me to officially move in with him."

Her mother's eyes flickered to her, and a smile crept up her cheeks. "And…?"

"And…" Kylie shrugged. "I don't know what to do. With this big dad question mark hanging over my head, how am I supposed to give myself to someone when I don't even truly know myself yet?"

Rhonda's expression was filled with compassion. "Do you love him?"

"Yes, I do."

"Then what's the problem?"

Her mother didn't get it. "The problem is that I haven't even told him that I love him, and he hasn't said those three little words either." When Rhonda opened her mouth again, Kylie held up a hand. "I believe he loves me too."

"I don't see the problem," Rhonda said gently.

Kylie pulled the picture from her pocket, watching her mom's eyes widen in surprise. "This. This is the problem. See the way Dad was looking at you? It's totally clear that he loved you, too, once upon a time. But what if I, like him, decide in a few years that Linc isn't everything I want? I don't want to put him through that. I don't want to be that person. But maybe I am, maybe it's in my genes, and there's nothing I can do to stop it. Maybe I need to turn Linc away before I hurt him like Dad hurt you and me."

Rhonda looked at her daughter for a long time. Kylie saw the tears shining in her mother's eyes. She was about to apologize and change the subject herself when Rhonda leaned in and said, "I raised a good daughter. I have to believe that, even if the impulse to run away was in her blood, she'd know better than to do it in a way that was so horrible."

Kylie smiled sadly. "I'm glad you think that about me, but I don't know what to think about myself. I'm scared. I know I have trouble controlling my impulsive behavior. And I just want to make sure, absolutely sure, that what I'm wanting now will be forever."

Rhonda's eyes traveled over the table. Set with a white linen tablecloth, it could easily hold another ten people, but Kylie couldn't remember a time they'd ever had more than two, or more recently, three, when Linc joined them. For so long, it had been just her and her mother, eating together, here. She'd often wondered, if her father were around, where at the table he would have sat.

With a long sigh, Rhonda pushed her lasagna away and laced her hands together in front of her. "What would you like to know about him?"

Kylie was shocked at the invitation. She'd waited decades to hear it. "Well…everything. Where did you meet?"

Taking a sip of her water, Rhonda said nothing until the glass was precisely centered on its precise spot on the place-mat. "Well, you know that after I graduated from high school, I went up to New York, hoping to get a bite of the big apple."

Kylie raised an eyebrow. "Yes. You lived in an apartment with a bunch of girls from your graduating class, right? You went to college there. And that's where Dad grew up, right?"

"Right. In Brooklyn. It was my senior year, just a couple months before I graduated with a Bachelor of Business degree. I was also waitressing at a twenty-four-hour diner, and that was where I met your father for the first time. He was one of my best customers. He was a garbage truck driver for Cityside Garbage Services, and the diner was on the way home from his route. He used to come in and flirt with me. I can still remember how bad he smelled."

Kylie leaned forward, hanging on every word. She raised an eyebrow. "Is that what made you fall in love with him?"

Rhonda laughed. "The smell? No. He was a charmer. Not only was he handsome, but he had this cute little Brooklyn accent. He made fun of me, called me a Southern belle. My girlfriends at the diner all thought he was a player, but he'd always give me a massive tip. Like twenty dollars on a five-dollar bill."

Kylie grinned. "So, he tipped his way into your heart."

Rhonda grinned back. "That makes me sound like a hooker, but no. What got my attention was that he clearly couldn't afford to be that generous, but he was with me. So, we flirted a lot, and one day, when I got off from work, he was waiting for me with a single red rose. When we started dating, he treated me like a princess. Then…"

Kylie could barely breathe. "Then what?"

Rhonda looked at her daughter with the same level of love she'd smothered her with all these years. "Then you came along. The minute he found out I was pregnant with you, he got down on his knee and proposed." Rhonda's eyes misted, and she lifted a napkin to just under her nose, blinking furiously. When she was composed, she met Kylie's gaze again. "So, you see, he wasn't afraid of commitment at all."

Kylie's eyes widened. Now that the door had been opened, she wanted more. "And then you got married?"

"Yes. Small ceremony. City Hall. We lived in his place above Able Body Hardware Store, which was just a couple blocks away from the diner. It wasn't fancy, but I don't think I'd ever been so happy," she said, getting a faraway look in her eyes as she stared at nothing in particular. "I think he was happy too."

The lasagna was now cool enough to eat, but Kylie couldn't even think about food. She fisted the napkin in her lap. If they'd been so happy, then what happened?

"And?"

Rhonda Hatfield's brow knitted, and a pained look flitted across her expression. "And…then things changed. Actually, he changed. At the time, I was too hurt to question it. But I still haven't the foggiest idea why, other than that it must've had to do with his new job."

3

Rhonda Hatfield sat at the head of the table, gazing at the candles that flickered at the center of it. It was much easier than facing her daughter.

Her daughter, who had been so starved for information about her father that she was practically salivating, begging Rhonda with wide eyes to go on.

It was Rhonda's own fault, trying to protect her by withholding all the information. She wished she'd been given a Single Mother Rule Book. She didn't want to bad-mouth the man who'd left her alone to raise their daughter, but she didn't want to wax poetic, constantly bringing up the painful memories of the past, either. So, she'd done what was easiest, and what she thought would keep Kylie blissfully unaware of the pain she'd endured at Adam Hatfield's hands.

It was a rare thing for her to mention Adam Hatfield at all.

Rhonda dropped her hands under the table and pressed them into her thighs to keep them from shaking. All her life, she'd coddled Kylie, bending over backwards to try to make up for her lack of a father.

She'd exceeded her credit card limit during Christmases to get Kylie the gifts she desperately wanted, volunteered as the only female coach when Kylie went out for basketball, and had even humored her through her extended years of undergraduate education. She'd somehow believed that Kylie's indecisiveness was because she hadn't had adequate male guidance to help her pick a profession.

Deep down, she'd hoped that she'd done a good enough job cobbling together a happy childhood for her daughter that Kylie never would question her about her father.

Clearly, she'd failed.

"But that's why I don't speak of him much," Rhonda lied, not making eye contact with her daughter. "I really don't care. It was so long ago. And I've moved on."

Of course, that wasn't true. Was it possible to move on from the love of your life? It might have been if there'd been anyone else in the twenty-four years since Adam Hatfield left. But she'd been too heartbroken to look at first, and then, when she'd gradually warmed to the idea of not spending the rest of her life desperately alone, finding a new man had proven as difficult as finding the right needle in a stack of needles.

Kylie had gone off to college, and her house was so quiet. She was so set in her life alone that she wasn't sure if she wanted a man, or one of those fancy new whole-house sound systems. Plus, she was forty-seven years old, and wasn't dating something teenage kids did?

Gradually, she'd just settled into life. Until recently, she'd worked as an administrative assistant for a manufacturer so close she could walk to her job. Her life had always been solid and predictable. She had a small circle of friends and neighbors, no excitement, no romance, no surprises from day to day…and she liked it very much. She needed nothing more.

Kylie eyed her doubtfully. "But you said he changed? How?"

Even now, Rhonda could see her earlier life vividly. The sights, the smells—which weren't all that appetizing, to be honest—but more especially, the feelings. How her heart pounded. How his fingers felt on her skin. His lips…

Rhonda mentally shook herself. All she needed to remember now was how it felt when he left.

But her daughter needed more, she knew, so she made herself keep talking. "I hate to even think of that awful city. How I even survived up there is beyond me. But I guess it was…him. He was my life. We were living in that apartment on Gold Street near Vinegar Hill. It was awful. Cockroach infested and probably not the best place to raise a child. But I didn't mind. I knew we could make it work. We were in love. You can turn a blind eye to many things when you're in love, right?" Rhonda even managed a smile at the end.

Kylie stared at her blankly. It occurred to Rhonda that her daughter might have shared her vivacious, outgoing person-ality and looks, but Rhonda had jumped feetfirst into her first relationship with Adam. Kylie was always cautious when it came to men, passing up dates and turning down boyfriends.

Even now, she was so wishy-washy when it came to Linc, and he was clearly a good man. Definitely the most solid and dependable man she'd ever dated. Was her caution because she'd never had a positive male influence in her life?

Probably. Another mom-fail.

"Anyway," Rhonda continued, tamping that worry down, "I might have been happy in our little place, but Adam sure wasn't. He was always talking about the future and thinking up schemes that might bring in more money. Trying one thing, then giving it up for another. I suppose that's where you got that tendency from."

She hadn't intended to make it a slight and was relieved when Kylie only nodded, accepting the truth in the words. In truth, that part of her daughter's nature often scared her. She'd spent many a sleepless night worrying that Kylie'd do something stupid on her career hunt, just because nothing seemed to make her happy. Rhonda had been so elated when Kylie accepted the private investigator job, even as dangerous as it was, because it finally looked like Kylie had found something she wanted to settle into.

"When I was six months pregnant, he came home and told me he'd gotten a different job, working in Manhattan. It was a supervisory level job in construction. I was floored. I asked him how he qualified for such a job, since he'd never told me he worked in construction before. But he was pretty silent about it. He told me that he'd made friends with the owners of the company, who were on his route, and this was an opportunity we'd be crazy to refuse. He wanted it so much, so we went with it."

Kylie tilted her head. "You moved to Manhattan?"

Rhonda nodded, thinking of the beautiful apartment she'd lived in for just a few short months of her life. It was the only time in her life that she'd ever felt wealthy. Doormen and crystal chandeliers and people calling her "madame," even though she'd been barely as old as Kylie.

"A couple of weeks after he started his new job, we moved into a beautiful place on the Upper West Side. I felt like I was in a fantasy. The only problem was that your father was barely ever around. Even when I went into labor, I couldn't get in touch with him. He arrived after you were born."

Kylie gasped, and Rhonda realized this was the first time she'd ever told her of this part. "You went through labor alone?"

It was terrifying.

"Yeah, but it was okay." It wasn't, but Rhonda needed to

keep that to herself. "He was bringing in great money at the time, and I was living like a pampered princess. He kept bringing home gifts for you and me, so I excused him. After I was released from the hospital, we went back to the apartment, and he'd set up the most beautiful nursery for you as a surprise. All pink gingham check and lace, and so many stuffed animals. He was so proud. I remember him saying all this stuff about how he was going to make the best father possible."

Tears flooded Kylie's eyes, and she used a napkin to dab them away. "And?"

"And well…you know the rest. Four days after you were born, he disappeared."

Kylie dabbed at her eyes again. "Do you have any idea why?"

Rhonda's heart picked up rhythm, almost like it was reliving those dark days. "I don't know, sweetheart. I was beside myself. I called the police. Called everywhere I could think of. Went looking for him. Nearly had a breakdown, since I was trying to take care of you at the same time and had no support system whatsoever in Manhattan. I almost checked myself into a hospital, I was so beside myself with worry. I really did think he must've been murdered. Then, a couple days later…I received a letter."

"A letter?"

This was part of the story that Rhonda had never shared with her daughter. In her mind, it was better that Kylie not know how casually they'd been tossed aside.

"You were colicky, so I had you strapped to my chest in one of those baby carrier things. It was a pretty day, so I'd taken you for a walk. We stopped at the mailboxes on our way back in, and I pulled out a manila envelope with no return address."

Kylie had started screaming again, almost like the infant

had known that the contents of that envelope would change everything.

"What did it say?"

Rhonda blinked out of the memory, but the feelings of that moment didn't depart so easily, and she hugged herself now as she'd hugged her baby then. "It was a deed to this house, and a ten-thousand-dollar check. There was a note that said he was sorry, that the marriage was a mistake, and that I should try to forget about him. That was it."

Kylie's expression was the very definition of sadness. "That's all?"

Rhonda shrugged with a nonchalance she didn't feel. "Yes. It was at that moment that I realized he wasn't dead…he just didn't want me."

"Or me," Kylie whispered.

Rhonda didn't have the heart to disagree. What could she say, anyway?

Should she tell her daughter of how she'd cried for days, barely able to take care of her also crying infant? How betrayed she'd felt? How rejected? How alone?

By that time, her friends had graduated college too and were living their own lives. She had no help, no support system. And the rejection, coming so suddenly and awful, had made her simply want to die.

Should she tell her precious daughter how, at one point, she'd poured the entire contents of the bottle of pain pills she'd gotten after giving birth into her hand? How she'd had them within an inch of her mouth, wanting to end it all, when she finally came to her senses?

No. Her daughter didn't need to know that. She didn't need to know how desperate she'd become. How Adam's games, playing house then disappearing, had almost become deadly.

Rhonda lifted her chin, gazing straight into her daughter's eyes. "But I wanted you, Kylie."

Kylie dabbed at her eyes again. "What did you do?"

"Well, I did the only thing I could do. I took it day by day. I stayed in the apartment for a little while, but I knew even with the money from the check I'd never be able to continue to live there. So, I packed you up and left New York, moved here."

"This house?"

She looked around. "Yep. This very one. I thought about selling it, but I kind of liked it. Turned out, Adam knew just what I would like. And it was perfect for the two of us. It gave us a fresh start."

"And you never heard from him again? Or tried to contact him?"

"No. I was too hurt to reach out, and to be honest, I didn't want to feel the rejection for a second time. I figured that he knew where I was. If he wanted me, he'd come back for me."

Kylie let out a sad sigh. "But he never did."

Rhonda shook her head.

"And you never sought a divorce?"

Rhonda knew it sounded pathetic, but she hadn't. She was normally a woman of action, but just thinking about Adam Hatfield rendered her queasy and immobile.

"I'd sooner just forget it. Whenever I thought about what I might find if I dug into it, what kind of new life he was living, without me...it made me physically sick. And I had you to raise. I poured myself into doing that. Plus..." She toyed with the stem of her wine glass. "Plus, I suppose there was a tiny part of me holding out hope that he would come back." She snorted. "Pathetic, isn't it?"

"No..." Kylie's voice was firm. When Rhonda looked up again, she expected to see a pitying look on her daughter's face. Or disgust. It was neither. It was worry. "You loved him.

Is that why you never dated anyone while I was growing up?"

"That, and because I had you," she said with a smile. "While thinking of your father made me ill, thinking of you, taking care of you…that made me happier than you could ever know. I threw myself into that, and eventually, your father didn't matter to me anymore. Nor did any other man, really. I can't say any viable alternatives have come along, making me want to jump back into the dating scene."

Kylie smiled. "I could set you up with Greg. He's successful, and he treats me like a daughter."

Rhonda waved that idea away. "For the hundredth time, no. He's such a grouch."

"Yes, but he's a nice grouch. You and your optimism could balance him out."

Rhonda finally picked up her fork and cut into her lasagna. "Sweetheart, I'm happy just as I am."

Following her mother's lead, Kylie picked up her fork as well. "Thank you for telling me all of that. I know it couldn't be easy. I've wanted to know more about him for forever."

Rhonda smiled. "You've always loved mysteries."

Yet another reason why she hadn't spoken of her disaster of a marriage until today. Her daughter was a digger. Not only that, she was on her way to becoming a very successful private investigator. She had a knack for turning up things, especially missing people. She'd probably have no trouble learning just what Adam Hatfield had been up to all this time.

But Rhonda wasn't sure if she wanted to know.

Actually, she was positive she didn't want to. She was content with her life. What was the point?

"Well, if you go digging and find something about him… don't tell me."

Kylie looked at her like she was insane. "Are you telling

me that there isn't even a small part of you that wonders where he went? The only man you have ever loved just leaves you without any good explanation, and you don't care why he did it or where he went?"

She shook her head, almost in slow motion. "Nope."

Kylie eyed her suspiciously, until finally, Rhonda cracked. She held her thumb and forefinger up so that they were a centimeter apart. "Okay. A small part, but I'm not willing to experience the pain that I know will come with that knowledge."

"But, Mom. He can't have remarried. You said it yourself. You never got a divorce."

She let out a long breath. "I know he isn't wondering about me, so what difference does it make?"

"How do you know that? Maybe he is. Maybe he's ruing the day he ever walked out on you and wishes he could make amends, but he doesn't know how."

Rhonda stared at her kind, glass-always-full daughter. "Sweetheart, you really think he can make amends? He can't. That ship has sailed. Nothing he can say would be of interest to me. He may have been the love of my life, but that part of my life is over, and there's no room for him any longer. Like I said, I'm in a good place right now."

"Oh, come on, Mom." Kylie gave her mother a disappointed shake of her head. "Don't you want a happily ever after?"

Rhonda gritted her teeth. Yes, she had once been an avid reader of romance novels. All those lonely nights, she had wondered what it would be like to have some Prince Charming come sweep her off her feet. She'd dared to believe that Adam was that someone, even years afterwards. She would dream that he'd only been confused or coerced in some way and would come crawling back for her. But those dreams had faded.

And that was fine. They were clearly ridiculous and deserved to remain buried. Maybe some people were just meant to live their lives alone, and maybe she was one of those people.

Rather than acknowledge her daughter's look of disappointment, Rhonda stabbed her fork into her lasagna. It was cold. She stood and picked up both plates. "Let me just pop this in the micro."

Kylie called after her, "Well, even if you don't want to know, I'm going to track him down. I have all the tools. It'd only take a little searching. I could know exactly where he's been and what he's been up to by tonight. I won't get in contact with him, but I just want to know what he's been up to all these years. Okay?"

Rhonda didn't answer. The moment Kylie had started asking about Adam Hatfield, she knew her child was going to chase him down. Her daughter never backed down where a challenge was concerned.

Her daughter had been shot, and she'd survived a car crash down the mountain. But Rhonda worried that her sweet girl wouldn't survive the disappointment of getting turned away by her deadbeat father.

4

Something changed in her mother that night.

Kylie felt it right away, in the way her mother didn't try to coax her to stay for another slice of Key Lime Pie. Not only that, she'd looked exhausted, like she'd just been through a particularly harrowing war.

When Kylie finished her slice, her mother hadn't begged her to stay a little longer. And she knew why. Their discussion regarding Adam Hatfield was the culprit.

And it was all her fault.

It surprised Kylie when Rhonda picked up the picture of their tiny family, and instead of tossing it into the trash, she used a magnet to stick it to the freezer door. She smiled at Kylie. "Maybe if I look at him enough, the pain will fade. A wound never heals if kept under a bandage."

She'd never been more proud of her mother than at that moment.

When she got to the door, she gave her mother a big hug. Rhonda hugged her back, tight as ever, but she seemed smaller, somehow. Kylie knew she was the nervous type and often suffered bouts of insomnia. She hoped their discussion wouldn't keep her awake all night.

"It's okay, Mom," she said, inhaling the familiar scent of her Estee Lauder perfume. "If you don't want to know what I find out, fine. I'll keep it to my grave."

Rhonda tucked a stray strand of hair behind her ear. "I don't. I just hope he won't disappoint you. God knows our family has suffered enough disappointment at his hands. I'd hate for whatever you learn to add to it."

"He won't," Kylie said, kissing her sweet-smelling cheek. "Call you tomorrow. With absolutely no news of Adam Hatfield."

She crossed her heart and held up her palm in oath.

Rhonda managed a smile, said goodbye, and closed the door tight behind Kylie.

Kylie walked down the steps with Vader at her heels, feeling like she'd wounded her mother. Rhonda Hatfield had never said goodbye with quite so little enthusiasm before.

Guilt flooded her as she walked down the street to the "hellayella" Jeep Wrangler she bought with the bonus she'd been given from her last big case. She loved it.

Greg had rolled his eyes, asking how she ever thought she'd be able to go incognito with "that Big Bird looking thing," and even though he had a point, she didn't have the heart to pick out a more neutral color. Plus, this was the mountains. Everyone drove a four-wheel drive and in a variety of colors, so she didn't stand out *that* much.

Vader loved it too, especially when she took the top down and his ears could fly in the wind. He'd also gotten much better about chewing, and so far, all the headrests and seat cushions were intact.

After the big Newfoundland mix peed on every bush and tree along the way, she loaded him inside and sat at the steering wheel for a long time, looking up at her mother's house.

On one hand, Adam Hatfield had been a bastard for deserting his brand-new family, but on the other, at least he'd taken care of them in a couple important ways, which was more than some men did.

Kylie studied the house. Why this one? Why Asheville?

Rhonda Hatfield was from a little town near Atlanta, Georgia and had been on her own since her parents died in a freak car accident when she was only nineteen.

So much loss.

It was strange to miss people she'd never met, but Kylie used to look through the photo albums containing picture after picture of her late grandparents, wishing they'd still been alive so that, if something bad happened and her mom disappeared, she'd at least have someone on this earth she could turn to.

Vader licked Kylie's face, and it was only then that she realized she was crying. She pulled the dog close and buried her face in his soft fur. "I'm not alone, am I, boy," she cooed to him. "I'll always have you."

And her mom. And Linc.

At least she hoped so.

Wiping her face, Kylie watched the light go on in her mother's bedroom. The same room her mother had never shared with a man, to her knowledge at least. She briefly wondered how long it'd been since her mother had sex, and then cringed and pushed away the thought. But she still found the idea sad that a woman as sweet as her mother lacked that kind of intimacy.

Her mother had done everything for Kylie, and never thought of herself. Though Rhonda Hatfield seemed happy, Kylie wasn't so sure how much was a facade. Something told Kylie that she was missing a part of life that would make her even happier, that she was lonely, and just scared of putting herself out there.

Her phone dinged with a text. She looked over at the lighted screen. It was from Linc. *Home now. You on your way?*

Home. He meant the sweet mountain farmhouse he'd inherited from his grandparents, where she'd been practically living the past several weeks. Sure, it was *his* home, but whenever she heard that word, she still thought of her apartment right outside of the UNC Campus. The home he wanted her to leave behind and permanently move in with him. But something about relinquishing it made her heart race.

She loved Linc, and she believed that he loved her too, although neither of them had officially said the words out loud.

There was no other reason for keeping the apartment other than that she was scared. Scared of being abandoned. Scared of having nowhere to go. Scared that she would suddenly get itchy and want to leave too.

And thinking of what her father had done, she now had a very good reason for those fears.

But she didn't have to make any decisions now.

She quickly thumbed in, *Yes. On my way.*

She turned the key in the ignition and the powerful four-wheel drive roared to life, making her smile. But the expression faded away as her mind quickly fell back into just what steps she'd need to take to track down her father.

He was probably still living in New York City. Kylie had always wanted to live there. She loved Asheville, but she sometimes wanted more excitement, more people, more everything. That was probably from Adam Hatfield's DNA, since her mother liked her peace and quiet.

When she was a kid, she'd imagined growing up and living in the big city after she graduated college. Then reality set in. When she was looking at colleges, she thought she might like to go away to the city, but quickly squashed that idea. With her gone, her mother would have no one.

Driving up the mountain, Kylie refused to look at the place where her Mazda met its demise. The guardrail was bright and shiny now, but she didn't think the sound of the old one giving way would be something she'd ever forget.

She pulled into the long, winding dirt and gravel driveway that led up to Linc's secluded farmhouse at around nine. He always said to her, "It's not my home. It's *our* home." But, so far, she hadn't been able to call it that. He'd given her full reign to do anything she wanted. She could put her toiletries where she wanted, decorate the rooms as she pleased…but had she? No. No matter how comfortable she got in his home, she couldn't help thinking that all of this was a temporary little blip in her life.

The porch light was on, spotlighting Linc sitting out on the porch with Storm, sipping at a beer, wearing his standard cargo pants and a tight t-shirt that stretched across his muscular frame. Her heart skipped when she saw him. He was just so damn handsome, it still made her insides flutter. He had one of those faces like a movie star; perfect at all angles, and so damn watchable that you couldn't help staring at it.

"Hey," he said, meeting her at the Jeep and wiping a shock of brown hair from his forehead. When she first met him, his hair was the high-and-tight military fashion, and she enjoyed how he was, literally, letting his hair down a bit.

"I hope you're hungry for lasagna and key lime pie," she said, holding up two big Tupperware containers. Her mother never let her go anywhere without leftovers.

"Of course, you know I love your mom's cooking," he said absently, like that was the last thing on his mind. He was staring not at the containers, but at her, in a meaningful way, like one would before giving a speech of great importance.

As she approached, he stood and began to reach into his pocket.

Her stomach lurched.

Oh, no. Wrong time. Definitely the wrong time. Kylie's thoughts were frantic. *Not here. Not now. Not when all I'm doing is thinking of my jerk of a father.*

When Linc looked at the ground, like he was trying to find a place to plant his knee, she quickly skirted past him and onto the porch, like a kid trying to avoid the classmate with cooties in the schoolyard.

What am I, twelve?

She turned around and faced him as he followed her. He was giving her a curious look. His lips parted, but before he could get a word out, Kylie jumped in. "You know. You need a haircut." As if to reinforce the words, she reached out and pushed back that same shock of hair, which had again fallen onto his tanned forehead. The hair was also starting to curl at his ears a little, giving him the first sideburns she'd ever seen on him.

She studied it, fully aware his eyes were on her, questioning, appraising. The temperature went up a thousand degrees.

"You just noticed?" he asked, taking an empty hand out of his pocket and running it through his hair. Whew. Crisis averted. "My barber retired last month."

She gave him a look. Sometimes, the man was so set in his ways, he let all common sense go out the window. "So, are you just going to let it grow until it reaches the floor?"

He shrugged. "Maybe. My barber knew how to get it just right."

Kylie sighed. "It's not rocket science. I'm sure any person

out there could get it right. I bet I could even do it. Do you have clippers?"

He nodded. "Yeah. Inside."

She tittered nervously and opened the screen door. At least cutting his hair would help her take her mind off her father, and maybe get him to second-guess giving her whatever was in his pocket. "Well, I didn't mean on your person. Come on."

She went inside, and he followed. A few minutes later, he was seated in the bathroom, and she had a pair of clippers in her hand. Was she insane? She'd never clipped a guy's hair before. Just the fact that he was sitting in front of her, allowing her to do this showed how much he trusted her. But she didn't trust herself. Her eyes slowly drifted to the bulge in his pocket. It was big enough to be a ring.

Oh, god.

"Are you okay?" Linc asked, nearly making her jump.

Her eyes met his in the bathroom mirror. She nodded and looked at herself. She was holding the clippers in a white-knuckled death grip, and her hand was visibly trembling.

"Oh, sure. Just contemplating how to start," she said, running a hand through his hair. She thought of what her hairdressers usually said to her before they started clipping. "What are we doing here?"

He let out a confused laugh. "Uh. Cutting it? The way it was before?"

"Yes. Right." She flipped on the clippers and brought the buzzing contraption to the back of his head. Even before it made contact, she was already sure this was going to be a disaster.

"Have you…ever done this before?" he asked.

She met his gaze in the mirror. "No, but how hard can it be?"

"Just…whatever. I can always wear a ball cap if you screw it up too much," he said with a shrug.

"Right." She moved the shaver up the back of his head and nearly had a heart attack when almost all the hair fell away. She looked at the clippers, remembering something about a guard. Looking back at the wide strip of nearly bald head, she mentally shrugged. Too late for that now.

"How was your search and rescue?" she asked to take his mind off what she was doing to his head.

"Fine. The administration was worried he'd been abducted but fortunately it wasn't the case. Kid wanted to get out of a math test, so he played hooky by taking what he thought was a shortcut back home. Then he got lost and couldn't find his way back. We found him about three miles out of the way. Shaken but okay."

She tried to listen but again she found herself thinking of Adam Hatfield. When she was done with this, if she could get away from Linc for a little bit, she could use her laptop and start pulling together information on him. Then she could—

"Whoa…that's short."

She blinked as that same shock of hair she'd touched earlier slipped through her fingers and landed on Linc's lap. She looked at his reflection in the mirror. He looked a little like Mr. Clean. "Oh. Um…"

To her immense relief, he laughed. "No sense worrying about it. Just do the rest like that. It's just reminding me of when I went to bootcamp."

She worried her bottom lip. "I'm so sorry. I didn't think about the guard until it was too late."

He smiled at her in the mirror. "It's fine. I'll just need to remember to wear a cap or sunscreen if I go outside. Otherwise, I'm gonna get burned."

She was practically in tears by the time she finished up the job. She actually liked his hair longer. He looked better that way, though he was handsome all the time. But her tears had nothing to do with the length of his hair. He was so good to her, not complaining. Most men probably wouldn't be so nice about it. All the more reason she shouldn't be afraid…

But no matter how much she told herself she shouldn't be scared of a lifetime with Linc, it didn't stop the roiling in her stomach.

She wiped the hair from his shoulders when she finished. "Looks good. Sort of."

He ran his hand through the remaining scruff, which was now no longer than the scruff on his jaw. "I wonder why, with all your career choices, you never decided to test out becoming a hair stylist? You clearly have the gift."

She winced as she looked at him. He did look a little bit awkward, like a shorn lamb. "I'm sorry."

"Relax. You didn't clip off an ear. I'm good," he said, standing up and lifting the chair out of the way. He folded up the newspapers where the rest of his hair had gone as Kylie watched him.

Her mother was right. He was the perfect man.

Of course, her mother had made a mistake with that kind of thinking once before. As did the approximate fifty percent of couples who walk down the aisle a few years before duking it out in divorce court.

She shook her head, trying to force the doubts away, just as Linc looked up. She mentally told those worry creases she could feel wrinkling her forehead to get lost, but not before Linc caught sight of them. "You okay?" he asked, for about the twelfth time that night.

She brushed some stray hairs from his shirt. "I'm fine, just tired." Which was true. Ever since her concussion, she seemed to lose steam faster than usual. "Hungry? Want me to heat up the lasagna for you?"

"Already ate," he said and followed her to the kitchen. "But I'll take some of that pie."

She hurried to dish him out a big slice, glad to have something to do.

For the rest of the night, her philosophy was this: It was impossible to pin down a moving target. Actually, she'd have been happy if all he wanted to do was pin her down. But every time her eyes drifted to that bulge in the pocket of his cargo pants, she had a feeling that his mind was on something much more serious. So she kept running around, first getting him the pie, then going out to make sure the dogs were okay, then doing dishes and tidying up the things she'd neglected while she recovered from the car accident.

By eleven, all she wanted to do was sit down and rest, but she was still worried that he'd corner her and drop to one knee.

"You should take a break," he said to her from the couch, where he was paging through his phone.

From the kitchen, she could see him silhouetted in the light of the fire, patting the spot next to him. She'd always thought that spot of the house, with that glowing orange fire, was so romantic. A perfect place for cuddling, kissing, and…

She *definitely* didn't want to go there.

"I'm good!" she called back.

When she finished the last of her self-imposed tasks, she saw him looking at her from the couch, and her heart rate sped up. She was getting physically tired, and walking this mental minefield was proving harder than she'd expected.

She needed to be alone. She needed to think. She needed to figure out why she was so innately terrified of having a close relationship with this man. And she couldn't do it with him staring at her like she was some complex mathematical problem he needed to figure out.

Maybe she could just be alone in the bedroom. Ever since

she'd met with her mother, she'd made up her mind to go online and put Adam Hatfield's name into Google. Upstairs, alone, she could finally do it.

She started to fake a yawn, but the moment she opened her mouth, a real one took over. She really was bone-achingly tired. "I think I'll take your advice and turn in for the night." She was so tempted to go over and give him a kiss, but she knew he'd draw her onto his lap…kiss her more deeply… take off all her clothes…make passionate love to her…then…

Pull the box out of his pocket?

She simply couldn't risk it.

Blowing him a kiss from the bottom of the staircase, she shot up them two at a time, hating herself all the way.

In his room, she sank onto the bed.

She didn't deserve him, she knew. She really didn't.

Kylie practically jumped out of her skin when Linc appeared in the doorway. He gave her another worried slash curious look as he pulled his shirt over his head. "Thought I'd turn in too. After a shower to get this hair off me. It's kind of itchy."

She eyed his head again. It actually wasn't all that bad since it gave him a kind of dangerous, Jason Statham vibe. "I'm sure it is." Beating him to the bathroom, she brushed her teeth and washed her face as he turned the water on and began to strip.

As each inch of his flesh was revealed, she grew more tempted to join him. When his jeans hit the floor with a slap, she couldn't pull her eyes away from the lump in the pocket. It was definitely a box.

Don't think about it now.

She needed to think less of the box and more about why it terrified her so much. Maybe she needed to make an appointment with the therapist Linc was seeing. She clearly had some unresolved abandonment issues that were seriously messing with her head.

Slipping from the bathroom, she climbed into her pajamas, and got under the covers before pulling her laptop onto her lap. Taking a deep breath, she typed *Adam Hatfield* into the search bar.

Half a million results poured in, including image results of men old and young.

She scrolled up to the bar and added *New York* to her father's name.

The results were about half that.

Thinking, she added *Construction.*

Better...only ten-thousand results. Kylie sighed and began scrolling through them, spotting plenty of older men who could've been the man in her little family photograph, but she wasn't sure.

Kylie also wasn't sure her mother had mentioned the name of the new company that her father had begun working for, but Cityside Garbage Services, the company he'd driven a truck for, had stuck in her mind. She typed it in and hit enter just as the faucet in the bathroom shower turned off.

Crap.

She scrambled to close the computer, but before she could, a headline caught her attention:

Head of Cityside Garbage Services nabbed on extortion charges, possible mafia ties.

She wanted to read more but she also didn't want Linc asking about her search and possibly commandeering her investigation like he did last time. This was personal for her, and she wanted it to stay just hers.

For now, anyway.

Kylie tagged the link to the article, then shut the laptop

down as the sink faucet turned on. She only had a minute while Linc brushed his teeth.

Feeling like the worst person on the planet, she replaced the laptop on her night table, grabbed her pillow, and pretended to sleep.

Which was as close as she got to real sleep for the entire night.

Her mind whirred all night long with thoughts of extortion...mafia...did her father know anything about that? Maybe he'd somehow gotten himself tangled up with some bad people and needed to leave...or go into witness protection because he was law enforcement's star witness?

She sighed, realizing she was doing what most kids did. Trying to think the best of their parents. Making excuses for them. But even knowing that the possibility of him sacrificing himself for his family was slim, she couldn't help but wonder...could it be?

Had her father been trying to protect her and her mother all these years?

But as half-formed thoughts and ideas swirled in her head, one big thing began to solidify.

The only way to find out what had happened to her father was by going to New York and tracking down Adam Hatfield herself.

WELL, that had been a big old bust.

After getting out of the shower, Linc picked up his pants from the floor. Reaching into the pocket, he pulled out the little box that had been practically burning a hole in his thigh all night long.

He set it on the side of the sink, frowning.

She'd had a crappy day. He could tell that much at lunch.

In his mind, he'd thought that she'd come home, tired, and he'd make her laugh by presenting her with an official key to his home in a little box. He'd even thought that he might kneel, like he was going to propose, but had thought better of it.

He didn't want to scare her to death. Hell, he didn't want to scare himself to death either.

Just inviting her to live with him was enough to give him the hives.

Kind of.

A little.

Shit. No, it didn't, which was the strangest thing. He wanted her by his side every night.

He opened the box, looking at the key to his home.

That's when it hit him. Had she seen the outline of a little box in his pants? Had she thought it was a ring? That he was going to propose?

He groaned and turned on the water, attacking his teeth with a toothbrush.

Was that why she'd been so zany this entire evening? He went right, she swerved left. It had almost been enough to give him a complex.

And was that why she'd cut off all his hair? Hoping to steal all his strength and noble intentions like Delilah did Samson?

He turned off the water and put his toothbrush back in the holder before pulling on a pair of boxer briefs, cursing himself for his stupidity.

A key in a box? What had he been thinking?

And what did he do next?

Go to her and reassure her that he had no immediate plans to propose? How would she take that? And how would he feel if she heaved out a sigh of relief at the admission?

It was a no-win situation.

But he had to say something to her. She'd clearly been on edge, and he deeply wanted her to feel no pressure. That was why he was going to give her a key, so she could come and go as she pleased. He might want her there all the time, but he wasn't selfish enough to pressure her into something she wasn't ready for.

Taking a deep breath, Linc psyched himself up for the conversation. But when he opened the door and stepped out of the haze, Kylie was already asleep.

Well, that answers that.

Moving quietly to the armoire, he tucked the box with the key into the back. Then he stopped and dug a little bit deeper. He pulled out the second box. The one he'd purchased just a week ago.

It had been impulsive. He hadn't been ring shopping or anything like that. He'd simply walked past a jewelry store and saw the two-carat beauty in the window and instinctively knew it would be perfect for Kylie.

Some day.

When they both were ready.

He'd thought long and hard before he made the purchase, then decided if he never gave it to her or if he found one he liked even better one day, he could always sell this one.

The ring didn't come with an actual ball and chain.

Linc looked over his shoulder, making sure that Kylie hadn't stirred, before stuffing the box back into its hiding place where he knew it would stay for a long, long time.

Then he sat on the edge of the bed and buried his face in his hands, elbows on his knees, thinking.

She'd been acting squirrelly for the past few weeks. Actually, ever since he'd gotten it in his head that he'd wanted her to move in with him, he'd sensed something was bothering her. At first, he'd thought that she was having second thoughts about being with him after his official diagnosis of PTSD.

But lately, he'd been thinking that she might just be getting bored of him.

He thought she loved him, and he knew he loved her, even though neither of them had officially said those three little words.

Which was stupid, he thought to himself, moving until he was under the covers and staring up at the ceiling as the full moon slashed through the blinds, painting lines across Kylie's sleeping form. Why hadn't they shared how they felt?

His therapist called it philophobia, the fear of love or any emotional connection.

At least the fear had a name.

But how to get over it? And more, how to help Kylie over her phobia too? As opposite as they were, they were so very good together. They filled in each other's cracks, became the glue to the other's personality.

A couple of things he'd done were not so bright. He'd mentioned to her once that he wanted to have kids before he was thirty-five. She's ignored that statement. Then, he'd told her that he was a traditional person. She hadn't said anything to that, either. Then, he told her that his grandparents had been married on the hill out behind the pasture, and it was a really nice spot for a wedding, especially if the wedding happened right when the sun was setting. Nothing.

He'd quickly come to learn that where Kylie was concerned, there were few things she wouldn't talk about. But those few things she refused to speak of? If they were brought up, Kylie would simply ignore them.

For example, football. It bored her to tears. Whenever he and Jacob got into a discussion on how the Panthers were looking for next season, Kylie went on talking about whatever subject she wanted to talk about as if they hadn't said a word.

Linc was quickly getting the feeling that marriage and kids were two of those subjects. Not that they were taboo. She just wasn't interested.

But hell, that couldn't be right. She was a woman. Women liked commitment, didn't they?

Apparently not Kylie.

What else could have spooked her?

Had she accidentally seen the receipt in his wallet? Or the velvet case tucked in his armoire?

They needed to talk. He needed to tell her that he wasn't ready for that level of commitment either. He needed to assure her that he was fine with just being together the way they currently were. And he needed to tell her that he loved her, so she could feel secure in that knowledge.

At least he hoped she would be.

He sighed as he looked at her, with her long brown hair slipping down her shoulders, scattering on the pillow. God, she was gorgeous. She had these green, expressive eyes, little freckles on her skin, and the most phenomenal body he'd ever seen. Not only was she beautiful, she was smart. Funny.

To think, she'd annoyed the hell out of him when he first met her. But all the things about her that had once ticked him off—her impulsiveness, her tenacity, her craziness—turned out to be exactly everything he needed in his life. And she was the right woman. He had no doubt about that at all.

Months ago, while dealing with memories of his past in Syria, he'd thought all he wanted was to be alone. Then, he'd met Kylie. The second he saw her outside the Asheville vet clinic, trying to haul an injured Newf out of her truck, he'd been smitten. She'd been clueless about handling dogs then; had no clue what she was getting into. But she was so damned persistent, cute, insane…a little firecracker.

She'd been the one pushing to be with him, constantly showing up at his house. If it hadn't been for her, he'd probably still be alone.

He smiled at the thought.

Since then, they'd slogged through a lot of shit together. They'd taken care of each other. She'd stuck close to his side during all of his PTSD episodes, making sure he was up to date on his counseling appointments and simply being there if he ever needed to talk.

She was the reason why he was here, functioning, and not a complete wreck. Hell, if she hadn't been there for him during the time when his nightmares had gotten really bad, he didn't want to think about what he might have done. He owed everything to her. Couldn't even think of life without her.

And she probably knew it.

She expected it.

Was that it?

Did she think he'd fall apart without her? Was she here out of guilt?

The thought made him sick to his stomach. He'd never considered himself to be a pity fuck.

Linc eventually fell asleep, but not until the wee hours of the morning. When he finally woke up, he felt the other side of the bed to find it cold. Opening his eyes in the orange glow of the sunrise, he looked around and discovered Kylie had showered, dressed, and left the room without waking him.

Was she still avoiding him?

Noises resounded from downstairs, so he pulled on a t-shirt over his boxer briefs and went down to the kitchen. He found her pouring coffee into her commuter mug. Again, he was struck by just how gorgeous she was.

She'd been dressing more professionally in ass-hugging

skirts and high heels, maturing from the perpetual college student to a damned classy woman. His eyes went over her hand, with its thin, flower-stem fingers, and he couldn't help thinking that this damned classy woman should be wearing his ring.

"What? Were you just going to escape without waking me?" he said with mock-hurt, though it was bordering on real hurt by now.

She smiled. "Sorry. Told you I had to get to the office early. I have a client to meet this afternoon and another case…" She trailed off as she looked around, clearly missing something. He smiled and lifted her car keys from the newel post at the bottom of the stairs. She rushed up to him and grabbed them, kissing him long and hard. "Thanks."

"Don't mention it," he mumbled, scratching his scalp. Holy shit. She'd really done a number on his head. She had to be deliberately avoiding him, because all he kept thinking was that she'd said how dead it was at work. Why was she now rushing to get there?

She'd already pulled the front door open but stopped suddenly and came back to him. "Sorry I have to run off. Are you doing anything interesting today?"

He shook his head. He'd hoped to be cuddling in bed with his girlfriend, but it looked like that wouldn't be happening. Again.

"All right! I'll see you!" She pulled his head down for another quick kiss before darting through the screen door, letting it slam behind her.

He followed her, stopping in the doorway, watching her climb into the tall Jeep.

She didn't even wave as she pulled away.

5

Kylie drove into work after ditching Linc, her fingers shaking on the steering wheel.

Yes, she actually felt like she'd ditched him. The way she'd tried to skulk out the door before he woke up…was terrible. Then, when he'd come down the stairs and caught her trying to slip away, she'd averted her eyes, guilty as charged, and ran as fast as she could to get away from him, like a criminal avoiding pursuit.

She'd ditched him.

And he didn't deserve that.

"What's wrong with me?" she asked the road. The road said nothing in return, just twisted its way down the mountain, the sharp curves feeling like a resemblance of her life.

When she came to the place where she and Vader had gone off the road, she carefully adverted her eyes once again from the shiny section of guardrail. Against her will, her heartrate increased, and she took several deep breaths trying to calm herself.

But her thinking didn't calm.

She couldn't stop from thinking of how terrible she'd been to Linc. She'd given him a terrible haircut, then avoided him the rest of the night. She'd tried to sneak away this morning and could barely look him in the eye when he found her before she could creep out the door.

They'd only known each other a few months, but they'd been through a great deal together during that time. On the surface, they seemed an unlikely pair. She was outgoing and bubbly. He was calm and contained. But instead of their personalities competing with each other, they complemented each other. His calm soothed her, bringing her back to reality.

Well…it would if she'd let it.

Heck, they still hadn't officially said those three little words that normally preceded a couple moving in together or getting married. Why was that?

Just more to think about.

But she didn't want to think. She wanted to work. She wanted a meaty case.

When she was working, she had something to focus on… someone to save…a mystery to solve. She was important.

Hmmm…importance.

Was that what she truly craved?

Significance. Influential. Relevant.

Or was she just hoping to not be the opposite?

Worthless. Trivial. Dull. Weak. Insignificant.

Like how insignificant you would have to be for your own father to leave you?

She sighed, tears pricking at her eyes. It all circled back to that.

Linc deserved so much better than her, it was ridiculous.

She knew he was the perfect man, but it felt like something was clouding her vision. He was perfect, but she wasn't. That was the problem. She wasn't good enough for him.

But did that matter?

She sighed. She didn't know.

Maybe what she needed was some time away from him. Maybe that would give her a sorely needed dose of perspective. Maybe if she went away and cleared her mind, she'd come home, ready to say those three little words and wholeheartedly mean each syllable, with all that came with them.

Hope. Family. A future.

An unending I'm-here-for-you commitment.

There was only one way she could do that. She had to find her dad.

Not just for herself. For them. Her and Linc.

Everything in her head seemed to be pointing her toward New York. She needed to make it happen. She needed to talk to her boss.

To her surprise, Greg was already in the office by the time she arrived, fiddling with the Keurig she'd gotten him for his birthday the week before. He'd had a regular old coffee pot that had to have been a hundred years old, and it'd spit out burned coffee that was barely fit for human consumption.

Kylie'd thought he would appreciate the upgrade. Unfortunately, Greg had a way of making any technology built in the last twenty years hate him. His computer was constantly giving him the black screen of death, and he hadn't been able to wrangle a single decent cup of coffee out of the Keurig. Kylie didn't understand it. She'd thought the thing was so easy a toddler could do it. Wasn't technology supposed to improve people's lives, not destroy them?

She dropped her purse on her desk as he fisted what was left of his bushy salt and pepper hair in his hands and let out a long string of curses. His normally doughy complexion was bright red.

"Um, dude," she said, walking up to it and noticing the problem right away. "You didn't fill the reservoir with water."

He grumbled something that sounded like *reservoir my ass* under his breath and went back to his seat. "That thing is the devil."

"It is not. Plenty of people love their Keurigs."

"Not me. I don't need coffee anymore. I need Xanax."

She studied him. He looked like he was about two seconds from having steam blow out of both ears like a tea kettle. Her heart sank. This wasn't the mood she needed her boss to be in on the morning she asked for a few days off. She'd just gotten back after a two-week concussion hiatus. She needed to smooth off his rough edges before she could ask.

She went and filled the reservoir at the sink in the back of the office, popped in a new K-Cup, and a few minutes later, delivered him a perfect mug of steaming black coffee, just as he liked it.

"How was your day yesterday?" she asked, gathering her courage. "You doing more surveillance for Impact?" She figured Impact Insurance was a safe bet because it was their biggest client, and he was constantly working with them, doing workers' comp fraud investigations.

He nodded. "Thanks. How was yours? You still working that Davidson case?"

Kylie lifted up a thick file with all the data she'd amassed thus far. "Yep. I'm finishing it up today. I'm meeting with Barbara Davidson this afternoon to turn the goods over to her."

"Good." He flipped on his computer.

The Keurig was strike one. She had to be quick before Windows 98 thwarted him and he started complaining about how stupid it was to buy the computers. She sat on the edge of his desk. "Can I ask you something?"

He looked up at her, eyebrow raised. "You ask me things constantly. Nothing's ever stopped you before."

Well, that was true. Though he was rarely in the office, when he was, she bombarded him with question after question, barely stopping to take a breath. She'd been so hungry to learn everything about the business. It was what she had to do, she thought, in order to become a world-class private eye. And though he was grumpy with his answers, he'd always been helpful.

"I mean, something that's not about the private investigations business."

He raised a suspicious eyebrow. "This ain't personal, is it?"

Kylie knew better than that. Greg didn't like talking about his home life at all. She'd worked for him for months, and she still wasn't one-hundred-percent sure about anything other than that he was a private investigator. "No. I guess it's semi work-related."

He pushed away from the desk and laced his hands over his pot belly. "Shoot."

"Well, you know I haven't taken any time off, except for when I was recovering from that gunshot wound, and the car crash and—"

"Are you asking for a vacation? Approved," he said, slamming his fist on the desk like a judge hammering down a gavel. Case closed.

That was it?

Kylie's eyes widened. "Wait. Really? I thought you'd say something about how I needed to ask for one in advance, because you really needed me, or—"

"In case you didn't notice, short stuff, we don't have any pressing life or death cases. And Jesus, you were nearly killed a few times, and you got your car torched, all in the line of duty. I'm thinking you're due a little break."

She smiled, not just because he'd approved her request but because of the backhanded compliment. "Really? So, it's not a problem? But what about the—" She waved her hand toward the... hmm, there really wasn't a very big stack of paperwork because she'd gotten things all caught up already. Maybe she wasn't a total failure at every part of her life after all.

"The filing can wait. Go." He waved his hand in a shooing motion. "Be young. Have fun with that dreamy boyfriend of yours."

Her stomach sank. Yes, she supposed that was what most people her age would be up to—having good, footloose and fancy-free times with their significant others. But no, not Kylie Hatfield. She couldn't just be happy with what was right in front of her. She had to go digging up the past, hoping the skeletons in her family's closet didn't jump out and kick her curious ass.

She was officially the worst girlfriend in the world. The craziest person on earth.

But maybe...just maybe...if she could have some type of closure around her father's abandonment, she could lay that fear to rest.

"Thank you," she said, going back to her desk and opening her computer. "I'll just be gone a couple days. Three at the most. I...I mean, we'll probably—"

"Whatever. Take the whole rest of the week, if you want to." He was stabbing his finger at the keyboard, and she smiled, affection for the grump nearly bringing tears to her eyes.

What was wrong with her?

For the rest of the day, she did her best to prepare for her two o'clock appointment with Barbara Davidson. Not prepare physically...she had all the research she needed and had spoken to everyone she needed to speak to. From a purely private investigator perspective, this one was open and shut.

Emotionally, though? Even as she walked into the coffee shop, she was still torn on what she should do. As she stepped through the door, she tossed up a prayer that she'd say the right words.

She found Barbara already waiting, looking very nervous. Equipped with her thick manila folder, Kylie sat across from the older woman and passed on coffee when the waitress came by. She was already too jittery.

"Did you find anything out?" Barbara asked anxiously, wrapping her hands around her coffee mug.

Kylie pressed her lips together, thinking of what that poor woman on the phone had said to her. She'd gotten into this business to help people, not ruin lives. She knew Barbara wanted to know…but did she really need to know this news?

Barbara's birth mother, Sarah, ran away from home when she was only thirteen years old, escaping an abusive father who'd been raping her since she was six. Alone and broke, Sarah was pulled into the world of drugs and prostitution. When her pimp found out she was pregnant, he kicked her in the stomach so many times that the baby shouldn't have lived.

The baby did.

In the hospital, Sarah was taken into protective custody and sent to a home for wayward girls. There, she gave birth and the baby was whisked away within the first minute of delivery.

"What did I have to offer a child?" Sarah had told Kylie when Kylie appeared at the woman's door. "And how could I ever face her? I was a drugged-up prostitute who didn't even know the baby's father."

But the woman wasn't any of that now. Which was why Kylie had been so puzzled and sad that she refused to meet her long-lost daughter. So far, in every adoption case she'd investigated, the biological parent had been open to see their child.

Not Sarah.

"I can't do it," she told Kylie. "I can't think about those dark days, of the grief and loss, of the fear and guilt. I can't do it, and I won't."

Sarah explained that no one in her new life knew that she'd had a baby that young. They knew nothing of the abuse, the prostitution. The drugs.

"I clawed my way out of that life and turned it all around. I married a preacher. I am a respected member of my church and my community. I have three other children."

In a nutshell, this could destroy her life.

Sometimes, knowledge wasn't power. Sometimes, it could be a bad thing.

And where was Kylie going? To New York to find a father who obviously didn't want to be found. And if she did find him and he had a story as heartbreaking as Sarah's, what would she do? What if she found her father and wished she hadn't? She couldn't simply unlearn the things she found out.

Fighting back the tears that seemed to be on the surface today, Kylie met Barbara's nervous gaze across the table. She needed to just give her the news, like ripping off a bandage.

"I found your birth mother, and I'm very sorry to tell you that she wouldn't give me permission to give you her information."

Kylie had warned Barbara at the beginning that this result could be a possibility. It was even written in the contract Barbara had signed too.

Still…the look in the woman's eyes was devastating. Kylie reached over the table and covered her hand with her own.

"I'm so sorry, Barbara. I spoke to her at length, and she told me that she didn't want you to carry the burden of knowing your birth story, but that she thinks of you every day and lights a candle on your birthday each year."

Barbara swallowed hard and squeezed Kylie's fingers. "Are you sure? Can you tell me the…circumstances of my birth?"

Kylie hated to disappoint her even more. "She was adamant that I not tell you because she said she wanted you to focus on your future, not your past. She told me to tell you that she wanted the best for you and that she knew she wouldn't be able to give you anything close to what you deserved, and she said that she hoped you would see her giving you up as an ultimate act of love rather than an act of abandonment."

That word again.

Kylie cleared her throat and reached into the folder and pulled out the letter Sarah had written her daughter and slid it across the table to the devastated woman.

"She wanted me to give you this."

Barbara took the letter in trembling fingers. She didn't open it, though, and Kylie didn't blame her. It was something better done in private, and Kylie deeply hoped it gave the woman some peace.

"I gave her your contact information in case she changes her mind."

Barbara simply nodded, staring at her named scrawled across the front of the envelope. Her mother's handwriting. The first time Barbara had ever seen something so personal from the woman who'd given her life.

Dreading this next part even more, Kylie pulled out another envelope. The invoice.

She felt terrible.

The retainer was nonrefundable and the fee plus expenses was due at the delivery of whatever information was found, regardless of whether anything was turned up. That was just standard operating procedure, Greg had told her, when Kylie questioned why they'd charge people if they delivered absolutely nothing. All the investigators charged similarly.

Business was business and all that, but still…

"What's that?"

Kylie nearly told her it was nothing and slid it back into the folder. Instead, she did what she was obligated to do… slid it over to the other woman. "I'm so sorry, but it's the invoice."

Barbara simply nodded and put it in her purse.

KYLIE WANTED to stay and talk to the woman about her feelings, but she wasn't qualified to be a counselor to anyone, even herself.

Plus, she could almost hear Greg talking in her head. *If you want to help people work through their family problems, that's a different line of work. Become a psychologist.*

"I'm sorry I couldn't deliver what you were hoping for," Kylie said.

Barbara took a sip from her mug. "It's okay. Maybe it was meant to remain hidden for a reason."

Kylie nodded. "Maybe."

And her own mother might have been right. Maybe no good would come from finding out about her dad.

But as Kylie left the coffee shop, she couldn't help thinking about the bad things that were happening in her life because she had so many questions about her father. She was so scared of whatever characteristics he might've passed on to her that she didn't know if committing to Linc was a good idea. She was on her way to ruining her relationship with the man she loved because of it.

It was worth the risk.

Barbara had risked finding out about her mother, but she seemed to be glad she'd tried anyway.

Kylie climbed in her Jeep, and as she headed back to the office, decided to make plans to travel up to The Big Apple tomorrow. She'd never been there before, and she'd have to book a flight and hotel in a rush, but she was convinced it would be worth it.

She was ready to find Adam Hatfield and get her answers.

6

_____

It was never more apparent to Kylie how much Linc loved her as he sat on the corner of the four-poster bed, silently watching her pack her suitcase. He had a lot of clothes, mostly t-shirts and cargo pants, but he'd cleared away nearly three-quarters of his drawer and closet space so that she could fit the pieces of her wardrobe that had slowly migrated to his place. And he did her laundry, too, folding everything so neatly, with military precision.

She'd never felt so guilty.

She wasn't exactly lying to him, but she wasn't exactly telling him the truth, either.

Linc was fully supportive of her finding her father, but when he said that, she knew he meant an internet search. A phone call. Not hopping on a plane and tracking him down in person. That, to Linc, would be too risky. But to Kylie? It was a necessity.

"I'll only be two days," she said, packing some jeans, some tights, some skirts…more than she could possibly need, but the weather was supposed to be warm during the day and cold at night, so she needed a little bit of everything. "Thank you for taking care of Vader for me."

He didn't say a word, but she could tell he wasn't happy. Or maybe he was just unhappy about his hair because he kept taking off his baseball cap and scratching at the fuzz.

"Adoption case, you said? Didn't you just finish one of those?"

She rolled a pair of jeans to tuck into a corner. "Yeah. This is, um, something similar. Kid trying to find their bio father."

He scratched his head again. "In New York City?"

"Yeah. Good place for people to get lost, I guess." She laughed, but it sounded nervous as hell, so she slammed her lips shut.

"Sounds like it. Sounds like Greg's really giving you a lot of responsibility."

She smiled, more genuinely this time. "Yeah, I think he is. He actually seems kinda proud of me and seems happy with what I've been turning out so far."

Linc stood and walked over to her, pressing his lips to her forehead. "He should. You've given Starr Investigations a lot of good PR these past few months."

She pressed her face to his chest. "Right. Good PR that people remember for about five minutes. Things are a little slow right now. Greg said the phone rang off the wall the first week, but I was out with the concussion so…" She shrugged and pulled away, lifting her face for a proper kiss before returning to her packing.

Kylie went to her dresser and picked up the airline ticket. A last-minute ticket meant she was in the middle seat, at the absolute rear of the plane. Good thing the flight was only a couple hours. "Are you sure you don't mind taking me to the airport? It's terribly early."

She had to be at the airport by five.

He took out his phone and took a picture of the ticket, making Kylie smile. "You think I'll lose it?"

Linc chuckled, that low, deep sound that did something twisty to her insides. "Nah…I'm a just-in-case kind of man, if you haven't noticed."

She winked at him. "I've noticed for sure."

Still smiling, he looked back at the ticket, and the smile slid away. "You ever been to New York? Big city. I'd feel better if you were going with someone."

Someone…like him. Ordinarily, she would have liked to have him along, but not this time. For some reason, this trip seemed too personal, and she didn't want to be distracted by anything.

"You been there?" she asked, heading into the bathroom to gather her toiletries.

"Hell no. Never want to go, either. Too big for my taste."

She met his gaze in the mirror. "So, what good would it be if you came with me? It'd be like the blind leading the blind. I'll be fine. I know New Yorkers have a bad rap for being unfriendly, but I'm sure they'll help me out if I get lost."

"Just make sure they don't help you out of your wallet," he said, reaching over and batting her purse. "Keep it close to you at all times."

She forced the annoyed look from her expression and focused on gathering the makeup she'd need into her travel case. Ever since he found out she was going to the city, he'd been peppering her with safety tidbits, making her more and more nervous and doubtful. He was probably right to be doing so. She could be careless and forgetful at times, but she was getting better.

"I'll be fine."

She wasn't really fine, though. Even after they made love, she wasn't able to sleep. Part of it was because she knew she had to get up at three-thirty to get to the airport and was afraid of oversleeping. The other part was that she kept thinking, in less than twenty-four hours, she could potentially meet her father. The man of the faded photo would cross the line into a living, breathing person.

It made her queasy, just thinking of what she'd say. What she'd do. And what would he do? Hug her? Cry? Tell her to go to hell?

It was almost a relief when her alarm went off and she jumped into the shower. As Linc drove her to the airport, he kept drumming his fingers on the steering wheel, a sure sign that he was nervous. It only added to her worries.

When he pulled up at the drop-off lane in front of her terminal, she leaned over the console and kissed his cheek. "Don't worry about me. I'll text you when I get there."

He caught her chin and gave her a proper kiss. "You're gonna be in one of the biggest cities on earth, Lee. Worry is a given."

"I'll text often," she promised, then wiggled her eyebrows. "Will you text me back?"

He was notoriously the worst communicator she'd ever known.

Linc ran his hand through her hair. "Yeah. Maybe even more than a word or two."

She opened her eyes in mock surprise. "What about an emoji? Will you send me an emoji?"

He looked horrified, but a smiled played on his mouth, giving his humor away. "You'll have to wait and see."

She kissed him again. "And on that note, I better go."

Kylie opened her door and wasn't surprised when he opened his too. He'd never let her wrestle her own bag onto the curb. As she slipped out of the truck, he came around, pulled out her case, set its wheels on the sidewalk, extending the telescoping handle for her. Such a thoughtful man. "Do well, then come back to me."

Emotion filled her chest, burning into her face and making her heart pound. She reached for him and did something she been wanting to do for a long time. She took his beautiful face in her hands and waited until he looked directly into her eyes.

"I love you, Linc. I know I'm not doing it right, and I know I'm screwed up and act crazy," her voice grew thick with emotion, "but I'm going to try to pull myself together and be the person you deserve."

He swept the tear that fell away with his thumb. "I love you too, Lee. And I know I'm screwed up and act crazy," he swept away another tear, "and I'm trying to pull myself together and be the person you deserve."

Kylie smiled through the tears, and hope...that awful, terrible emotion she was afraid would break her heart...filled her. She was still afraid, deeply, deeply afraid, and she'd probably faint if he dropped to his knee at this moment, but she loved him and he loved her. The words had been said. That was a start, and that was enough. For now.

"See you soon," she said, rising to her toes for another kiss.

When he let her go, she found it really hard to turn away, put her hand on her suitcase, and walk to the entrance. Before she stepped through the door, she looked back, saw him leaning against his truck.

She waved, and he waved back.

He was so damn good. Too good for her.

But she was working on getting better, just like his therapy sessions for his PTSD were working for him.

This was her therapy, she realized as she went through the security checkpoint, got herself a coffee and a muffin, and found her gate. She'd find her father, probably get her heart broken just as she'd broken Barbara's heart yesterday. Then, she'd move on.

Her phone dinged, and she smiled when she looked at the screen.

It was a text from Linc, and it contained one thing. A hearts-for-eyes emoji.

She sent him the blowing-a-heart-kiss emoji in return.

Sipping her coffee, she was still smiling when she began research on her phone, looking at all the places she was hoping to visit. Most of the hotels inside her budget were booked solid at this late notice, so she'd made a reservation at a hotel near the dive in Brooklyn where her parents once lived, and only hoped it wasn't in a terrible area of town.

It probably was. But it was close to Cityside Garbage Services, which would be one of her first stops. She'd also looked into the Brooklyn Diner, where her mother had worked, but the restaurant had burned down about a decade ago. That was okay. This hotel room was in the middle of the action, and that's where she needed to be.

She heard Linc's voice in her head: *Are you crazy? You're just asking for trouble.*

And maybe she was. She planned to buy some pepper spray the minute she found a store since she wasn't able to carry any on the plane. She'd packed a rape whistle and had brought the crossbody purse with the long strap so she could wear it over her head and not have it easily snatched. She was prepared.

Of course, Linc would probably tell her she wasn't prepared enough. He was always coming up with dangers she never thought about. Living in his mind must've been a crazy experience, considering how many "what ifs" he came up with on a daily basis. It was a wonder he could still function in this world.

Then she sighed and berated herself. She was thinking

about Linc again when she needed to concentrate on her father.

The two-hour flight to Newark International was uneventful, but when she stepped out into the taxi line, she started to wonder if she had bit off more than she could chew. Everything she knew about New York made it seem like, well, a wonderful town, as Frank Sinatra would say.

Most of her impression of the city had been amassed by watching movies where people fell in love at the top of the Empire State Building and had amazing adventures running through Times Square or Rockefeller Plaza or under the lights of Broadway. She hadn't really expected it to be so... cold and depressing. There were people swarming around, filling every available space. Nobody made eye contact with her. A man bumped into her and didn't even acknowledge the contact, much less say he was sorry.

As she moved up in the line, she started to wonder if she had made a mistake. She knew that was what Linc would've said. After all, there was no telling whether her father even still lived in the city. It had been nearly twenty-five years, and people moved around all the time. Maybe he'd left years ago.

When she finally got into a cab, she heaved a sigh of relief, and then realized the driver was looking at her expectantly, a slightly annoyed expression on his face. "I'm sorry. The Piedmark Inn in Bushwick, please. That's in Brooklyn."

Without saying a word, he nodded and started to drive into a sea of traffic.

She checked her phone. It was just after ten. She leaned forward and said, "How long do you think that might take?"

He lifted both shoulders to his ears. "Depends. Half an hour to forever."

The snark made her smile. It seemed that all the taxi drivers in movies had that cocky little bit of snark, and for some odd reason, the thought brought her a bit of comfort. In movies, the guy started out gruff but eventually warmed up and imparted some life-saving bit of advice to the main character that would save her life.

So far, unless mumbled cursed words helped her out in a pinch, she was screwed.

Kylie was excited when they went through the Holland Tunnel, but it proved to be less interesting than she'd hoped. After that, it was stop and go, all the way to Brooklyn. Kylie felt like she could've walked it faster, but if she had, Linc surely would've had something to say about it. Every block they passed looked like a bad area of town, and instead of getting better, it only seemed to get worse. When the cab driver pulled over to the curb at a run-down building, Kylie looked up at it and prayed that wasn't her hotel.

The driver got out and went to the back of the car to get her bags.

Oh, god. It *was* her hotel.

She stepped out and took a closer look, hoping to glimpse some of the charm she'd seen while booking the place online. She couldn't. Where had those thick prison bars on the windows come from? There had been *flowers* in the windows in the picture on the internet, not bars. In fact, she was pretty sure the building on the internet was different altogether.

She sniffed and inhaled a strong whiff of what smelled like sewage. Gagging, she looked down the street, past discarded trash of all sorts rolling around in the stiff breeze, at a gang of men who were eying her up like it was dinnertime and she was on the menu. The buildings cast sinister shadows down upon her and the rest of the street, blocking out the sun. She felt a little like Snow White in a concrete forest.

"Thank you," she said to the driver, handing over her

cash. He didn't respond; the second she slammed the door, he sped away from the curb, tires screeching.

She quickly rolled her suitcase across the walk into the lobby of the Piedmark, trying her best to ignore the sixties paneled walls and lime green shag carpet, the peeling paint on the ceiling, and the strong smell of urine. It looked like the living room of a serial killer.

Can't wait to see what my room looks like.

The woman at the desk had three-inch black roots under her platinum dye job, and the complexion and bloodshot eyes of a meth-head. She actually snarled at her. "What do you want?"

"I have a reservation? Under the name of Hatfield?" For some reason, everything she said was coming out as a question, probably because she was now questioning positively *everything* about this trip.

The woman looked down at something. "Yeah. Check-in's at three, but what the hell. You're room's ready."

Kylie pushed her credit card over to the lady, promising herself she'd check online for errant charges later that night. The woman ran the card and handed her a worn key on a plastic keychain, then pointed the way to an elevator.

The elevator was more like a death trap. At one point, it made a groaning sound and stopped, and Kylie thought she might be stuck in there, with four walls covered in gum and graffiti closing in on her, for the rest of the night. Finally, it opened on her floor, and she found her room.

It was just as she'd thought—more sixties fixtures and a mattress so misshapen that it looked like it still had a body sleeping in it. Or dead in it. This room had an upgrade, though. Instead of smelling like cat pee, it bore the pungent aroma of stale cigarettes.

Exhausted, Kylie wanted to lie down in bed and rest. But not that bed. Instead, she sat on the very edge of the bed and wondered if she should've sprung for a nicer place in Manhattan. Then she wondered, for the hundredth time, whether she should've come at all.

Sighing, she got to her feet and freshened up at the cracked, rust-stained sink while looking into a mirror that had someone's cherry-red lipstick kisses smeared on the glass. After that, she felt better. It was still early, so there was plenty of time to do a little exploring. If only what she'd seen out the window of the taxi hadn't been so, well…frightening.

Still, she'd be fine. Those people outside might have looked tough, but that didn't mean they were going to mug her. Her parents had lived in this neighborhood, and they'd survived. Sure, it was a different time, but it would be okay. People were people, and in her optimistic viewpoint, mostly good. She could do this.

She texted Linc: *In the Big Apple! Just got to my hotel. So far, so good.*

Total overstatement. She promised she'd take a picture to send to him, one that didn't make it look like she was two seconds away from getting murdered.

She looked around. She'd have to do that later.

Her phone dinged. He'd responded exactly as she thought he would: *Stay safe.*

She went back outside to the sidewalk and looked up and down. Still nothing she could snap a picture of that wouldn't make this place look scary beyond belief. Wasn't there a single person in this city who didn't look like the Big Bad Wolf? Everyone and everything seemed foreign and sinister.

As she was trying to orient herself to the direction she needed to travel, she spotted two of the same gangbangers, possibly in the middle of a drug deal. They headed her way.

Oh, hell no. She turned to leave but then one of them said, "Hey, mama. Where you going? Talk to us."

She didn't want to be rude. But she also didn't want to be dead. Instincts warred within her.

Finally, she whirled, a big, bright smile on her face.

"Hi," she said in her gruffest voice. "Either of you know where Cityside Garbage Services is?"

The guy in the Mets cap and a scraggly beard grinned and picked the toothpick out from between his lips. "Sure do. What's a pretty thing like you doing looking for a place like that?"

"Yeah," the other said. He was bald and wore a wifebeater that showcased a sleeve of tattoos up each arm. "You don't look like you belong there. But if you want dirty, we've got it right here."

Adrenaline shot through her system like a hurricane, causing her heart rate to pick up by about a hundred beats. Still, she did her best to give them a nonchalant shrug, even though her whole body was trembling. "I have business there."

"Oh, you do?" Mets Cap Guy asked, punching his friend playfully on the arm. They both had huge biceps and Kylie's eyes were drawn to the tattoo Mets Cap Guy had snaking up his neck and to the side of his face, though she couldn't figure out what it was. Another one of the tattoos, this one on his hand, had a skull and said something about blood. "She's got *business*. That sounds serious, mama."

The man with the wifebeater came up close to her, so close she could smell the cigarettes on his breath. He was looking at her, and not in a friendly way, his eyes scraping over her body like claws. His gaze stopped at her cleavage and he licked his lips.

This was not good.

Kylie sucked in a deep breath. "Do you mind telling me the way? I'm late," she said primly, surprised that her voice never wavered.

Because what she was really thinking was, *These guys are going to rape me, murder me, and stuff me in a trash bin, and I'll never see Asheville again.*

And Linc will probably stand at my grave and say, "I told you so."

Damn him. He was right about her. Again.

She really did need to learn to look before she leaped.

7

"I can't thank you enough," Kylie said to the two men, Tomas and Jose, as the two of them flanked her like an entourage, delivering her right to the front door of Cityside Garbage Services. They were brothers, it turned out, and they both worked for the company as trash collectors and had just gotten off their shifts.

She still couldn't believe how their attitude had changed the moment she'd tapped the Facebook app on her phone and started a live video.

"Hey, friends and family," she'd said into the phone's camera. "I'm live in the big city of New York and have just met two really nice men who are going to help me get to where I'm going."

The moment she'd turned the camera on the two men, their entire personalities had changed.

Whew. That had been close.

As it turned out, Tomas and Jose were pretty nice guys when they weren't being jerks. When she'd asked them to introduce themselves to all her Facebook friends, they'd spoken of their big families. Wives and lots of children whose names they went through so quickly, Kylie couldn't remember all of them. The two of them insisted on escorting her door to door, and never stopped talking the entire way.

"De nada," Tomas said, bowing to her. "Hope you get that business of yours done soon, girl, because this ain't the place for a girl like you."

"I'm stronger than I look," she told them with a hint of pride. "You know, I single-handedly brought down a serial killer."

They both laughed, slapping their thighs.

"I'm serious!" she said, her hands on her hips. "I'm a private investigator. I've solved murders."

They snorted again. She could tell they still didn't believe her.

"Right, mama." Jose winked at her. "You need us to wait for you?"

"Thank you," she said, shaking their hands. "You're really the first two nice people I've met in this city. I was scared I'd have to go home to Asheville empty-handed."

Or that I wouldn't go home at all. I was afraid you two were going to kill me, honestly, and I'd never get back there.

"Asheville?" Tomas asked, scratching his head. "Where's that?"

"North Carolina."

"Ah! You hear that, Jose?" Tomas said, shoving his brother's beefy shoulder. "She's a real Southern belle."

Jose laughed. "A murder-solving Southern belle. We don't get girls like you around here."

Southern belle. It reminded her of the story her mother told her about her father. She smiled, and then shivered, thinking of what answers might lie right behind the doors of this one-story, crumbling brick building. The place backed up to a bunch of old burned-out buildings, and the yard with the fleet of green garbage trucks was surrounded by barbed-wire fencing.

It didn't smell the greatest here either. In fact, this smell scoured her nostrils. New York was definitely a city of interesting smells, and none of them had been particularly pleasing so far. She'd never take the air in North Carolina for granted again.

"Again, thank you," she said as she waved to them and climbed the steps. They started to walk back the way they'd come, and Kylie felt positive for the first time since she'd boarded the plane. Maybe she would be able to make a good connection or even find her father after all.

When she opened the door to the dark office with the low ceiling, she saw a series of desks, scattered with paper. No people. The place stunk of old cigarettes and someone's burnt microwave popcorn. She called out, "Hello?"

"Hold your horses," a voice grouched to her from behind the stacks. An older woman with crazy salt and pepper hair and thick glasses poked her head up. She looked Kylie over, a scowl of disgust on her face. "You a bill collector? We're closed. Come back tomorrow."

Kylie pointed to the door behind her. "Door was open, and I only have a few questions. Is the owner here?"

The woman snorted. "Owner? Owner's on his golf course in Jersey. As usual. I'm the one in charge when the cat's away. What questions?"

"Well," Kylie began, reaching into her messenger bag. "I have—"

"Are you selling cosmetics? Does it look like I wear cosmetics?" she said, her eyes traveling over Kylie like a scouring pad.

"No." *Does it look like I sell cosmetics?* Kylie wondered. "I'm trying to track down a former employee of Cityside Garbage Services, and I was hoping to get some information."

The woman wheeled her chair closer, then stood and came to her full height, which Kylie realized was tiny. She was barely four and a half feet. She peeled off those thick glasses and looked up at Kylie with watery green eyes. "I've worked here for over thirty years. I know everyone we've employed." She tapped the side of her head. "Photographic memory. Who're you talking about?"

Kylie knew there was no such thing as a truly photographic memory, but even so, a woman with a great memory was a good sign. "His name is Adam Hatfield. He might have worked here about twenty-five years ago?"

The woman's pinched, pockmarked faced wrinkled some more as she shook her head slowly.

"Doesn't sound familiar. Hatfield, you say?" She started cleaning the lenses with the hem of her bright yellow t-shirt from a place called Crazy Eddie's Electronics.

Kylie nodded. "He was tall, slim, had dark hair. I believe he was one of the collectors here."

Her eyes widened. "Wait…Hatfield. I'm starting to remember."

Kylie's heart leapt. "You do?"

"Yeah, Adam Hatfield, first name William, I think."

Kylie got excited. She'd seen her birth certificate a couple times, of course, but her mom always kept it in the safe deposit box the rest of the time. Anytime Rhonda ever spoke of her father, Adam was the name she used. But his first name was William, so this had to be him!

"Most people around here called him Bill or Billy." The woman scratched her head, little flakes of dandruff drifting down onto her shoulders. "That was definitely at the beginning of my tenure here, though, but I remember him. He was a total dish. I was just a little thing back then, barely out of my teens, but he had all the ladies on leashes. Used to flirt incessantly. I remember his partner was a little miffed that they always got off late on their route because he was too busy charming the women in the office. He was a smooth talker, that man."

The woman sounded like Kylie's mother, the way her eyes glazed over and her voice got high and faraway. Kylie jumped on the lead, her heart speeding up. "Do you happen to remember what he looked like?"

"Oh, he was a total dish. Just like you said. Thick dark hair, medium build. Could charm the panties off any girl. That's what I remember about him. Never tried his luck with me, though. He was dating some girl, if I remember correctly. Got married. Moved away. Or something." She shrugged. "Long time ago. I don't remember."

Kylie tapped the camera screen on her phone and pulled up the photo she'd taken of her little family picture, though she'd cropped herself and her mom from the image. "Could this be him?"

The woman squinted at the screen. "Yeah." She tapped the glass. "That's him, sure as shit."

Kylie's heart picked up speed. "Do you remember anything else about him at all?"

"I can check my files if you want."

"Yes, please. I appreciate it."

She disappeared behind the stack of papers as Kylie looked around, drumming her fingers on the counter. The place looked like it hadn't been renovated in many years, so it was possible her father could've leaned against this exact same counter with its cracked plastic overlay.

Underneath the plastic was a faded calendar and a brochure that said CITYSIDE GARBAGE SERVICES – Waste Management at its finest! Even though the counter was coated in something that looked like caked on dirt, she ran a finger over it, imagining him standing in that very spot over two decades ago.

The woman came into view again, holding a yellowing index card. She tilted her nose up to peer down through her bifocals. "Yes, here it is. Hatfield, employed with us twenty odd years ago. He quit work suddenly and left no forwarding address. From what I seem to remember, it was pretty abrupt. Like he just didn't show up one day and we had to scramble around to find a replacement. That's not unusual, but I remember it because so many of the girls in the office were heartbroken."

Great. My father was a massive player with no work ethic.

"And you don't know where he might have gone?"

The woman looked up at the ceiling, deep in thought. "Now that I come to think of it, he was in thick with the former owners. Very thick."

"Former owners? Who were they?"

"Yeah. Joey Gallo. They owned the place, but like the current ownership, were pretty hands-off. Hung out on the golf course, probably, and managed from afar, so I never saw 'em. Supposedly Gallo got sent to jail, and so the family decided to sell." She looked both ways and whispered, "He and his boys were into some illegal things, I think. Owned a lot of this city but acquired it in kind of fishy ways."

Kylie's eyes widened. Did that have anything to do with her father's weird disappearance? "Do you think this Hatfield was into illegal things too?"

She hitched a shoulder. "Who knows? Wouldn't put it past a smooth-talker like him."

Kylie nodded, wondering if that was why he'd disappeared without a trace. It felt like she was chipping away at an answer, but instead of a picture of her father becoming clearer, it was only opening up more questions that Kylie was dying to answer.

Kylie stood on her tiptoes and leaned over the counter to try to see if there was anything else on the card, but the woman hugged it close to her chest. "Wait. What you want with him?" The old lady's eyes were narrowed in suspicion.

Kylie gritted her teeth and picked one of the excuses she'd thought of on the plane. "Just trying to track him down. I'm from Publishers Clearing House, and he may be our next big winner." Kylie told the lie with a straight face.

Before Kylie's eyes, the lady grew excited, her pinched face brightening in a way Kylie wouldn't have believed was possible. "Really? I enter those all the time. My friends say they don't think people win, but I always believe. Do you have one of those big checks for him?"

She nodded as the woman dropped the card on the table between them. Kylie inspected it for more information. Other than his sparse work history and old address above the Able Body Hardware Store where her mother said they lived when they were first married, there wasn't much else.

"Yeah. In my car," she said absently, pulling out her notebook and scribbling down the name, *Bill Hatfield.* "Do you happen to remember any rumors about where he liked to go, things like that?"

She shook her head. "Sorry, girlie. I'm a dead end."

Right. "Well, thank you." Kylie forced a smile before turning to leave and decided to head down to Able Body Hardware. Climbing down the steps of the old building, she entered the name of the store into the GPS on her phone and found it wasn't more than a block away.

She walked to the end of the block, where the barbed-wire fencing became a bunch of burned-out row homes. Then she passed a sinister-looking bar called The Happy Owl—the people outside looked anything but happy and glared at her like she was an unwanted guest.

Across the street, she saw it. The Able Body Hardware Store. The glass windows were soaped up, and a sign had been propped up in the door: AVAILABLE. It looked as though the place had been closed for a long time.

Kylie's eyes trailed upward to the second floor, where her parents had once happily lived. Her mother had called the place a dump even back then—and Kylie had to admit, it hadn't improved. The two tiny visible windows had been boarded up, and the staircase leading to the door on the second-floor landing was nothing but a pile of splintered wood. Weeds grew like a jungle in the vacant lot next door, tangling through oil drums and discarded tires.

Kylie knew she would find no answers there. Maybe if she called the number on the sign, but that would likely just get her to a realty company. She doubted they'd have any details about who'd rented the place before, and if they did, they probably wouldn't give them to a stranger over the phone.

She tapped on her chin, wondering where else she could turn, when she noticed the curtains in the apartment across the street open and close. Great. The last thing she needed was to get shot for loitering.

She meandered down the street when it occurred to her that she had no idea where she was. She looked around, realizing that the neighborhood had gone from ghetto to something that looked more like a war zone. Hugging her purse tight to her side, she looked up and tried to reorient herself so that she could get back to the Piedmark.

Her neck prickled. Without Tomas and Jose, she was lost.

By the time she walked another few blocks, her feet had started to ache. She really was stupid to come all this way without solid leads to go on. Greg would've told her this was a waste of time and money, since he never allowed for travel expenses unless there was a solid lead. And what had she had? A name. A city. A company. From twenty-five years ago. It wasn't a lead. Wasn't even half a lead. It was…nothing.

No. Not exactly nothing. Her father, she was sure, had worked here. Had left here. But where had he gone?

As she was about to sit down on a curb and pull up Google Maps, she looked up, and all the air in her lungs went out in a whoosh.

Across the street, there was a building lot surrounded in chain-link fence. A sign attached to the fence said *D & H Construction—Builders of Manhattan's Most Distinctive Properties! Revitalizing Downtown Brooklyn!*

She almost turned away before reading the rest, but then the words hit her. Owners: Dennis DeRoss and William Hatfield.

She stared, mouth open, then stood up straight and started to walk toward it as a truck rumbled by, blaring its horn at her.

Holy shit, she thought. D & H Construction. DeRoss and Hatfield.

Excited now, Kylie wrote down the phone number and address underneath the logo and went to hail a cab. After a few false starts, she finally managed to get one to pull over. She climbed inside and gave the driver the address.

"Sure thing, girl," the dreadlocked man said in a thick Jamaican accent that immediately made her smile. "Anything to save you from dat hellhole. Why you off in a neighborhood like dat?"

She was happy this driver seemed more pleasant than the other one. "I got lost."

"Ya tellin' me. Ya get your butt to Manhattan, girl, where ya belong."

"I'm actually from North Carolina."

He laughed, the sound strangely lyrical. "Aw, Dorothy, ya ain't in Kansas no more. You gotta watch where ya step!"

She thanked him, and as he took off, she punched in the phone number for the company, not sure what she was going to say. Was her father really William Hatfield? Was this really her father's company?

A receptionist answered. "D & H Construction, how may I direct your call?"

"Yes. Hello," Kylie said, thinking quickly. "I had an appointment today with Mr. Hatfield regarding a project I'm working on, but I had my purse stolen with my datebook and can't seem to find the time. Can you help me?"

"Of course. Let me pull up his schedule. Are you Willis at one? Or Brown at three?"

Kylie checked her phone. It was just after twelve. She wanted to get in with him as soon as possible. She thought about lying and saying she was Willis, but if she showed up at the same time as the real Willis, things could get awkward.

"Oh, dear," Kylie said. "I'm neither. I was certain that it was today. I'm already traveling in from out of state."

"That's all right," the receptionist said professionally. "I can book you in for two. What is your name?"

"Ky—" she blurted before remembering that she should be using an alias. "Kyleen…Ravenclaw." Where the hell had that come from? *Harry Potter*? She hadn't read that since sixth grade.

"And what is this in reference to?"

Yes, that was the question. She knew *whether or not he's my dad* probably wouldn't fly, nor would anything regarding wizarding. "I have a large project that I need his help on. My brownstone is—"

"You understand that D & H Construction only handles commercial construction?" the woman said, still kindly, but Kylie could tell she was losing patience. "Most of our projects are billion-dollar undertakings."

No, she hadn't known that at all because she'd come up with this idea on the fly instead of doing her research first, like an experienced private investigator would do. She could see Greg wagging his thick finger at her now.

"Yes. As I was saying, I was planning to knock down my old brownstone and put up a…shopping mall." Kylie immediately felt dumb. Not because of the half-assed excuse, but because her voice had suddenly taken on a snooty English accent. The cab driver looked at her through the rearview mirror and shook his head, confirming she probably sounded dumb.

"All right. I'll put you in for two," the woman on the other end said.

"See that you do," Kylie said primly, rolling her eyes at her own ridiculousness. "I shall look forward to it."

She cringed. She needed to hang up before *Kyleen Ravenclaw* punctuated this whole act with a *Cheerio!* Ending the call, she looked outside. They'd cruised into downtown Manhattan's Financial District, where many people were dressed in suits and ties. She looked down at herself. She was wearing her comfy jeans and blouse.

Oh, this simply will not do, Lady Ravenclaw.

She leaned forward and addressed the driver. "Can we stop at a store?"

He shot her a curious look. "What kind of store, baby?"

"For like, clothes?"

He laughed. "Baby, ya be goin' to Midtown Manhattan. Ya be havin' your choice of clothing stores. Ya see a place, shout it out, and I'll get ya there."

She wanted to beg him to just take her by the hand and lead the way. She had no idea what she was doing. Her favorite clothing store was Target, and she'd never spent more than fifty dollars on any one piece of clothes in her life.

Then she saw it. Nirvana.

"There…" She pointed excitedly. "Take me there."

Chuckling, he let her out in front of Saks Fifth Avenue,

then pointed down the street to the sign for D & H Construction.

"Good luck, Kyleen Ravenclaw from North Carolina," he said to her with a wiggle of his eyebrows as she handed over her cash. "Something tells me ya gonna need it."

She looked up, up, up at the imposing tower. The building was massive and foreboding with its all-black windows and shiny steel. Whoever William Hatfield was, he was clearly successful and powerful. And handling only billion-dollar projects? If she was going to meet with him, she'd need to dress the part. If only she knew how to dress as hoity-toity as that accent she'd faked would imply.

At least, she thought she needed to dress the part, until she went into Saks, priced out an outfit, and realized it cost more than her monthly salary. She still had some of the bonus money left over from her last big case, but Kylie was too thrifty to spend it on something she wouldn't wear a hundred times.

For a moment, she considered wearing the expensive outfit and then returning it, but knowing her luck, she'd probably spill something down the entire front. As she was wandering down the sidewalk, she looked up and saw a Jackie O style dress suit in the window of a thrift store.

Lady Ravenclaw would totally wear that, she told herself, even though she wasn't sure.

Fifty dollars later, she walked out wearing the dress and a gently used pair of pumps, carrying a giant black bag. Stuffing her old clothes into the bag, she stood in a store window and put her hair up into a severe bun. The dress had a moth hole in the sleeve and wasn't perfect. And maybe, just maybe, it was a little too pink. But it would have to do.

She was ready to meet her father.

If this was even her father. Maybe it was just a man who shared his name. But something inside her rippled as she crossed the street with the flood of bodies and walked to the imposing revolving door of the D & H Construction building.

Even if her father wasn't in this building, she felt like she was on the right track. Even if she had to be Kyleen Ravenclaw and sacrifice her dignity again and again, she would find him. This had to be done.

8

At two in the afternoon, Kylie walked into that imposing, all-black building with her chin up high. The receptionist's desk was massive, as was the security stand near the elevators. The four security guards didn't look suspicious of her, so that was a good sign.

"Hello, my name is Ravenclaw," Kylie said, still sporting that ridiculous British accent. Why, when she decided to pretend she was rich, had she also decided to pretend she was from across the pond? Now she was stuck speaking like this, and everyone was giving her double takes. "Kyleen Ravenclaw. I am here to see Mr. Hatfield, if you please."

She gritted her teeth. She sounded so ridiculous, she wanted to smack herself.

"Yes. Please wait one moment." The woman lifted a phone to speak into the receiver. When she whispered, "Ms. Ravenclaw is here to see you," Kylie cringed with embarrassment. Two points to Slytherin.

To keep herself from staring at the receptionist, she walked around the expansive entrance. The entire place sparkled, with its modern chandeliers, floor-to-ceiling

Japanese artwork, and a giant glass fountain. Mr. Hatfield was clearly an important man. She strolled back up to the receptionist and peeked over.

The woman's smile was tight. "Mr. Hatfield's assistant will be down to fetch you momentarily."

"Thank you." Kylie knew she was only minutes from getting booted out, but she pressed her luck anyway. "Pardon me, but is this entire building owned by William Hatfield?"

The woman narrowed her eyes. "Mostly. It's a joint purchase between Mr. Hatfield and Mr. DeRoss. They lease a few floors out to other companies, but it is a D & H property. One of six in the city and there are many more in the boroughs," she said, seeming pleased with her employer.

Wow. Mr. Hatfield wasn't just important. He was a bazillionaire.

Was her father a bazillionaire? And growing up, she'd sometimes had to spend Christmases with some lame thing she told her mother she wanted that didn't cost too much money, and she and her mother ate ramen noodles more times than she could count...why, again? If he was really that rich, and he'd just left them to rot?

Kylie felt her blood grow warm but calmed herself. There was nothing saying this was her father. As she'd learned from her searches, Hatfield was a fairly common name.

"Ms. Ravenclaw?" a voice behind her said.

She turned to find a small man, not much taller than she was. He was about her age, too, despite the misfortune of being nearly completely bald on top, with a very shiny, red pate. "Yes." She held out her hand like she'd seen in movies, limply, palm down, like a proper English lady should. "And you are..."

He studied her hand curiously, then shook just the tips of her fingers. "Mr. Wiener. Mr. Hatfield's assistant."

"Mr. Wiener. Charmed, I'm sure," Kylie said.

He ran a suspicious eye over her. "You say you had an appointment?"

"I did, but I seem to have misplaced my datebook and can't recall the precise time. But I was interested in your shopping mall work."

"Well. We've done extensive commercial work such as that, but if you'll forgive me...Mr. Hatfield might be a little unprepared for your questions. Ordinarily, he prepares quite extensively for his engagements. He didn't remember having an appointment with you. And I have to say, since I book in all of Mr. Hatfield's appointments, neither do I."

"Well," Kylie said, sweat trickling down her rib cage. "It might be possible I booked in with his...partner."

The man raised an eyebrow. "Mr. DeRoss?"

Kylie nodded, relieved to find out he actually *had* a partner. "Yes. That name does ring a bell. Perhaps it was with him. But Mr. DeRoss did say that Mr. Hatfield would be present. This project requires his insight. I was very adamant I speak to the great man himself, so do see that he's available."

Kylie caught his dubious expression reflected in the shining glass of the elevator doors and told herself to shut up and not say anything else. Even so, Wiener seemed to buy it.

"I will be sure to. Mr. Hatfield is very hands-on," he said as they stepped into a sparkling, circular glass elevator and the tiny assistant pressed the button for the top floor.

When the doors slid closed, Kylie kept her eyes on the climbing numbers above the door, but she could feel the little assistant's eyes on her, quietly assessing her. It was probably the accent. She'd been straddling the lines between British, Australian, and snooty American the whole time. How much longer did she have to keep that up?

They climbed to the eighty-second floor of the building, and Mr. Wiener stepped aside to let her pass through the open doors. "To your right. Double doors. Feel free to go right in. Mr. Hatfield is waiting for you."

Kylie's knees wobbled as she looked at the doors. She managed one step, then another, wondering what the man on the other side would look like, be like. Was he her father? The man who had wooed her mother? Held her when she was a baby? Left them both without any explanation?

She froze. For a second, she had the strangest urge to run away, straight back to Asheville and Linc, and never return.

As she stood there with her feet planted, the door opened, and a tall, slim man in a three-piece suit stepped out.

And Kylie knew it at once.

The hair was shorter, grayer. The skin sagged from his face, giving him slight jowls, and a squarer face. He had a gray goatee. But it was him.

It was the man in the picture on her mother's refrigerator. Adam Hatfield. Her father.

She took a deep breath as he neared her, her legs still unable to move. He extended his hand and smiled broadly. "Ms. Ravenclaw?" he said in a voice much more gravelly than she'd expected in the millions of times she'd imagined him speaking to her.

"Yes," she said, her British accent long since forgotten.

He waved her on. "Fantastic to meet you. I hope you weren't waiting long. Come on inside. My office will be much more comfortable," he said, bringing her into a large space with a massive wood desk silhouetted against a series of floor-to-ceiling windows.

She followed him, stumbling a little in her too-tight shoes as he closed the door. She sat down in the chair across from his, just as he lowered himself into a tufted leather executive chair. He looked down at a piece of paper on his desk, where a few words had been scrawled. "There's a brownstone you want to transform into a shopping mall? Where is this located?"

Brownstone? What the hell was he talking about? Didn't he recognize her? His own daughter?

Quickly, the story flooded her. "Uh. Yes. In…" She couldn't think.

He leaned forward, smiling in such an accommodating way, and all she could do was think that this was the man who had left her and her mother, without any excuse.

She could bear it no longer. Linc had said she had no patience, and he was right, because the second she thought of her poor mother, she exploded, her voice dry and full of accusation. "I'm here about Rhonda." She strained to remember her maiden name. "Rhonda Whitman."

He stared at her, a smile frozen on his square face. He looked younger than her mother, mid-forties, maybe. Trim and tanned and handsome too. He clearly hadn't had any of the worries her mother had. "Rhonda Whitman?" he asked, his brow wrinkling.

"My mother," she said, her voice clipped and full of annoyance. "Your *wife*."

"I'm sorry. Your…" He stopped, and Kylie could pinpoint the exact moment when realization crept in, because his face turned pale, and his eyes widened. "And you are…"

"Kylie," she spat out. "Kylie Hatfield. Her daughter. *Your* daughter."

His eyes slipped over the shiny surface of his desk. He didn't seem to know what to do with his hands. Finally, he laced them together and leaned forward, lowering his voice to a whisper. "Why are you here?"

With that one question, any hopes Kylie had for a happy reunion disappeared.

She frowned at him. "Because you're my *father*. Isn't that a good enough reason? What, you really expected to just walk out and never hear from us again, after the way you left things? You didn't think I'd come looking for you? That I'd have questions?"

He closed his eyes and sighed. When he opened them again, he looked at her like she was invading his personal space. His voice was just as clipped as Kylie's had been. "You've made a mistake, my dear. I'm sorry, but—"

"Why did you leave us?"

"I…I don't know what you're talking about," he said, his eyes darting to the door. The man looked terrified. "You need to leave." He lowered his voice to just above a whisper as he hissed, "I'm serious. You need to leave. You're not safe. Leave New York now." His voice went loud again as he pushed to his feet. "Please don't—"

The door flew open, and a gorgeous blonde woman barreled in, carrying along the scent of an entire rose garden with her. She carried herself like an older, more sophisticated woman, but her body was tight and toned, and whatever wrinkles usually came with age were nonexistent, so Kylie had trouble placing her true age.

She had very short, stylish platinum hair and was dressed head-to-toe in red. With five-inch platform heels, she looked like a real NYC fashionista, not a fake one, like Kylie so desperately felt like right then.

"Oh, Will, I missed you at breakfast, and what's this about having an appointment at two? You told me you were free—" She stopped and looked at Kylie, her hand flying to her chest. "Oh, dear. You're already here. And what is the meaning of this, taking over my hubby's free time so that his wife can't even come in and visit with him?"

She batted some thickly mascaraed eyelashes at Kylie. The woman was clearly trying to be cute, smiling sweetly, but as she stared at Kylie, her eyes narrowed in suspicion.

And had she just said "hubby?"

Kylie just stared, every cell in her body frozen in place. "Uh…"

William Hatfield stood up and strode to the woman, taking her hand and stroking it gently. He looked calm, but his voice was anything but. "Yes, but we'll only be a minute. This very important meeting came up, and I couldn't get out of it…with Miss…" he looked at Kylie pleadingly, silently begging her to keep up appearances, "Ravenclaw."

Dear? Hubby? The dots connect with a crash, and Kylie felt her face grow hot. It couldn't be…it sounded like…

Kylie had been knocked speechless by the mere thought. Was her father married to this woman? Had he dumped her mother for this piece of plastic garbage? How could that be? He and her mother never officially divorced. Or had they?

She was so very, very confused.

The woman eyed her down to her toes and back. "Raven-claw?" she asked, doubt dripping from the word. No doubt she could see every false, knock-off item in her wardrobe for what they really were. "And what do you do, Miss Ravenclaw?"

Kylie lifted her chin. "I'm building a shopping mall." It was on the tip of her tongue to scream out her name.

She should have. It would be immensely satisfying to blow the whole thing in front of his sham of a wife. The more she turned it over, the angrier it made her. It'd been a mistake, he'd said in his letter to Rhonda. So why was marrying this blonde bimbo *not* a mistake? What, in his eyes, made her better wife material than Rhonda? And according to the law, wasn't this illegal? She wanted to scream that at him, but all she could do was stare.

Her father, who had completely written them off, moved on, and was now married to…someone else. Even though he was still married to her mother. The last Kylie'd checked, that was called bigamy, a federal offense. So her dad, in addition to being an all-around awful guy who couldn't live up to his promises, hadn't reached out to his firstborn a single time while she was growing up...was also a bigamist?

She'd come here expecting disappointment. After all, he'd left them, and never sought them out in all this time. But she didn't know she'd learn her father was the worst scum of the earth that ever lived.

What an asshole. What a fucking asshole.

"Oh, a shopping mall?" the woman said with dramatic flair, as if she didn't believe a single word Kylie was saying. She wrapped an arm tighter around him, kissed him on the cheek, and gave Kylie a superior glare. "So sorry, sweetheart. I didn't know that this was such an *important* meeting. You know how I like to stop in during your free time and catch up. But shopping malls must be built. If you'd like me to—"

Kylie shot to her feet. The woman was definitely on to her. And the more she spoke, the older Kylie placed her. Now, she thought that the woman was at least fifty. Hefting her purse onto her shoulder, she mumbled, "No. We're all done. Don't let me keep you."

So very, very don't.

Coming here to find him was the biggest mistake Kylie had ever made in her life.

She didn't even look at her father, or at the woman, who she practically felt clawing a suspicious eye over her. Kylie simply walked to the door, opened it, and went out. She didn't even have the heart to slam the door.

9

William Hatfield had had a feeling, when he woke up this morning, that today was going to be a doozy. He didn't like surprises, so he did his best to keep a strict schedule: gym in the morning, breakfast at six, in the office by seven, desk work in the morning and meetings in the afternoon.

Wiener, his assistant, understood he liked to have everything planned to a tee, which allowed for fewer unexpected wrenches to be thrown into the mix. It worked well that way, letting very few surprises intercede and tear apart the entire day.

But when his penthouse bedroom on the Upper West Side lost power and his alarm clock didn't sound on time, forcing him to get up at five-thirty instead of five, everything had been thrown off. He'd had a rushed workout and hadn't been able to attend yoga, missed breakfast with Christina, and ended up traveling to his office right in the middle of rush hour.

Definitely a doozy.

And now he felt like a wrench had hit him square in the head.

He'd already known it wouldn't be an ordinary day. He had a lot of meetings scheduled, so he hadn't minded adding one more to his afternoon. A Ms. Kyleen Ravenclaw.

Kyleen Ravenclaw. He snorted at the ridiculous name. He should've known.

Although, how could he? He'd walked out on them almost a quarter of a century ago, making a clean break and wiping his hands of them. He'd thought that by now, they would've forgotten him entirely.

Though, truth be told, he hadn't done a good job of forgetting pretty little Rhonda Whitman.

She was the prettiest waitress at the Brooklyn diner. She looked so cute in that candy-cane striped waitress dress, with her long legs and her sunshine-blonde hair spilling down her back. Every one of her male customers tried to flirt with her, but she didn't give them the time of day. She'd go along, delivering their breakfasts with a bright smile all while putting the men in their place if they ever tried to get too personal.

William had probably been the only one of her regular customers she'd let try his luck. And it hadn't been easy. He'd been going in there for months before she'd finally scribbled her phone number down on one of his checks.

He thought of sweet, beautiful Rhonda now, as his wife blabbered on about things that didn't concern him. Though he kept Christina in the lap of luxury in their penthouse overlooking Central Park, she always had to drop by his office to keep tabs on him.

Missing breakfast had been a no-no—it hadn't allowed her to get her fill of what he was up to. Oh, she kept a close leash on him. The other wives shopped to their hearts' content during the day, went for spa appointments and fitness classes, and ate expensive, long lunches with too many glasses of wine.

Christina did all those things, but she also seemed intent on coming to visit him in his office at least three or four times a week. She didn't make appointments; she just dropped in unexpectedly, as if she was hoping to catch him in the middle of something.

"I said that cream is a more sophisticated shade than vanilla, but I wanted to run it by you," she said, lounging in the chair and cocking a thin, manicured eyebrow in his direction.

"I'm sorry, what?" he asked, leaning back in his chair. Christina often used the pretense of "running it by him" to make him feel like he had some control in their relationship, but she always went and did her own thing. He wasn't sure what she was talking about now—probably some renovation project that he could care less about. He'd been thinking of that day, nearly twenty-five years ago, when he'd left their apartment for good.

Christina clucked her tongue. "The drapes in the living area. I think the warmth of the cream counterbalancing the stripes of the red wallpaper will really set off the light from the sconces…"

His wife's words jumbled together as his mind drifted away from their meticulously kept showroom of a penthouse on the Upper West Side. Kylie had come to see him. Kylie, his firstborn child. Of course, she would. He was her father, and the way he'd left had been too sudden, and completely wrong. Rhonda probably had a million questions about it, which she'd undoubtedly passed on to their child.

But Kylie wasn't a child anymore. The tiny baby had transformed into a beautiful woman. The type of woman who had everything going for her. She had his dark hair and her mother's sparkling green eyes. She'd been flustered and scared, but what child in her position wouldn't be, especially when he practically threw her out of his life.

Again.

Jesus. The years had gone by in a blink of an eye. It seemed like only a year ago, he and Rhonda were married at city hall and living in the rat trap over that shitty hardware store in Brooklyn. And now, here he was, with a *kid* the same age he'd been then, when he'd been full of romantic dreams and hope and a feeling like he could conquer the Big Apple, if he just made the right connections.

He'd made connections, all right. And he'd conquered the city.

Except for dollar signs, he hadn't won a thing in this game called life. Not a damn thing.

He was jarred from his thoughts when Christina raised her voice. "So?"

William shook his head. "I…uh…I think you should just do what you'd like."

"Seriously? That's all you have to say?" she spat out, leaping out of the chair, her hands planted on her hips. "That powder room is extremely vital. It's the one your clients will use when we entertain, since it's right across from the dining room."

His eyes trailed to the door, as if he expected his firstborn would come waltzing back in. "Well, I—"

"Who was that woman?" Christina blared in his ear, eyeing him cautiously. Even the most beautiful could be ugly when they wore that look of disdain. "I thought you didn't have a two o'clock."

It pissed him off that his wife knew his exact schedule so intimately.

He tried to push aside a memory of Rhonda, the first woman he'd ever loved, and said, "I didn't. She was added in today."

Christina's face tightened, and he knew she'd be wrinkling her nose if the Botox had allowed the movement. "For what? A roll in the hay?"

He gritted his teeth and adjusted his tie. "Of course not."

"Then, what?" she hissed. "I don't trust that shopping mall story as far as I could throw that girl off her knock-off Louboutin pumps."

His beautiful rose, Christina, was all thorns now that they were alone. That was usually the way. After twenty-four years, he'd come to expect it. She was all style and sophistication in public, but a mean, nasty bitch behind closed doors. He knew the best way to end this argument wasn't to try to win.

Winning didn't happen with her.

"No. Of course not. She…" He coughed. "You're right. She was an imposter. Gave me a fake story about wanting to build a shopping mall, but she was really trying to get us to switch our payroll vendor. I told her by no means. We're happy with what we have."

She raised an eyebrow. "Really!" William could tell by her utter indignation that she'd bought the story. "The nerve of some people. You should've told me, and I'd have kicked her little ass out the door. Wasting your time like that. Did you tell Wiener that he needs to screen these calls a little better? I wonder what she said to weasel her way in here?"

She stared at him expectantly, tapping her designer shoe on the shiny marble with her normal impatience. She wasn't going to let this go.

He didn't feel like explaining the ridiculous excuse Ms. Ravenclaw had given to get an appointment with him. Christina was naturally suspicious and could detect bullshit a mile away. "Yes. He's been talked to. And it's not important." Forcing a smile, he rose and stepped close to his wife, giving her the full attention she craved. "How was your day?"

"Don't try to change the subject!" She pushed against his chest, but the gesture was weak. It was just part of this dance. "Are you sure that whore wasn't trying to get into your pants? The way she looked at you…" Her hand moved down to his belt.

He pulled her close against him, gritting his teeth at her closeness, but willing his dick to get hard just the same. Again, just part of the dance.

"I already told you, Tina. She's a saleswoman, and no one of consequence. She wanted to get into the business, not into my bed. And you're right, the cream is perfect with the red."

It was exactly the right thing to say. She beamed up at him, pure pleasure transforming her into a beautiful woman. "I'm so glad you like it. And please remember that Ty has a basketball game tonight at the high school, and you promised him you'd be there. He's one game away from the championship."

He managed not to groan. His sixteen-year-old son, Tyler, his youngest, had begged him to watch the game. Ty was the captain, and this was varsity, but William had missed all the games so far. Ty was a good kid and he been looking forward to attending the game, to being the good, present father, until Kylie had come back into his life.

Kylie, his one glaring reminder that no matter how hard he tried these days, he'd never win father of the year.

Christina was still staring at him, expecting something, so he nodded firmly. "I'll be there. What time?"

Christina scowled. Yes, she had told him the time on at least twenty occasions. "Seven."

"I'll be there," he said, reaching over to pat her hand, which was planted on the desk, baring the massive five-carat diamond he'd bought her many years ago in Las Vegas, right before they were bound in holy matrimony.

Fauxly matrimony. He nearly laughed at his own humor.

But she pulled her claw-like hand away at the last second and made a clicking sound with her tongue. "I guess we'll see about that," she said, turning and heading for the door. She slammed it so hard behind her that he expected the wood to crack down the middle.

He flopped into his chair and stared up at the ceiling. What the hell?

This day had definitely been a doozy.

I STOOD in one of the floor-to-ceiling windows of D & H Construction, watching the little girl with dark hair walking back and forth on the sidewalk, poking at her phone.

I was seething.

Who did she think she was?

That girl didn't belong in this city. You could tell by those cheesy knock-off shoes and her bright pink suit. Who the hell'd be caught dead in a get-up like that on the streets of Manhattan? Most people in this city tried to outdo each other, flaunting their wealth, even if they had to go deep into debt to do it. But this girl? Her getup said *look at me, here I am, I'm tacky and proud of it!* even while every other part of her body was trying to shrink into the cracks on the sidewalk. That, and by the way she tried to hail a cab, holding her hand up tentatively, as if she wasn't sure she was doing it right.

Oh, that little girl had a lot to learn.

She was all sunshine and rainbows and whiskers on kittens. She'd made the wrong choice, leaving whatever hovel she'd grown up in to come here. I wasn't quite sure what her game was, but I sensed it…she wanted a piece of William Hatfield, and thought she could get it. But she was wrong. This city was going to chew her up and spit her out, for sure.

If the city didn't, I would. I was going to make damned sure of that.

What did she think she was doing, dropping into William Hatfield's office like that, like she was important or something? Like he owed her a minute of his time. He'd humored her, of course, because she was a nice piece of ass, but that was all. Clearly, she needed to be put in her place.

I'd have to take care of that too.

I watched her exhaling in relief as she finally succeeded in getting a cab driver to notice her. She slipped in and peered out the window, running those wide eyes over the skyscraper she'd just exited. Then she said something to the driver, and the cab sped away.

It was midafternoon. The beginning of New York's rush hour. Wherever she was going, it'd take a while. She likely didn't have a clue where she was going. Or what was coming after her.

Good.

This would be fun.

It was her fault, though, coming here. No one lied their way into William Hatfield's office and got away with it. No one. He was off-limits. He was not someone people messed with. I'd had to prove that, time and time again, to people a lot savvier than this little girl.

What the hell was she after? Did she know she'd just stepped her little Payless-clad feet into the lion's den?

Well, whatever her game was, I was going to find out. The poor little thing wouldn't even know what hit her by the time I was done with her.

I lifted my phone and called Nico. Nico, my right hand. Nico, the man who'd be the subject of all that little girl's nightmares for the foreseeable future.

"Don't talk. Just listen," I said when he answered. "I have a job for you. Write this down."

I smiled as he told me he was ready. Nico was always ready. He loved doling out punishment, and I had the feeling this punishment would be nice and easy, and just as sweet as that little girl.

Oh, we would have fun. I was sure of that.

10

——————

Kylie took a cab back to her motel in Brooklyn, stewing the entire time. The guy, William Hatfield the Asshole, didn't just leave them. He'd gone and married Queen Plastic Bitch, and was now living the high life, managing his own company. He was a billionaire, and had he even paid one dollar toward Kylie's expenses while she'd been growing up?

Kylie clenched her fists so hard her fingernails dug into her palms. Growing up, she hadn't felt awfully denied. They'd had lean moments, but they'd been happy. She knew her mother worked hard to provide for her and give her a happy childhood, sometimes going without, often overspending her credit card limit, and always living paycheck to paycheck. And what had he done? Absolutely nothing, from his little penthouse in the richest zip code in the world!

To think, she'd wanted to live in New York City when she was young. Now, she just wanted to get the hell out. Everything about this town annoyed her. She couldn't even imagine staying in town for another two days, as had been her original plan. And that hotel? Even the thought of laying her head down on a pillow in that roach motel made her stomach roil.

She opened her phone and started searching for earlier flights. If she could find one leaving early enough, maybe she could get out and be home in Asheville by late in the evening. Maybe she could even sleep in bed with Linc.

That sounded like heaven.

There was a nonstop from Delta leaving at six-thirty, which was only a few hours away. If she hurried, she might be able to make it. She quickly booked it and leaned into the cab's vinyl seat, stretching her back. Her muscles were tight and painful from tension, and her head was starting to pound.

She was still steaming as she paid the driver and stepped out at the Piedmark. She'd let her hair down, ripped off the floppy bow on the blouse of her ridiculous Jackie O suit, and opened all the buttons on the jacket. She didn't want to set foot in those uncomfortable heels again, so she carried them in her hands, not even caring about setting her bare feet on the dirty street. As she stormed toward the door, a couple of guys called to her from one of the stoops nearby. "Hey, mama!"

Kylie turned. It was Tomas and Jose, drinking beers. She waved at them but couldn't bring herself to smile. They slipped off the stoop and walked over. Jose ripped one from a six-pack and handed it to her.

"Let me guess, mama," Tomas said. "You didn't find what you were looking for?"

She sighed, shoved her shoes in her bag, and took the beer in both hands. "Oh, I did. I guess you could say I found more than I bargained for."

Jose actually looked concerned. "You don't look so good. Maybe you party with us tonight?"

"Would love to," she said, looking around. "But I feel like a bomb was dropped on me."

They stared at her, waiting for an explanation, but she didn't want to talk about it. In fact, she just wanted to go home.

"It's nothing. I think I'm just homesick. I miss my dog and my boyfriend," she said with a shrug, perilously close to tears again. "Things just haven't gone the way I'd hoped. I'm probably going to pack up and go home."

She cracked open the beer and took a long drink.

"Sure you don't want to hang with us tonight?" Jose asked.

She patted his arm, so glad she'd been able to see past her initial impression of the men. And glad her initial impression had been wrong. "I think I've had enough of the big city for now. But I can't thank you two enough for your help."

"All right, mama," Jose said, seeming disappointed. "If you're leaving in a little we'll get a cab for you. You take care of yourself."

Since the elevator was a death trap, she went into the stairwell. It smelled even worse in there, like cat urine and pot. Her footfalls plodded heavily on the steps as she went upstairs, thinking. Who knew that meeting Jose and Tomas would be a highlight of this horrible day?

No, she hadn't expected her dad to break down in tears and cry about how much he missed her, how he'd been searching for her but had never been able to find her, but... okay, a little part of her had hoped for that.

He'd essentially told her to get the hell out. He'd wanted nothing to do with her.

And she'd thought the feeling of rejection she'd felt from her father couldn't get worse.

She'd been wrong. Now, instead of a hole in her heart, it

felt like a massive chasm. By the time she reached the door of her hotel room, her chest hurt.

She hadn't unpacked her things yet, so she simply changed out of the suit, threw it in the trash, and pulled on her jeans and boots. Pulling her hair into a ponytail, she threw her toiletries into her bag, zipped it up, and headed down to get a cab to take her to the airport so she could catch the flight.

Tomas and Jose were nowhere to be found when she got back to the street, but there was a cab waiting. She smiled, silently thanked them, and opened the door.

When she slid inside, she dialed Linc. He didn't answer, and her heart ached more. She wanted desperately to hear his voice.

Linc would be happy to see her home. Maybe almost as much as she was to get there.

Home.

Why was she fighting moving in with him so much?

She'd come to New York to get some answers, they just hadn't been the answers she'd been hoping for. But she knew one thing for certain now.

She was nothing like her father.

Even more, neither was Linc.

Surely that knowledge could be enough to reduce her commitment fears? Surely it would.

When Kylie got home, she'd slip into bed with Linc, wrap her body around his, and tell him everything.

She imagined herself relating the whole sordid story. Imagined him digesting the whole tale without judgement. He'd understand. Maybe he could help her to decide whether she should tell her mom that her father was a bigamist.

She was so lost in thoughts of Linc, and of home sweet home, that she didn't even notice the car that was following directly behind her.

❄

LINC WASN'T ATTACHED to his phone like most people, so he didn't always carry it around in his pocket. He'd been having a busy day, repairing the kennels and working in his garden.

All through the day, Kylie hadn't been far from his thoughts, but he knew from the way she was acting that she wanted distance from him. She'd sent a message that she'd arrived in New York, and that was probably the most he'd get. She was a prolific texter normally, but when she got deep into her work, she could think of nothing else. Besides, unlike him, she seemed genuinely excited by the prospect of exploring the city. With her bubbly personality and innate curiosity, she was probably having a grand old time, checking out the sights while she wasn't working.

Night had fallen, but since he hadn't had a lot of time with the pups and didn't think he'd get much sleep without Kylie next to him, he decided to play catch with them. He wasn't sure when he started sleeping better with Kylie than without her, but now, he knew he'd probably spend a good chunk of the night wide awake, staring at the ceiling.

It was better than the nightmares that still haunted him many nights of the week, but still, he dreaded the sense of aloneness. His therapist had told him that it was a good sign that he wanted to be close to someone again. That he was opening himself up to being happy, finally beginning to feel as if he might possibly deserve that happiness.

He wasn't there yet, and may never arrive there fully, but he was more open to risking it. With Kylie. Because there was something about her that made him feel whole again. Alive.

Which was terrifying and thrilling all at once.

As he threw the ball into the yard, he heard a car coming up the long driveway. Since he knew it couldn't be Kylie, he waited, expecting to see either his best friend, Jacob Dean, or his mother.

He pulled his ballcap down farther on his forehead when an unfamiliar bright blue RAV4 appeared around the bend. He headed its way. Probably someone who was lost and needed directions.

Linc grabbed the tennis ball from Storm's jaws as the small SUV came to a stop, the headlights shining directly at him. The driver's door opened and a woman with long, sunny blonde hair stepped out, and he blinked, moving to where he could see her better.

Holy shit. It was Faith Carter.

"Hi, stranger," Faith said shyly, giving him a half-wave.

Linc just stared, speechless. They hadn't always been strangers. In fact, once upon a time, before he'd gone into the military, they'd been quite cozy. He'd met her his first year at Duke Law, and they'd dated into his second. Not only was she beautiful, she was damn smart, always showing the rest of them up with her grades and her arguments.

At one time, about a million years ago, he'd thought she was the one. Until he went on his first deployment, and she sent him a warm, apologetic, but no less stinging Dear John letter. He'd been gone less than a month before she'd given him that little send-off, with an *I just don't think I'm cut out for the long-distance thing.*

And now she was here. In front of him.

He hadn't seen her since before he left.

She was prettier than he remembered too. She'd filled out. She was wearing a long-sleeved denim dress that bared her pale legs, even in the cool October air. Her hair was longer, and her face had matured.

But why in the total hell was she here? Why had she shown up, out of the blue, after all this time?

"Faith," he started, intending to ask her all of those questions.

Before he could say more, she came around the side of the car, and without a word, wrapped her arms around him, pulling him close and pressing her breasts against his chest.

Just as another car came crunching up the driveway.

Well, this was turning into a regular traffic jam, he thought as Faith whispered in his ear, "I've missed you."

"Faith," he said again as the other car approached. He blinked in the bright headlights. It was another one he didn't recognize. "Why are you…"

Then the car stopped, and the back door opened.

And Kylie stepped out.

11

K ylie had been thinking of Linc, expecting she'd find him in the midst of one of two things when she arrived at the house: Either playing with the dogs, or on the couch with a beer. He was steady and dependable that way; not one to do anything outside the norm.

So, when the Uber she'd ordered so as not to disturb him and make him come all the way to the airport for her sorry ass pulled up into the driveway of the farmhouse, she was more than surprised to see he wasn't doing either of those things.

No, instead, he had his arms around a tall, willowy blonde in a little denim dress.

Welcome home, sucker, Kylie thought, breathing out all the air in her lungs. It was dark now, so she nearly pressed her nose against the glass, trying to get a better look. Maybe her eyes were deceiving her.

But no. It was him. And a beautiful girl. Embracing. In front of the house that she'd been thinking of all the ways she wanted to redecorate on the plane ride home.

"Woooooooo!" The Uber guy, a total hick in a cowboy hat, said, adding a long whistle for emphasis. "Can I stay around for the fireworks?"

She scowled at him. Really? So it was *that* obvious what was going on here? "That's his...cousin," she muttered.

At least, she hoped it was his cousin, although he'd never mentioned having a beautiful cousin before. And did cousins even hug like that? The woman had her arms all around him, her big, bountiful breasts pressed into his chest.

Worse, they looked like they'd held each other like that before. They looked...comfortable. Was that why he hadn't answered his phone? Had he been in bed with her?

Kylie's stomach roiled at the thought of Linc sharing his bed with anyone but her. She knew he'd had other lovers before—after all, he was thirty— but he'd never mentioned them, so she'd thought they were old news. Seeing this woman with her arms around him was enough to make her want to tell the Uber driver to turn around and drive away.

Steeling herself, she reached for the door handle and willed herself to be calm and collected and not make a scene, which she always managed to do when her blood started to boil like this.

When she stepped from the car, they quickly disentangled, or at least Linc did, like someone who'd gotten his hand caught in the cookie jar. He was rubbing the back of his neck, like he usually did when he felt bad or guilty about something. He didn't make eye contact.

Pain and utter humiliation sliced through Kylie, and her blood reached the point of explosion.

The blonde wasn't touching him anymore, but she was still glued to his side like she belonged there. They made a striking couple. Kylie wanted to rip her head off, so she knew she needed to get away before she did something that would land her in prison.

He opened his mouth as she approached and said, "Kylie, this is—"

"A mistake," Kylie muttered, rushing past him, up the stairs, and into the house. She grabbed her car keys and Vader's leash, then ran outside and clipped it on the dog's collar. He licked her knees. At least he was happy to see her. But when she tried to pull him toward her car, he planted his feet, refusing to budge.

"Fine, traitor," she said, dropping the leash. "Stay here with your new best friend. I'm out."

"Kylie," Linc's voice was far too even and calm for her liking. Why did he always have to sound like the voice of reason? It made her feel even more insane. And she'd done nothing wrong. All she'd wanted to do was come home and climb into bed with him, feeling his arms around her.

She was such a sucker.

She ignored him, grabbing her bag from the cowboy, who was enjoying the whole display, a big stupid smirk on his face. She stomped off toward her car and made one last, desperate attempt to wave Vader inside. It was a no-go.

"Wait, where do you think you're going?" Linc asked as the blonde bimbo watched.

Kylie turned abruptly, and he plowed right into her, causing her to drop her bag.

His hands came down on her shoulders, steadying her, and she almost sank into his warmth. Which pissed her off even more.

She pulled away. "I'm going to my place. I'd hate to interrupt." She ran an eye over the blonde. Hell, she looked even prettier up close. There was no way he wasn't tapping that.

Linc reached for her again. "Wait…"

But Kylie's eyes were watering. She was about to burst into tears, so she turned on her heels and left before he could say more, leaving her suitcase where it had fallen. She'd have to come back for her things eventually anyway. What was one more thing to add to the load?

She was close to breaking, and she couldn't let anyone see her like this. She just wanted to go home and sleep in her own bed. Alone. She couldn't even get Vader to be with her, that's how unlovable she was to all males in this world.

A sob escaped her lips at the thought, and she pressed them together, refusing to give in to the grief and pain swirling inside her.

She did a quick three-point turn in front of the barn, kicking up dirt and gravel as the Jeep's tires tried to help her get away. Kylie cursed when she ended up on the ass of the cowboy Uber driver, who was pulling out of the driveway. She wanted to beep at him to hurry the hell up because she just wanted to get as far away from Linc as possible, but he crept down the winding road, which was probably the only thing that saved her from crashing down the ravine again.

The tears started coming as soon as she hit the road down to Asheville. The headlights of the occasional passing car made it nearly impossible to see on the way home, but she wasn't thinking of that. She was thinking of the past few months, completely wasted.

How could he do that to her?

Had he lied when he said he loved her just this morning?

Had he changed his mind when the pretty blonde showed up?

Yeah. That was probably it. Kylie wanted to stab herself in the heart for how stupid she felt. *Of course he wouldn't want to be with you. You're a Hatfield. Men run in the other direction.*

It was getting close to midnight by the time she trudged into her old apartment building. Her downstairs stoner neighbor was throwing another one of his raucous parties. Normally, the noise never bothered her, but this time, everything did.

Her mailbox across the foyer was filled with mail—bills, probably—but she ignored it. She stalked upstairs, ignoring Baron's calls to her to come and join the fun, and when she was inside, slammed the door.

The place looked so empty and unlived-in, considering she'd systematically moved so many of her things to Linc's house. She'd have to go back and get those things, if this was the end.

Was this the end?

Now that she was in her little place, she knew she'd most likely overreacted. Hell, she hadn't even given the man time to speak. But…

Wiping her eyes, she sank down on her bed. But she'd just felt the sharp knife of rejection from her own father, the one man who was supposed to love her endlessly.

Sighing, she looked at her phone. No call. No text. No little heart-eyed emoji.

Mentally shaking herself, Kylie changed into boxers and a camisole before flopping back onto the mattress. She pulled up the blanket and wrapped herself in its warmth, then stared at the ceiling.

Was that what men were made for? Destroying women? Wasn't there a single man on earth who was trustworthy? Or was it just Kylie who had that effect on men?

No.

She thought of the files upon files of cheating spouse folders in the file cabinets of Starr Investigations.

She thought of her high school and college friends who'd gotten married just moments after walking across their respective stages. More than half of them were now divorced. Others were Instagram happy, but she wondered what happened behind closed doors.

She thought of her father. He was handsome and distinguished, the epitome of success. But he hadn't wanted her then, and he didn't want her now.

Unable to sleep, she reached into the tote she thankfully hadn't dropped and pulled out her laptop. She turned it on and opened a browser, then typed into the search bar: D & H Construction.

A number of results came back, including a slew of image results. The blue company logo, photographs of men in hard hats studying blueprints, and several of the powerful man himself. Her father. She stared at him, her fingers shaking on the keyboard. Now, she wasn't angry. She just felt sad.

What about her made men think they could treat her like trash?

No. Not just her.

Alongside the cheating spouse folders were hundreds of other equally vile people who were happy to tromp over others for their own personal gain.

The first web page was for her father's website. She clicked on it and read: *Twenty-five years ago, William Hatfield came to Manhattan from Brooklyn with a dream—to fill the NYC skyline with unique, sophisticated commercial properties. William Hatfield is a true self-made man and living the American dream, showing how ingenuity and tenacity can bring success. Now responsible for hundreds of projects in the tri-state area, the D & H Construction name is synonymous with style and substance. Take a look at our most recent projects below and kindly contact us if you would like a consultation about your latest building project. D & H Construction specializes in making your dream a reality.*

Kylie clicked on some of the projects, but she wasn't interested in the buildings. She wanted to know more about the man. There was a tab that said: About Us. She clicked on it and a list of employees came forth. At the top was her father. His picture stared back at her. In it, he looked warm, friendly, charming.

What a crock.

She read: *William Hatfield's ties to the area run deep. He was born and raised in a working class neighborhood in Brooklyn. From these humble roots, early on he discovered a deep interest in construction. With talent and perseverance, he was soon creating some of the most talked about and exciting properties to grace the Big Apple's skyline. He started D & H Construction twenty-five years ago, which has since grown into one of the most successful developers in Manhattan, with over 3,000 employees and $25 billion in assets. He is one of the city's most benevolent philanthropists, donating millions of dollars in money and substantial resources toward ending homelessness in the city. He lives in uptown Manhattan with his beautiful wife, Christina, and their three children.*

Kylie stared at that last sentence. Their three children. William Hatfield didn't just have a wife. He had three other children.

Kylie's half-siblings.

She gnawed her cheek raw. She didn't even know them, but she already hated them. After all, they'd grown up with a mother *and* a father. In Uptown Manhattan, living the high life, benefiting from his billion-dollar company.

And what the hell? He was a philanthropist? He gave millions of dollars to the homeless and to those less fortunate that he didn't even know but hadn't given a single cent to raising his first daughter after essentially bribing her mother with a house and a check.

Kylie balled her hands into fists to ward off the urge to throw her computer against the wall. When the urge passed, she typed in Christina Hatfield, and brought up pictures of her father's second wife. Apparently, her maiden name was DeRoss, so she must have been a relative of her father's business partner.

From what Kylie could tell, they'd "married" not long

after Kylie was born—a year, tops. They had a daughter named Sophia, who was only two years younger than Kylie. Sophia was beautiful, with long, striking red hair. She'd gone to Columbia and now worked in fashion in the city.

I hate you, she thought, scowling at the picture of a stylish girl with the life Kylie'd always dreamed of for herself. *I hate you. I envy you. I...*

Kylie threw herself back against the headboard of her bed with a bang, shaking, not even feeling the pain that shot down her spine. She couldn't remember ever feeling this angry and out of control before. It felt like everything in her world was falling apart. She was usually so optimistic and could pull herself out of the worst funk simply by looking at the bright side of things. But this time, she couldn't see a bright side.

Everything was shit. Her father, his perfect family, her boyfriend, her life. All shit.

She reached over to pet Vader, then she remembered that even her best friend was a traitor. Red-hot anger coursed through her veins anew. William Hatfield. Christina Hatfield. Sophia Hatfield. What a happy family.

She wanted to punch something.

Closing her computer, she picked up her phone again, hoping for a message from Linc. Of course he'd have texted by now. Yes, he was awful when it came to texting, but the way they'd left things? It definitely called for some form of communication. A call. A text. Something.

But there was nothing on her screen except a low-battery warning.

He hadn't tried to get in touch with her at all.

If that didn't scream "we're over" loud enough, she didn't know what else would.

Dropping her phone on the nightstand, she pulled the

covers over her head, like she had when she was a child and hoped to keep the monsters at bay.

There were no monsters, she knew.

There were worst things lurking in the dark.

Human beings.

THIS WAS NOT GOOD.

Linc was opening drawers and slamming cabinets, looking for his damned phone.

"I hope I didn't come at a bad time," Faith said from the kitchen doorway.

He slammed another drawer. "You need to go, and I need to call Kylie."

Faith leaned against the doorjamb. "Is she your girl-friend?" When he shot her a *no shit* look, she raised an eyebrow. "Well, she definitely got the wrong idea, and I'm really sorry about that. I just came into town and thought I'd stop by and say hi. The hug was totally innocent. Is your girl-friend that insecure?"

He opened the refrigerator, thinking he might have left his phone there. It wouldn't be the first time, he hated to admit. He also hated Faith coming in here and assuming things about Kylie that were all wrong. "No. Not at all. She's just going through some shit right now."

Faith did that little hair flip thing that always used to turn him on. Now, it just annoyed him. He wanted Kylie back.

Speaking of…why had she come back so soon? And at absolutely the wrong time? He'd been thinking constantly of her, up until the moment that Faith stepped out of the car. Then…

Shit.

He needed to call her.

He tried to think back. He'd taken his phone out when he was giving the dogs a bath earlier in the day, and he'd set it...where?

He couldn't remember.

Great.

He headed to the porch. "Faith. I haven't seen you in years. Why would you just come by here unannounced? Don't you think I might have my own life now?"

"I know, it's been so long," she said, smiling. "I thought you and I could catch up."

As far as Linc was concerned, there was nothing they needed to catch up on. Not now that Kylie was racing away from their house, with the completely wrong idea. And what had Faith done? She'd just stayed silent, letting her continue on with the impression. He scanned around the porch area in the darkness, looking for any shadows that could've been his phone.

"Catch up? Great, let's catch up," he said as he stalked to the barn. "What have you been up to?"

She either didn't catch or ignored the sarcasm as she trotted beside him. "Oh, not much. Been in D.C. for a little, then in Virginia. Now, I'm working in New York. Such is the life of a lawyer. That's an...interesting haircut."

He scrubbed his hand over his head, remembering the shearing Kylie had given him. He'd gone into town earlier and had gotten another barber to even things out. It'd be thick and full in a couple days, anyway, so it didn't matter.

"You get downtown often? Any of the old gang a—eek!"

He smiled as Dolly the llama spit at Faith. He'd have to remember to give her extra feed tomorrow.

Where was his damned phone?

He'd given the dogs a bath. Vader had gone first because he was the one who hated getting bathed most. Then, he'd...

Linc groaned, slapping a hand over his face. He turned on his heel and headed back toward the house. He knew exactly where the phone was.

Faith followed him into the kitchen and went straight to the sink. She had a disgusted look on her face as she washed her hands, then tore off a wad of paper towels to get the spit off her dress.

He went straight to Vader's bed, and sure enough, there was his phone. It was caked in dried slobber and didn't power on when he hit the button. Shit. Back in the kitchen, he tore his own wad of paper towels off and began working on the device.

As he worked, Faith looked at him expectantly. What had they been talking about? The gang?

The "old gang" she was referring to was their classmates at Duke Law. He never liked going out with them—she was the social one—so he'd lost track of them the second he dropped out and enlisted. He had taken her out to the movies in Asheville a few times with Jacob and his flavor of the week, though. She'd always liked Jacob. "Don't know. Jacob's still around."

"Really?" Her face brightened. "What's he up to?"

"Detective with the Asheville County Sheriff's Department," he said, opening the screen door and turning on the porch light. Now that he'd found his phone, Faith needed to go. "Been nice seeing ya. Take care."

Get the hell out.

Hurt flashed across her face, and he took a deep breath. "Listen, Faith…"

She held up a hand. "You know what? I can tell that you're busy. I just wanted to let you know I'm back in town. So, if you ever want to grab some coffee or…?"

No way in hell.

"Yeah. Sounds good. I'll see you."

She didn't come in for another hug. She waved goodbye, and he watched her get into her Rav4 and drive away. He felt nothing toward her, aside from the anger at her bad timing. They were just different, although he'd been crazy about her once.

He'd hated everything about law school, but she'd made it tolerable, with her easy sense of humor and the way that she made every professor love her, so that those who were in her circle were favored by association. She'd loved the law and had been due to graduate at the top of their class. Wanted to go into the federal government or possibly do something with criminal law.

She'd told him he was crazy for wanting to drop out of school and enlist. He'd only realized how crazy she thought he was when he got that Dear John letter a couple weeks after making it to Syria for his first tour.

In her letter, she'd said something about their lives going in different directions. Back then, he'd been upset. More than upset. He'd spent a good two to three months moping around, wondering if he'd made a big mistake by stepping off the path he knew he'd been born to take, sending his career off on such a wild, uncertain trajectory.

She'd been right. Their lives had gone in separate directions, and he was happy with what he had.

He was happy with Kylie.

Tossing his phone into a bag of rice, he considered just jumping into his truck and heading to her apartment. Then he hesitated, and with that hesitation, a new emotion bloomed.

Anger.

Just that morning, Kylie had told him that she loved him, and he'd said the same in return. Did she really think he'd... what? Cheat on her, just hours after making such a verbal commitment?

Was that how highly she thought of him?

Linc sat down on his steps. He had a great deal to think about.

12

William Hatfield arrived at his penthouse on the Upper West Side later that evening, feeling like he'd been hit by a truck.

The doorman opened the door for him and greeted him as he always did, with a reverent, "Good evening, Mr. Hatfield."

He nodded to him, strode through the opulent lobby, and waved at security as he pressed the button for the elevator. When he stepped inside, he willed the numbers over the door to climb much more slowly.

Christina would be there, and who knew what would be on her bitch-list this evening. He hoped he'd be able to make it into his study, his domain, and swallow down a few stiff scotches before she realized he was home.

Looking at his reflection in the mirrored doors, he adjusted his tie, thinking of what his first-born child must've thought about him. Certainly, she must've seen how successful he'd become over the years. That was obvious to anyone, especially since the company bore his name. He hadn't aged too awfully, either.

But could she have seen the other things? The misery? The feeling of having a noose around his neck, twenty-four-seven? All of this world he'd built for himself was a sham. It'd been that way for twenty-five years.

There was a time, not very long ago, that he'd thought this kind of life—being waited on hand and foot, eating at the choicest restaurants in the city without a reservation, heading off to the islands whenever he wished, having limos deliver him wherever he liked—would be the ultimate.

He used to lie in bed with Rhonda, his hand on her stomach, feeling for the baby's kick, and he'd tell her that one day, he'd have this. *They'd* have this.

He didn't care what he had to do. He'd make it.

And he had. He'd done precisely what he intended to do.

But he hadn't done it for them. He'd done nothing for them but provide them with misery. And now, twenty-four years later, he questioned everything he'd once valued.

The doors to the elevator slid open, and he strode into the foyer, bracing himself for Tina's appearance. Gripping the handle of his briefcase in sweaty hands, he crossed his sprawling penthouse home, past the kitchen, into the living room with a sweeping view of Central Park, and into the hallway. Why did everything have to be so sparkling white? Not a thing was out of place in this house; it could've been a museum. Sometimes he wished for a little bit of mess, a little bit of imperfection.

He'd almost made it to the double doors of his study when he heard her heels clicking on those sparkling polished tiles behind him.

"Forget something?" she said sweetly, her voice echoing through their cavern of a foyer.

Shit. The sweetness made his heart begin to pound. With his wife, he'd learned the more pleasant she sounded, the more trouble he was in. And judging from the way the honey practically dripped from her tongue, he was in some serious trouble. He turned, plastering a smile on his face. "Hello, dear. Nice to see you."

She walked toward him, her hands on her hips, which swung back and forth with a bit of sass. Since he'd seen her last, she must've had her hair done—she'd always worn it short and boyish, but in her younger days, it had been a cute pixie cut. As she'd aged, it became more severe and spikier. Now, she reminded him of a dominatrix. "Don't hello me. You should have said hello to your son…at his basketball game. Remember?"

Damnation. He knew he'd forgotten something. But seeing Kylie had upended everything. He could barely remember his own name. All he kept thinking of was memories of the past, of those early days in Brooklyn. Funny, he'd thought those days were so shitty, compared to what he had now. Always scrimping, saving, having their electricity cut off every other month because they couldn't pay the bills.

But if those days were so bad, then why did he keep thinking of them so fondly? Why would he have given anything to be back there again?

"Jesus," he said.

Poor Tyler. Their youngest. William had set out wanting to be such a good dad, but the fact was, he'd been absent for all of his kids. Work always took precedence. Tyler had made varsity as a sophomore, which was a huge honor, but William hadn't made it to any of his games last year. Then he'd been chosen as a captain his junior year, and William had promised to do better. So far, he'd missed every one of those games too.

"I'm sorry. I'll make it up to Tyler next week. Did they win?"

She sniffed. "Do you care? It's hard to believe you care about anyone in this family but yourself."

He scrubbed a hand over his tired face. "Sorry, Tina. It's just been a really tough day," he said, turning and opening the door to his office. He went inside and poured himself that drink he so desperately needed, hoping against hope that she'd leave him alone. But she didn't. When he turned around, she was standing in the doorway, drumming her fingers on the wall. He slumped into his chair and took the first calming sip of his scotch.

"What's the problem?" she asked him, sugar dripping from the words in spite of her obvious irritation. "You seem like you're dealing with an awful lot. Is it about that woman today? You seemed rattled, even then."

He waved it away, and quickly came up with an excuse. "The financing for that place in Brooklyn. The bank's giving us trouble again."

She came up behind him and started to massage his shoulders. "That's nothing the great William Hatfield can't handle."

It was true. He wasn't worried about it at all. He always dealt with financing issues but managed to get them worked out. No, the tension she was feeling in his back had nothing to do with the company. He forced himself to take a small sip of his drink instead of downing it like he wanted to. "Yeah. I'll get it sorted out."

She kissed him on the top of his graying head. "I know you will. I'm sorry for barging in on you today when you obviously had a lot on your mind. And missing the game isn't the end of the world. I'm sure you'll make the next game."

The look she gave him was a challenge. *I dare you to miss the next game.*

He managed a smile. "Don't worry about it. Is Tyler awake?"

She shook her head. "It's after eleven. He was exhausted. He went to sleep an hour ago."

"All right. I will make it up to him," he stressed again.

"You'd better," she said, sweet as could be, her hips swaying as she sashayed to the door. In the doorway, she stopped. She lowered her voice an octave and purred sexily, "Come to bed soon, okay? I bought a new negligee I want to test out."

His balls practically crawled inside his body, but he forced a grin. "Yeah. That sounds good. Just got a couple emails to send."

When she'd left, he powered up his computer. Bringing up the search engine, he went into incognito mode, and typed Rhonda Hatfield into the search bar.

He wasn't surprised to discover she lived in the same house he'd bought for her all those years ago, with the money he'd gotten from his first big job. He was surprised that she apparently kept his name. She was living down there and had worked as an administrative assistant for a small manufacturing company. From her Facebook profile, she seemed to be happy. Had a lot of friends, a quiet life. There were dozens of pictures of her, and in each one, she was smiling that infectious, bright smile that had caught his eye the first time he'd gone into the diner.

He leaned closer. No significant other in sight. That was interesting.

And she was still a beautiful woman. His heart whirred in his chest. If things had been different...

Shaking his head, he noticed the pictures of the girl who'd come to visit him earlier today. His firstborn child. Rhonda had tagged her in a few pictures, so he easily found her profile. Though it was set to private, some photos came up. She was indeed beautiful, with his dark hair and her mother's pretty features, including those sparkling green eyes and that infectious smile. He paged through it, noting she had quite a few real-life friends. Her profile listed her occupation as Assistant Private Investigator at Starr Investigations.

Holy shit. His little girl was a private investigator? He smiled, wondering if they taught bad cockney accents in PI school.

The memory almost made him laugh. She'd probably just been nervous. He knew he'd been the moment he learned who the badly dressed woman in front of him was.

Nervous and excited.

He'd thought of his baby girl many times over the years but hadn't allowed himself to search for her.

He couldn't.

Tossing back the rest of his drink, he knew he shouldn't even be looking at her profile now.

Even in incognito mode, he wondered if Christina would see his search history. Hell, he had little doubt that she'd installed some type of key tracking software so she could see his every move.

Searching her had been stupid.

Clicking out of the browser, he cleared his search history —just in case—before sending those emails he told her he was going to send.

Pouring himself a second drink, he sipped it slowly as he trudged down the opulent hallway and toward the master suite. He needed the fortification before facing his wife and her new negligee.

He'd never felt more like he was heading off to a dungeon than he did at that moment.

WILLIAM HATFIELD WASN'T QUITE AS bright as he thought he was.

He was leaving a little trail of breadcrumbs to his old life, and all I needed to do was to follow him around. He was making this all too easy. First, having that mid-day meeting with his little whore, and acting all day like he'd gone and lost his head.

The phone buzzed while I was getting ready for bed. Nico. At this time of night?

I hurried into the bathroom to avoid prying ears and took the call. "Talk to me," I said. "And this better be good, you disturbing me here."

"Oh, it is," Nico said. "You're gonna be thanking me. He's on the computer right now, looking them up."

I raised an eyebrow. Nico had told me he had "ways" of finding things out, but I'd been skeptical that he could hack into William Hatfield's computer so easily. After all, the company was a billion-dollar enterprise. Hadn't their IT department set up a firewall to deal with such things? I was used to dealing with computer nerds. They were all talk, little action. But apparently, Nico was right, D & H Construction's IT department needed to be canned.

"Tell me what you see."

"Uh-huh. He just typed in Rhonda Hatfield."

I scowled. *Hatfield*? Who the hell was she? And why was he searching for her? "And?"

"And she lives in Asheville, North Carolina. Now, he's searching Kylie Hatfield. From the pictures he's bringing up, it's a match to the woman you sent me pictures of today. She's the woman he saw in his office this afternoon."

I gritted my teeth. The girl in his office was a Hatfield? "Are you sure?"

"Definitely. I followed her all the way to Newark International this afternoon, watched her walk through security. She's gone."

"Obviously."

"Hatfield," the guy breathed in my ear. "You know. From

what he's bringing up, it looks like this Kylie Hatfield is Rhonda's daughter. They look a little alike, and they're friends on Facebook."

What did that all mean? And what other secrets was he keeping?

"It jives with what I learned earlier when I accessed the recording from William's office. This girl believes that he is her father and called Rhonda Whitman Hatfield his wife."

I tapped on the edge of the sink, staring at myself in the mirror, thinking hard. Could this be true? "Find out everything you can about them."

"Then what?"

My reflection in the mirror blurred, then cleared. "Kill them."

Nico didn't even question the order. Didn't even ask me if I was sure.

I had a bad feeling about all this. The more I thought about the girl, the more certain I was becoming.

I quickly ended the call and went back to my room. Setting my phone on the nightstand, I poured myself a drink. Actually, this wasn't a problem. This would work just fine for my purposes. William just needed to remember who was in charge.

In this life, playing games would get you nowhere.

In this life, games were deadly.

William Hatfield would be reminded of that when his wife and daughter ended up dead.

13

It was nearly impossible for Kylie to wake up the next morning. She rolled around in bed, writhing in pain that wasn't just physical.

She'd gotten practically no sleep, staring at the ceiling. Her mattress had felt weird and lumpy, not the nice soft one that Linc had. She hadn't even had Vader to cuddle with. As the light filtered in through the closed shades, she wanted to burrow deeper into her mattress and never come out.

When she had slept for about twenty minutes at around four o'clock in the morning, she'd had weird dreams. Linc was holding the blonde bimbo's hand, and they were running away from her. When they turned toward her and started to make out, she realized that it wasn't Linc at all.

It was her father, and he was with that horrible woman with the short platinum hair.

She'd woken up with a start, her night clothes damp with sweat, thinking the world was coming to an end.

Rubbing her eyes, she climbed out of bed and trudged toward the bathroom. She took a shower, dressed without looking into a mirror, then drove herself to Starr Investigations.

The second she walked in, Greg looked at her, his brow furrowed in concern. "Uh, what gives, short stuff?"

She trudged to her desk and sat down, powering up her computer. Maybe, just maybe, a juicy case would be waiting for her, demanding all her time and attention. "What do you mean?"

He laughed. "You wanted to take a vacation. You were gone one day. That's not a vacation. That's not even a breather. What's the deal?"

She looked at him, her eyes drooping. "I don't want to talk about it."

He bent forward and looked at her feet. "Wait…where's Vader?"

"He chose a new best friend," she grumbled.

He held his hands up. "Oh, god. That ain't good. Trouble in paradise?"

"There is no paradise. Paradise is an illusion," she muttered, her eyes shifting toward her screen. She was ready to do all the work. Be the best damn investigator North Carolina had ever seen. But when the computer finally finished puttering and showed her the home screen, she realized something: She didn't have any pending cases. Not a single one to get herself lost in.

With nothing to do, she was hit with an urge to google the hell out of her father and his perfect second wife again.

She needed to suppress that. Down that road dwelled madness. She'd done that last night and all she had was a pounding headache to show for it. She didn't think she'd ever recover.

"Greg," she said hopefully. "Do you have any new cases for me?"

He shook his head. "Sorry. Slow time, kid."

She clung to the edge of the desk in desperation. "Don't you have *anything* for me to do?"

He smirked and pointed to a pile of filing.

Oh, hell.

She stood up and walked to it. It was the thing that she'd initially been hired to do. The thing she detested more than anything. But it was something to fill the time. She picked up a stack of papers.

For the first time, she was happy to do it. It didn't really help her to stop thinking about yesterday, but at least it kept her itchy fingers from their urge to google herself into complete psychosis.

An hour in, Greg got a phone call. He spoke to whoever was on the other end for a few minutes, then hung up, and started to pull on his ratty old blazer. "Sorry, kid. Got my walking papers. I've been called away."

That was nothing unusual. "For the day?"

"For the rest of the week, at least. Impact has me working a fraud case in Raleigh. I might be over there for a while."

Lucky bastard. She fought the urge to throw herself at his feet and scream, *Take me with you!* "Well, I guess I could…" she looked around helplessly. Short of finishing the filing and answering the one phone call they got each day, there really wasn't much on the docket.

"Hey, kid?" He gave her one of his serious, fatherly looks. "You look like shit. Take my advice. Extend that vacation. Even if you're not spending it with Mr. Dreamy. You might just need time for yourself. To think. Relax. Get that sweet little head of yours some perspective. And maybe…a makeover."

A makeover? She looked down at herself. She'd accidentally buttoned her blouse wrong, but other than that, she didn't think she looked that bad. She quickly fixed the buttons and spied her reflection in the glass of the old storefront. Okay, her hair did look like she'd stuck her finger in an electrical socket. And she'd totally forgotten makeup. Her clothes were mostly wrinkles.

Yeah. She probably looked like she could've used more than one day of vacation.

"I don't really have anywhere to go," she said. *Or anywhere I want to go. Especially alone.* "Would you mind if I worked from home? I can forward the incoming calls to my cell."

He shrugged. "Have at it, but I expect you to give me a report every day."

"I w—"

Greg held up a hand. "Actually, don't give me a report. Go off the grid. My company's been around thirty years. It ain't gonna suffer much if you check yourself out for a few days. Relax. Seriously. That's an order."

She sighed. She wished she could check out and relax, but she knew she'd just end up doing what she'd done last night —moping. "Okay," she mumbled, powering down her computer and reaching for her bag.

She told him goodbye and went out to her car. When she slipped into the driver's seat, she sat there for a very long time, her hands on the steering wheel. Then she glimpsed her face in the rearview mirror. Pale skin, bloodshot eyes, hair from hell.

Greg was right. She did look like shit. Everything had gone to pot in less than twenty-four hours.

Sighing, she threw her Jeep into reverse, pulled out, and headed back to her apartment, wondering if she'd need a date with a couple of Linc's Ambien in order to get some decent sleep tonight.

Then she realized she was going back to her place, and the sleep meds were at his. And she knew she'd be memorizing every little crack on the ceiling, again, tonight.

❄

LINC GOT a late start that morning, all because of one furry little troublemaker, who was almost as much of a problem as his owner.

Vader. No matter how many obedience lessons he gave the dog, he had a mind of his own, and a little bit of a mischievous streak too.

Just like his owner.

Linc wasn't one to be tied to his cell phone. He didn't feel naked or jittery without it, the way Kylie did. In fact, he often left it lying around when he went out, and only realized he didn't have it when he wanted to use it for one of his infrequent calls or texts.

But when he woke up that morning, he practically tore open the bag of rice to see if his phone would power on. Nothing.

And now things were at a desperate level. He really needed to get in touch with Kylie. Knowing her, she was probably so angry at him, she'd spit in his face. Worse than that. Knowing her, she'd give him the silent treatment... forever. This was Code Red.

He tossed the dead phone on the counter and looked at a mystified Storm. "What should I do, girl?"

She simply walked to her water dish and had a drink.

"Guess that's an 'ain't got a clue.'"

Awesome.

"Guess I better put a trip to the phone store on my to-do list for today too, huh?"

But first, Kylie. As he grabbed his keys from the kitchen counter, he checked the clock on the microwave. It was after nine. She'd probably already made a voodoo doll in his likeness and was getting ready to prick the hell out of it.

They needed to talk. She'd probably give him the silent

treatment to end all silent treatments, but eventually she'd come around. It'd be hard to apologize, and he dreaded the thought of doing it, but it couldn't wait any longer.

He'd thought about the situation all night.

Kylie'd come home early, and she'd taken an Uber to surprise him. Ordinarily, he'd have been thrilled to see her, but then he started to wonder why she'd come home so soon. Had the work trip ended sooner than she thought? Or was it even a work trip? Had she actually thought he was cheating and had been setting a trap to see if he'd take the bait, and then Faith and her bad timing had shown up, confirming Kylie's wayward suspicions?

Was his luck really that terrible?

Did she really not trust him?

A couple weeks ago, he'd asked Kylie to move in with him. Hell, he'd practically begged her, promising her cart blanc if she'd just let him take care of her. He'd even delivered the lamest line in the world.

If you want to protect me and I want to protect you, living together makes sense.

God, he was pathetic.

Since then, he hadn't brought it up, and even when more and more of her stuff showed up in his house, he never said a word, just made more room for her.

Even while they'd gotten closer, had this crazy idea of him cheating been brewing in her head the entire time? Had Faith showing up at that exact wrong moment only solidified those feelings in her head?

Probably.

Shit. Maybe this was worse than he thought. Maybe she wouldn't talk to him. Maybe she wouldn't come around, no matter what he said. Maybe this was the end.

And maybe that was for the best.

He was still working on himself, after all. Trying to get on top of the guilt and sorrow he still felt from his last days in Syria. The days he'd repressed for so long. The nightmares that made them still seem so vivid.

Getting into his truck, he turned the key in the ignition and as it roared to life, gazed out at the mountain ridges that seemed to go on forever. The reds and golds of fall in their spectacular glory. The view was magnificent, even with the clouds that obscured the sun.

He'd hoped to share all this with Kylie, but now…?

He drummed his fingers against the steering wheel as he headed down the mountain listening to Garth Brooks, then shut off the radio entirely as he pulled into a parking space across from Starr Investigations. It looked dark inside. That, and he couldn't see Kylie's new Jeep anywhere on the busy street. And the yellow thing was a hard thing to miss.

He climbed out of the truck and jogged over to the old brick storefront. As he did, he noticed a young man peering in the picture window. He wore a leather jacket and sunglasses despite the gloom of the overcast day. With his hair slicked off his face, he reminded Linc of a weasel.

"Can I help you?" Linc asked as he approached.

The man spun in the other direction and walked away at a fast pace. A thousand possibilities for that guy to be staking out the place whirled through Linc's mind, all of them bad. He tried to think more like Kylie, who never assumed the worst.

Maybe he was just checking his reflection in the glass?

Linc didn't buy it. He was overly suspicious, precisely because Kylie was sometimes so oblivious and too trusting. That's why they made a good team.

If they even were a team now.

The guy picked up his pace, not looking back, then jaywalked across the road and disappeared down one of the side streets. Linc turned to look in the window. The lights were off inside. The shades were down in the doorway, the *Sorry, We're Closed* sign hanging crookedly at its center. Even so, he tried the door, because she should've been there.

If she wasn't, where else would she be?

Her apartment, maybe? But it was the middle of a workday. She might have gotten a new assignment and was out tracking down leads. Or she might be out buying the materials to finish his voodoo doll.

He reached into his pocket and looked at his dead phone. He'd have better luck calling. There was a phone store right around the corner. He could probably get the phone fixed or exchanged quicker than he could run all over town looking for her.

When he got there, the place was empty. The service tech looked the phone over and proclaimed it DOA. "You might as well just give it back to your dog," the man said. "Seeing as how it's his new favorite chew toy. It's beyond repair."

Linc scratched at his jaw as the man started showing him the latest and greatest new models of phones, phones that could do a hell of a lot of things that Linc didn't give a shit about, but many of those apps came in handy once in a while. "Just fix me up with the latest iPhone."

"You got it," the man said. "Have you backed up your data recently?"

Of course he hadn't. "No."

"If you want me to transfer all your data over, that'll be about an hour. You're welcome to wait here or come back."

Linc looked around. At the waiting area, there was a television blasting the day's news, and he knew that would only upset him. Since his PTSD had come to a head, he'd been careful to avoid all the things that stressed him out too much, and stories of death and gloom on the news qualified. He remembered the coffee shop next door. "Thanks. I'll be back."

He went one door down and pulled open the door to the

little shop, and a bell dinged overhead. As he waited in line, thinking of what he'd say when he got his new phone and called Kylie, he looked over at the bar and…there was Faith, waving at him from over her latte.

Holy shit. He hadn't seen her in nearly ten years, and now…twice in less than twenty-four hours? When the bell on the door rang, he looked back, expecting to see Kylie. Because…of course he would.

But it was just a kid with too many facial piercings, looking like he wanted to destroy the world with the beams of his ice-blue contacts.

Linc turned back to order his coffee, then waited at the pick-up station, keeping his back to his ex, not caring if he was being a bastard or not.

Coffee in hand, he turned and nearly plowed Faith over. "You following me?" she asked with a grin.

She wasn't serious, but he felt like fate was trying to throw them together, and by now, he was regretting the position it'd put him in. "Nah."

"Come sit with me. I have something important to talk to you about."

Linc looked around, expecting Kylie to be somewhere nearby. When he didn't see her, his eyes trailed over Faith's things as she moved them over on the bar to make room for him to sit next to her. She had a fashion magazine open. Clearly, she was still really into that, since she looked like a magazine cover herself.

Faith was big on not having a hair out of place, which he'd never been able to understand. The first thing she used to do every morning was put on her *face*, something she never needed because she was naturally beautiful. But, in her words, she wanted to be perfect.

To Linc, perfection wasn't only unattainable, it was downright exhausting to attempt to achieve.

No, thank you.

Faith was just different. In law school, she'd spent most of her time competing with Linc to get better grades than he did. She also had to win every argument, even if she was on the wrong side of it. The woman was exhaustingly always trying to prove to the world that she was the best and had the best of everything. She probably kept her multiple social media feeds full of selfies, constantly seeking the validation of others.

But as competitive as Faith was, she could still be a very sweet person. Even her Dear John letter had been a nice, overly apologetic one. She'd mentioned falling for one of their classmates—a Jim Something, who was kind of a douche. In the few times he'd thought about her since their break up, he'd expected they'd get married and open a law firm together and have had a half-dozen children by now.

Warily, he sat down next to her, sipping his coffee. "Dog killed my phone, so I had to buy a new one. That's why I'm here. They're transferring the data over next door."

"Ah," she said. "That's why I was always more of a cat person."

And that's why I should've known we'd never have lasted.

"Whatever happened to that guy? Jim? You marry him?"

She wrinkled her nose. "No." She wiggled her ringless left hand. "Still single. He was kind of a jerk."

Linc sucked on his teeth, bordering on regretting asking. Time to change the subject. "You said you had something to talk to me about?"

She gave him a worried look. "I want to apologize for showing up at the wrong time. That woman last night was… Kylie? Your girlfriend?"

He nodded. "Yeah."

She winced. "Oh, boy, then she *really* got the wrong idea, that you and I were…I'm sorry."

He offered up a chuckle but didn't find any of this funny. "You said that last night."

Color rose to her cheeks. "I know, but I wanted to apologize again for just showing up like that. But she wasn't wrong. We were together once."

Linc sipped his coffee. "The operative word being *were*."

She looked down into her mug. "Yeah, well. I wasn't wrong, was I? When I said we weren't cut out for each other?"

"No, you were right on the money," he admitted, shrugging.

When he went to push to his feet, she grabbed his arm, stopping him. "How's your parents? Your brothers?"

Faith had always fit in with his family of lawyers better than Linc ever had. They'd adored her. Even though she'd broken up with Linc, his father still blamed him for the end of the relationship.

"They're all good. Still ask about you from time to time."

She smiled. "They're such good people."

Linc raised an eyebrow. He knew they were, in their own way, and it bothered him a little that his ex had always had more of a connection with his family, who he had nothing in common with, than he ever did.

Faith was right. They did have very little in common, and it only made him miss Kylie more.

"So, what are you up to now? I read in the paper about your return from Afghanistan," she said, closing her fashion magazine. "You're a hero. Got the Purple Heart, huh?"

"Syria," he muttered. If there was anything he liked talking about less than his time overseas, it was all the awards they showered upon him after... Shaking the thoughts away, he took a sip from his coffee. "Now, I do search and rescue and train rescue dogs."

"Oh, really?" Faith said in what he knew was mock interest. She never had struck him as a dog person, much like the rest of his family. "That's great. It's really great."

The small talk over, Linc was sure it'd just dissolve into awkwardness. If he'd become a lawyer and they'd gotten married, it would've been utter misery. He took a big gulp of his coffee and checked his watch, intending to find a way to beg off so he could leave, when a familiar voice called, "What's this? A party I wasn't invited to?"

Faith turned around with a start and smiled broadly, then jumped off her stool and ran up to Jacob, nearly knocking the big guy over with the force of her hug. Linc watched her embracing his best friend, wondering why his own reception had been so much more sedate. The two of them hugged so long that Linc almost felt like he was peeping in on something he shouldn't be watching.

"Should I let you two get a room?" he muttered, and they slowly parted, as if they hated to do so.

"What are you doing here?" Jacob asked, his voice an octave higher and clearly thrilled. He still had yet to look at Linc.

Faith's voice was also higher, her words tumbling out a mile a minute, like her latte had been laced with strong speed. "I just came in! I'm working in New York, but I stopped by for a week. I was going to look you up. I tracked Linc down last night, and he said you're an Asheville detective. Really?"

He nodded and started to go on about his job. Linc stood there, hands in his pockets, a third wheel if ever there was one. The few times the two of them had double-dated at the movie theater in town, she and Jacob had gotten on famously. Back then, he'd thought it was great. His best friend and his best girl were in tune with each other, like brother and sister.

But when he looked down and noticed that Jacob was still

holding her hand, stroking the back of it very lightly, he started to wonder. What was going on?

When Jacob leaned down, murmuring something in Faith's ear, and still hadn't acknowledged him, Linc cleared his throat. With what looked like great reluctance, Jacob dropped Faith's hand and faced his friend, his smile transforming into a *what the hell is going on* frown.

Jacob clearly wanted to know what was going on too.

"What's up, man?" Jacob looked from Linc to Faith and back again, a confused look on his face. "How did you two...?"

Linc had known the big, burly ginger since kindergarten. They'd been through a lot together. Jacob may have been in-tune with Faith, but he loved Kylie just as much. What Jacob was trying to imply was simple: *Don't tell me you're two-timing Kylie with your ex. If you're gonna do that, let me have your leftovers.*

"It was innocent. We just ran into each other. That's all," Linc said, finishing off his coffee and pushing in his barstool. "You here for a reason, or are you just playing hooky from your job, Detective?"

Jacob grinned. "Just in the neighborhood to take a witness statement for an accident. Same boring shit, different day. You leaving?"

Linc nodded. "Got to pick up my phone next door and meet Kylie." *If she'll let me.* "You guys have fun catching up. I'll see you around."

They waved at him, but by the time he reached the doorway and looked back, the two of them were deep in conversation, smiling at each other, heads almost touching. Linc almost had to pinch himself to make sure he actually existed, because it was clear he hadn't needed to be there.

That's interesting, he thought, heading to the phone store.

But that was Jacob. He didn't miss the chance to flirt with

a hot girl. And Faith was outgoing and bubbly and hot and fun.

They were both nothing like him.

Neither was Kylie, for that matter. But whatever it was about Kylie, he felt like he was missing a big something without it. Without her.

As the store clerk showed him his new phone, all Linc wanted to do was grab it, call her, and hear her voice. The second he got it in his hands, he tapped her number.

It went straight to voicemail.

He gnashed his teeth as he got into his truck. He'd spent a good chunk of his first deployment beating himself up over fucking things up with Faith, but Faith had seen what he couldn't. They didn't belong. Kylie, though? Kylie belonged with him. It had taken him time to know what was right, and he'd never been so sure as he was at that moment.

Kylie was everything he wanted.

14

R honda Hatfield loved going out on her rounds when she wasn't working.

These days, her rounds involved stopping at three different supermarkets near her house, trying to get the best prices for her food. She'd clipped coupons and saved maniacally when Kylie was growing up, so now, securing good buys and spending less was a sport for her. She enjoyed it almost as much as some people enjoyed binge-watching their favorite shows or playing their favorite games.

First, though, she had to stop at the pharmacy and get her prescriptions for her blood pressure, and the post office to get stamps.

Unlike most people, she loved running errands. Rushing about and checking things off her to-do list. Also unlike most people, she'd never go out without a full face of makeup and dressed to the nines. How people could go out in their ratty clothes and curlers was beyond her. She might not be actively looking for a man, but it didn't mean she had to look like she didn't care.

It was all so exciting for her. So, when she had the chance

to dress up and go out, she did so to the nines, wearing her full makeup and a pretty outfit she'd gotten from the Chadwick's of Boston catalog.

After she picked up her medication, she drove to the little post office on Main Street. This one was less crowded than the one by her home, but that was because parking was awful. The only parking was on the busy, narrow street itself, which made for a lot of accidents and close calls. Rhonda decided to brave it, considering the other post office wasn't on the way to Harris Teeter Supermarket.

As she slipped out of the car, a truck roared by, going way above the speed limit. There was a time, when she was Kylie's age and in New York, that no truck driver could pass by her without giving her a beep. It was funny, she thought, that things like that annoyed her daughter. Rhonda would've loved to get some positive male attention these days. It'd been decades since she'd gotten even a compliment from a good-looking man.

Sighing, she thought of her daughter and her new mission to find her dad. If she was looking for positive male attention, she wasn't going to find it by way of Adam Hatfield. That, Rhonda was sure of.

The smooth-talking New Yorker had certainly pulled the wool over her eyes in the year they'd been together. She'd come to think of Adam as caring, good, a little sloppy for her tastes, but a diamond in the rough. She thought he had a good heart. But the way he'd left? Only a monster could be so cruel.

That was what Adam Hatfield was. A monster.

As much as Rhonda attempted to shield her daughter from what Adam Hatfield had done to her, her life had been utterly shredded by his disappearance. She'd been unable to get out of bed for weeks, and her self esteem still hadn't gotten over his betrayal.

She didn't hate him. Not now. But she had. For a long time, and very deeply.

But even though her hate ran deep, she couldn't help thinking that if he showed up and explained himself, she'd have taken him back in an instant. That was how much she'd desperately wanted things to work out between them, how much she wanted Kylie to have the stability of a father.

It was too late now, but if Kylie somehow found him and brought him into her life...what would she do? What would he say? What could he possibly say to make what he did all right?

Nothing. He could never be a part of her life now. Any explanation he'd give wouldn't matter.

She picked up her book of stamps and was so deep in thought as she crossed the street that she didn't notice the yellow sports car until the brakes started to squeal. It had almost stopped by the time it made contact with the backs of her thighs, sending her flying up onto the hood.

After the initial shock, she was more embarrassed than hurt, since her flowered skirt had flown straight up, baring her undies to the world. Rhonda hurried to push it down. The young woman in the driver's seat just stared at her with wide-eyed shock.

Rhonda started to apologize profusely as she climbed down off the bumper, shaking in time with the revving motor underneath her. Only when she took the first few wobbly steps toward the edge of the road did she feel the pain.

She limped across the rest of the street, focusing on getting to her car where she'd left her purse, thinking the cops would be there soon and would need to see her identification. Or something. She touched her temple with trembling fingers, trying to think.

Rhonda expected the woman to either ask if she needed

medical assistance or demand she fix some dent in the vehicle. Instead, the yellow car lurched forward and disappeared around the corner, tires squealing. Rhonda leaned against the side of her car, heart beating madly, trying to catch her breath.

"Are you all right, ma'am?" a voice said from behind her.

Rhonda turned her spinning head to see a man running toward her on the sidewalk. He was tall and distinguished in a tailored dark suit, his neat gray beard and a full head of white hair seizing her attention. Suddenly, despite wearing her best outfit, she felt underdressed, like her underwear was still on display.

When she said nothing, his look of concern grew, and he took her arm. "Can you walk?"

She nodded, still a bit dazed as he helped her onto the sidewalk.

"I saw the whole thing," he said, touching her hands, her arms, her shoulders. "I missed the license plate of the car that hit you, but…where do you hurt?"

She pointed vaguely toward her thigh and her hip. Her shoulder felt a little strange too. They were starting to ache now that the adrenaline was wearing off and she was shaking from the shock of her close call.

She tried to smile, tried to reassure him that she was okay, but as she gazed into his kind blue eyes, words escaped her.

He lifted a phone to his ear. "You should be checked out by professionals. I'm calling for a—" He paused and listened, then spoke calmly but authoritatively into the receiver. "Yes. I witnessed an accident. A woman's been hurt. Please send an ambulance to the corner of Main and Third. Thank you."

Her daughter had always been so embarrassed when Rhonda used the word "hunk" to describe Linc. Maybe there was a more modern word for it, but if there was, she didn't know what it was. And it didn't matter. Because right now, there could be no more fitting word for the man in front of her.

He was a tall, white-haired hunk. A silver fox if ever she saw one.

Rhonda was normally a woman of many words, and she hadn't had a man strike her speechless since...Adam. When she did gain control of her vocal cords, she cleared her throat. "I'm all right."

"You don't know that. You might be in shock," he said, leading her toward the passenger side of her car. "Why don't you sit down in here, where you can catch your breath? Can I get you anything?"

He opened the door for her and guided her onto the seat, then crouched in front of her, right at her knocking knees.

Despite the Autumn sun beaming down on them, she was shivering. It probably was shock from the accident. Or maybe quite a different kind of shock. She couldn't tell. She said, "No. Thank you." She reached into her purse for her phone. "I should probably call someone and let them know I've been in an accident, so they're not worried about me."

"Yes," he said. "I can imagine you're very shaken up."

She searched through her purse, slowly first, then frantically. "Oh. I forgot my phone."

She was always doing that, despite Kylie's urgings to keep her phone with her at all times. She'd lived so much of her life without one, and spent so much of her time at home, that she was always leaving it on the kitchen counter.

"Well, here," the man said, handing him hers. "You can call your husband from here."

She smiled and held up her left hand. Was he fishing for information about her? "No husband. I wanted to call my daughter."

"Oh, I'm sorry." His smiled grew wider, and Rhonda

noticed that he wasn't wearing a ring, either. "A beautiful woman such as yourself, I just assumed…"

"Thank you," she said, on the verge of giggling. She hadn't giggled in how many years? She needed to control herself. The last time she'd giggled, she'd ended up pregnant with a husband who promised to love her for the rest of her life. *Well, at least I can't get knocked up now.* "I'm really…I'm fine. You look like you have somewhere to be. I can manage by myself."

"Don't be silly," he said, leaning against her car. "What kind of gentleman would I be if I left you here? I was just headed to the hospital myself."

She blinked. "Oh! Are you hurt too? Or visiting someone?"

He laughed. "No. That's where I work. I'm an ENT."

A doctor? Her mouth went dry.

She'd gone through her entire life regretting falling so fast and hard for Adam and had resolved that it would never happen again. And this man—this perfect stranger—was making her want to toss all that out the window.

Had she hit her head? That was the only explanation she could come up with.

"Oh. How nice."

He shrugged. "I wish I could be more help in your current situation, but trauma isn't my specialty." He pointed to her knee, which was starting to turn an unflattering shade of purple. "May I?"

She stared, confused, as he crouched down and gently folded her skirt back and touched the purpling skin, his fingers like a gentle breath.

He had to have noticed the goose bumps that popped out all over her. And she thought goose bumps were just for school kids. She was wrong.

He met and held her gaze. "My name is Jerry Phillips. Pleased to meet you…"

"Rhonda," she breathed, as he still gently touched her skin. "Rhonda Hatfield."

"Rhonda," he said. She'd never heard her name said that way. So sensually, in such a way that the deep, rich timbre vibrated inside her.

Then, much to her own dismay, she opened her mouth and actually giggled like a schoolgirl.

15

I t felt better to get home and change into comfortable boxers and a camisole, but once Kylie sat down on the couch and looked around, she decided the rest of the day would be for moping. Not relaxing. Not binge-watching her favorite television shows. Not cleaning or catching up on errands. Not any of the things she wanted to do whenever she was working.

Moping. The end.

Her mostly empty apartment was so lonely and depressing, since she was surrounded by all these "rejects"—the things she hadn't needed or wanted enough to take them on the nights she stayed with Linc. It was a perfect place for the activity.

She felt a little like a reject now too. She knew she'd only feel worse if she allowed herself to dwell on it.

But dwell, she did.

Grabbing her laptop, she opened it up and started to google everything she could possibly think of regarding William Adam Hatfield. When she'd exhausted herself by looking at every picture of him and his new family on the internet, she threw herself back against the couch, half-hating him, half-mourning his lack of presence in her life.

What was it that lady at Cityside Garbage had said? Something about the owner of the company being arrested? Her father had been in thick with the family, and they'd been criminals. He'd wanted Kylie to get away. In fact, he'd seemed desperate to get her out of his office. Maybe that had something to do with his odd behavior. Maybe that's why he'd wanted to get her mother away, all those years ago. Maybe he was protecting them.

Scratching her head, Kylie thought back to the man's name. Joey Gallo? She typed it in, along with Cityside Garbage.

Hundreds of results poured forth. The first one was an article from *The New York Times*. *Cityside Garbage Services Top Man Nabbed for Extortion, Possible Mafia Ties.*

Kylie's eyes widened. Mafia?

Kylie clicked on the article, but it told her that she needed a subscription. She found another one, down farther, for another New York newspaper that was similar and clicked on it. It was a later article, mentioning that the case had never been brought to trial, and Gallo had been released because of some no-show witnesses. At the end of the article, it said, *Gallo is suspected of having ties to one of the city's most notorious crime families, the Colombo syndicate.*

As she read, that spidey sense inside her, the one she always got when something was wrong, started to buzz. The Colombo crime family?

Gallo's arrest had happened just about the time that her father had switched to the new job in Manhattan. Around that same time, he'd told Kylie's mother that he wanted to succeed in life and provide for the baby and seemed ambitious enough to go after it. Had his ambition gotten him involved in the mafia? Was he still involved now? Was that the reason he'd left her mother with no explanation whatsoever?

She googled the Colombo crime family and got millions of results. They were one of the five families, the most powerful mafia syndicate in the city. Murder, extortion, gambling, prostitution...you name it, they were involved. Had her father really been that stupid and desperate to provide for her that he'd gotten tangled in that?

And if providing for her had meant that much to him, then why did he just disappear? Was it for her protection?

A finger of ice stretched down her spine. She pulled a blanket around her shoulders and stared at some mug shots of a few of the most notorious gangsters in the group. They were all tough looking, frightening. Linc would've gone nuts if he'd known how close she'd gotten to them.

Linc.

If she hadn't been so angry at him, she'd be calling him right now, asking for his opinion. Her spidey sense was going off, but she usually needed a good dose of common sense from Linc to round her out and stop her wild theories from growing inside her head and becoming half-cocked and ill-advised action.

As she was contemplating what she should do, her phone rang on the coffee table.

Linc was her first thought. She lifted it up and frowned at the screen. Not Linc. It was a number she'd never seen before. Coming in through her direct line, not through Starr Investigations, where she'd forwarded the calls.

The number was local, and she didn't usually answer those since damn robo-callers so often spoofed local numbers. She let it go to voicemail, intending to block the number if they didn't leave a message. Not that it would stop the scammers from trying a different number, but what else could she do?

Gnawing on her thumbnail, she set her laptop down on the coffee table and absently went to the kitchen, searching for something to munch. She always ate when she was stressed, and only when she opened the fridge did she remember she hadn't any food at all in the apartment.

That meant she'd have to go out. Unless...Chinese. Lots and lots of Chinese.

She picked up her phone and called the place on the corner, ordering enough food for several days. As she hung up, she saw that the robo-caller had left her a voicemail.

Probably a salesperson, trying to get her in on an in-ground pool or some other thing that was completely useless to her life. She was about to delete it but decided to listen anyway. She heard a familiar voice, which she quickly realized was her mother.

"Hi, hon. I don't want to worry you, but if you want to call me back, just call the hospital. I left my phone at home, but I'm here. Everything's okay..."

Kylie felt a bit lightheaded. Her mother was in the hospital? Why hadn't her spidey sense sprung up, telling her to answer the phone when her mother was in trouble?

Was she in trouble?

Kylie played the message again. The tone of her mother's voice was odd. No, Rhonda didn't sound very much like she was in trouble. She sounded almost...thrilled. Did she have a concussion? Or was she on pain meds that made her giddy?

Kylie quickly exited out of the voicemail and redialed the number, hoping that the owner of the phone her mother had borrowed was still nearby. A moment later, a deep male voice came on the line. "Hello?"

"Hi." Her voice was breathless, so she inhaled, forcing her nerves to calm. "This is Kylie Hatfield. My mother, Rhonda, just called me from this number and told me she was in the hospital. Is she still with you?"

"Yes, she certainly is." He sounded a bit like a radio announcer. "One moment, and I'll put her on."

Who was that man? Whoever he was, there was no doubt Rhonda was probably pouring her charm on him. No wonder she'd sounded so happy on the phone, as if she'd just gotten a visit from Linc. Kylie knew it. Her mother was smitten.

"Hello!" her mother sang in her grand, boisterous way. Kylie could just see her, insisting on looking her best, even in a hospital bed. She'd probably been applying lipstick when Kylie called.

"Mom!" she said, gripping the receiver. "Are you okay? What was it? Your heart?"

Kylie'd constantly worried about her mother's ticker, ever since she was diagnosed with high blood pressure a few years before. It was from all the good food she cooked, and the fact that her mother never exercised or watched her fats. Kylie didn't, either, but she had time on her side. Her mother was her only living family; she needed her to take care of herself.

At least, the only living family she cared about.

"No," Rhonda said. "Not at all. I was hit by a car while leaving the post office."

"A what? Oh, my god! Are you okay?"

"Yes, it's just a bruised knee and hip, sprained wrist. Nothing broken, thank goodness."

Kylie let out a sigh of relief. "Well, good. How did that happen? Did that man whose phone you borrowed hit you?"

"No, it was a hit and run, believe it or not."

"Really? Bastard. Then, who is—"

"I'm using Jerry's phone. He's been so nice. Stayed with me the whole time, and he's just been a doll."

For all of Kylie's life, Rhonda'd kept herself off the market. Barely dated. Insisted she liked being alone. Why was she suddenly doing backflips over a guy she just met? "Did you hit your head?"

Rhonda tittered. "Not at all. Jerry saw the whole thing."

"Jerry?"

"Yes, he's very…" she sighed, "nice."

Kylie pressed the heel of her hand into her eye. That was all she needed. Her mom going nuts over some dude she just met. She needed to investigate this Jerry dude, and stat. "Well, tell Jerry that he can leave, and sit tight. I'll be right over."

Before her mother could protest, she hung up and grabbed her purse. As she was about to leave, she remembered the Chinese food. She scuffed into her flip-flops, closing the door and running downstairs as she called to cancel the order. As she did, her stomach grumbled.

It was only when she got to the hospital that she realized what a mess she was. She was only wearing a camisole and boxer shorts, and she'd piled her hair on top of her head in a messy bun. She didn't even look fit enough to go to the corner and pick up Chinese food. She didn't look like she belonged anywhere but in bed.

Reaching behind the seat, she pulled out a UNC sweatshirt that she kept in the back for emergencies. It practically came down to her mid thighs and would cover the boxers well enough. She put it on, took the tie out of her hair and fluffed it, and then hurried into the hospital.

She found her mother in the non-urgent side of the ER, looking exactly as she had expected her to look: Perfect. She had a sling on one arm and a bruise on her temple, but other than that, she looked fine. "Oh, Kylie!" she said. "Come here, darling."

As Kylie walked in, her eyes trailed over to the man sitting in the corner of the room. He was an older, well-dressed man with silver hair. Quite debonair and handsome, reminding her more than a little of Sean Connery. At a glance, Kylie understood exactly why her mom was acting that way. Her mother probably had forbidden him from leaving.

Kylie still didn't trust him. She wasn't sure she'd ever trust any man again.

"Mom," Kylie said, sitting on the edge of the bed. "Are you all right?"

"Of course. Just a little tap."

That was surprising. She knew her mother and got the feeling that, if Mr. Connery hadn't been sitting nearby, she'd be giving her a rundown of everything that ailed her. That was her mother. Never complaining and going out of her way to make others comfortable. She wished the man would just go so she and her mother could talk, but he appeared entirely too comfortable.

Kylie looked at him. "You saw it, right, Mr—"

Rhonda gripped her daughter's forearm. "Kylie, please let me introduce you to Dr. Jerry Phillips. He works in this hospital as an ENT. That's an Ear, Nose, and Thr—"

"I know what that is," she snapped, looking over the man. Oh. So now the infatuation was becoming clearer. He was a *doctor*. "But I'm here now, so he can—"

"Don't be rude, Kylie. He insisted upon staying because he's a witness, and the police may want to speak with him."

"Dr. Phillips," Kylie said carefully, studying him. He was dressed so well, almost too well. Kylie had always been suspicious of men in general, but men who dressed like they were going to a wedding every day of their lives made her doubly suspicious. "You saw the accident? Was it just a tap?"

He looked at her mother fondly. "Not quite. I was coming from the other side of the street and saw the whole thing. Your mother received quite the jolt."

"And this person just drove away?" Kylie touched her

mother's leg, and Rhonda yelped. Startled, Kylie lifted Rhonda's skirt, then gasped at how swollen and bruised her mother's knee was. "Nobody knows who did it? There has to be some way to find him!"

Rhonda pushed her skirt back down to cover her knee. "Nonsense. I could've been more careful. I shouldn't have—"

Dr. Phillips took Rhonda's hand, giving it a couple soft pats. "The woman driving the car was speeding and was probably distracted by her phone. Plus, running away from the scene of an accident is never okay," he said, echoing exactly what Kylie was thinking. She could feel him look at her, but she couldn't take her eyes from their joined hands. "The police are on their way over to take a statement. I do think whoever this person was needs to be brought to justice."

Kylie felt her suspicion toward the man soften. No, she wasn't going to get all googly-eyed like Rhonda, but he'd definitely won points by being here and taking such great care of her mother. "Thank you. I agree."

"Now," Rhonda said, looking over her daughter. "What is with that ensemble? Didn't you come from work? Please tell me I raised my child to know better than to dress like that in public?"

Kylie looked down at herself. "Well, I—"

"Darling, your makeup's all smeared. Have you been crying?"

Kylie winced. She hadn't cried...that much. Just a little in the car on the way home from Starr Investigations. And a little more as she was sitting on the couch, contemplating burying herself under the cushions for life.

Had she even put on makeup that morning? Or maybe it was left over from where she hadn't washed her face last night? She wiped a finger under her eye, and it came away black.

She felt her face flame hot, and her mother shook her head. *Forget it, sweetheart. You're a lost cause,* the gesture said.

Kylie smoothed her hair back into a ponytail and then dropped the long strands when she realized she didn't have any way of holding it back. "It's not a big deal. No one's here to see me, and this isn't a fashion show. I'll just—"

"Is that Kylie Hatfield I'm hearing?"

Kylie turned toward the hallway and saw a giant, redheaded form filling the doorway. He gave her a lazy smile.

Kylie smiled in return. She would've smiled brighter if she knew she didn't look like crap. "Jacob!"

"Should've known," he said, coming in to wrap her in a hug. "Where there's trouble, there's Kylie. Don't you look like shit?"

Kylie could always count on Jacob to tell it like it was.

"Gee, thanks. It's not me this time, I swear," she said, shoving him in the chest as she released him. "It's my mom."

"No, you definitely look like shit," he said to her with a laugh, then looked past her, raising his voice. "So, what's this I hear? All the Hatfields are troublemakers? You must be Kylie's sister. I can see the resemblance."

Kylie rolled her eyes as her mother blushed at the compliment. Rhonda actually seemed to be enjoying herself, so she simply stepped back and watched the men blanket her with their attention.

"How are you feeling? I'm Jacob Dean, county detective. I was already at the hospital, so I told the boys at the precinct that I'd take your statement."

She shook his big paw with her good hand. "Thank you for coming, Mr. Dean."

Jacob shook Dr. Phillips's hand, and he introduced himself as a witness. "Always good to have a witness. What's this about a hit and run?"

"I saw the whole thing," Dr. Phillips said. "It was a young woman in a yellow sports car."

Rhonda opened her mouth to speak, but then her eyes went to the door and her face lit up. "Linc!"

Kylie whirled to see him standing in the door.

And she didn't think she could feel much worse about her appearance. She looked like something that girl from last night would probably have on the bottom of her shoe.

"Sorry," he said, his voice tentative. "Jacob texted me that a Hatfield was in the hospital, and I wanted to make sure you were all okay."

Now she really wished she didn't look like an old bag lady. All she could think of was the woman he'd been embracing. That woman probably didn't go around with crud under her eyes, ever.

Kylie cringed as Rhonda said, "How kind of you, Linc! It's just me. Your girlfriend is fine."

Kylie hugged herself as his eyes fixed on her. She couldn't meet his gaze.

He went over to the foot of the bed. "You're all right, Ms. Hatfield? Nothing I can get you?"

"I'm very well, thank you. They're taking good care of me," she said. "But my daughter might need help. Look at her. Doesn't she look awful?"

Kylie shot her eye daggers. Then her gaze flickered to Linc, who was watching her intently. He came close to her, close enough to touch, but he didn't. He whispered, "Can I talk to you?"

She hitched a shoulder, like she didn't care. "Fine."

He let out a breath. "In private?"

She rolled her eyes at him like leaving the room was the hardest thing she'd ever have to do, then started toward the door as Jacob sat by Rhonda and started to take her statement.

This better be good, she told herself, trying to put on her tough front.

But really, he'd had her already, with those big brown puppy-dog eyes of his. Maybe it didn't matter what he did; she'd always want him.

She wondered if that was the same quality that had made her mother hang around, pining for William Hatfield all these years. The same quality that had practically ruined her mother's life: When she fell, she fell so hard that she lost more than anyone.

Kylie's stomach turned. As if she needed another reason to feel bad about herself.

16

K ylie walked out into the hallway, not stopping until she entered the empty waiting room, still trying to put on a tough front, though that strong exterior was cracking with every step she took. When she turned around, Linc was right behind her, hands in his pockets, looking like that sweet puppy-dog that made her insides flutter.

He was such a good guy, the very best man she'd ever known, and if he said nothing happened, then nothing happened. She would believe him and knew she should have given him time to explain last night. Shouldn't have been her typical self and jumped to conclusions, expecting rejection and pain.

It was time she started to expect love.

As she turned and looked up into his handsome face, she knew one thing for certain. She wanted to be with him. She didn't even want an apology, she realized. Or an explanation. She just wanted what came after. Him.

Did that make her weak? Did it make her like her mother? She didn't care. He'd come back to her. And she needed him.

He opened his mouth to speak, but she held up a hand. "Don't. It's okay. I don't care."

He gave her a confused look. "Let me explain what—"

"No." She put her finger on his lips. "I don't care. Because you have me. I don't care what you do or what you did, it won't matter to me. I need you so much that nothing you can do would make me change my mind. I'd still take you back. So, congratulations, you win. I'm yours."

He stared at her. "I...win? Since when was this a competition?"

She'd expected him to be happy. When he wasn't, she shook her head sadly as a thought occurred to her. "You are here to ask me to take you back, right? Or are you here to tell me to get my stuff from your house?"

"No, not that," he said, leaning forward so that their fore-heads were almost touching. "But I do think I owe you an—"

"Don't. I'm too tired." She wrapped her hands around his neck, her thumbs rubbing the scruff of his hair. "Just kiss me."

He did as he was told. She was just settling into the feeling of his mouth on hers when it occurred to her that she still looked simply terrible.

She pulled away and pressed her face into his chest. "I look awful. See, this is what not being with you did to me. Why did you wait so long?"

She realized at that moment how pathetic she sounded. It wasn't long at all, not really. Only a day. But to her, it'd been an eternity. Before she'd left for New York, she had some semblance of her life together. Now, a day later, she was a total wreck, and a lot of it had to do with him.

He gave her his crooked smile. "Believe me. I didn't want to. I tried to call you the second you left, but Vader stole my phone and hid it, and when I found it, it was broken." He held up a brand-new phone. "So, I got this thing, and when I tried to call you, your phone went right to voicemail. I also tried to visit you at work this morning, but you were gone. So...yeah, I tried."

She smiled and kissed him harder. "I love you," she said into his neck as he gathered her close. "I really, really love you."

"I love you too," he said, rubbing the pad of his thumb under her eye.

Her face grew warm as she remembered the makeup that was all over her face. "You must, if you haven't hit the road yet. Look at me. I'm a disaster. That girl...she was so beautiful, and I'm...me."

"You're beautiful. Perfect. Even now. That girl was Faith. She's my ex. She came to visit, very unexpectedly. But I swear, there's—"

She silenced him with another kiss. "I really don't care," she said against his lips. "Just kiss me more."

They kissed until footsteps had them breaking apart. They were in a public hospital, after all.

"Vader stole your phone, huh? And you left him alone in your house since this morning?"

He nodded.

"Bad idea. You know he hates being without one of us," she said, fixing his collar. "He's probably going bat shit. First, it was your phone. Next, it'll be your whole living room."

"Yeah? But he's gotten better—"

She planted a hard kiss on his lips. "You should go back and make sure he's okay. I'll be back as soon as I make sure my mother's all right. Okay?"

He tucked a stray strand of her hair behind her ear. "Yeah. No problem."

"And...would you do me a favor?" When he nodded, she went on, "Would you mind stopping by my apartment on the way? I left so quickly, I don't know if I locked up."

"Sure thing." He kissed her forehead, and she leaned into his touch, feeling warm and settled. "So…who's the dude with your mom?"

Kylie shrugged and wiggled her eyebrows. "Mysterious and attractive dark stranger who rescued the damsel in distress, I guess. He hasn't left her side since witnessing the accident."

Linc's eyebrows shot up to his hairline. "Whoa. Well—"

"Sorry. You're second in her heart now." She picked an imaginary piece of lint from his shirt. "Don't be too disappointed."

He pulled her even closer. "As long as I'm first in yours, I don't care."

She was practically floating as she watched him leave, thinking he wasn't just first. He was the only. Her heart was so full of him that she felt it might burst.

They were going to be okay.

Back in the tiny ER room, she watched her mother answering Jacob's questions in a dreamy voice, distractedly unable to take her starry eyes away from the handsome doctor. She looked so lovesick, Kylie was almost embarrassed for her.

And then Kylie realized that she probably looked the same way. And she was probably worse off, because she looked like a bag lady. It was a wonder security hadn't come to escort her out yet. She really needed to chill. And go and get herself a shower and a change.

Jacob stood and closed the cover on his spiral pad. "Well, thanks, you two," he said to them. "I'll put out a bulletin with this information and we'll see what comes in."

"You think someone might recognize it?" Kylie asked.

He nodded. "It's possible, and I'll review any cameras in the area of the accident."

Kylie went to tuck her hands into her pockets but then

remembered she was wearing boxers. "Okay. Well. Thank you for coming out. We really appreciate it."

She started to walk Jacob to the door and realized that her mother was talking in a very hushed tone to Dr. Phillips, and he was typing something into his phone. The middle-aged lady was blushing like a teenager. Were they trading digits?

Kylie's mouth opened. Jacob noticed as they went out. "Looks like your mom found herself a hot date, huh?"

Kylie cringed. She'd never thought she'd hear the words "mother" and "hot date" in the same sentence. Her mother didn't do that. Aside from her fawning over Linc—who was safe considering he was so much younger—her mother was practically a saint. "Uh. I guess. It's a little freaky, to be honest."

"Want me to run a background check on him?"

"Oh, no!" Kylie knew he was only joking, but she'd actually been thinking of doing just that. She didn't think her mother could afford to have another whirlwind romance let her down. And there were so many creepy guys out there. She wrinkled her nose as she listened to them laughing. When was the last time she'd heard her mom sound so happy? "He seems a little too good to be true, doesn't he?"

Jacob nodded. "I have it on good authority that I'm the only guy in the Asheville area who's the total package. So yes, I'd proceed with caution."

She smacked his massive bicep lightly. "I *could* do a background check…" she murmured.

"Ah. Kylie. You're a strange girl. He's probably fine. And your mom is old enough to look out for herself, isn't she?"

Maybe. But she hadn't been twenty-five years ago. And her mother was so trusting. She just didn't want her to be hurt again. A background check wouldn't hurt anyone. She'd do it in secret. Everything was probably fine with him. But just in case…

"I'm sure. Thanks again, Jacob," she called to his back.

He did a three-sixty spin, saluted her, and kept walking. "Take care, sweetheart. Don't you go getting yourself in any more trouble."

Smiling, she went back to the hospital room, where Dr. Phillips was putting on his jacket. "If you'll forgive me," he said to both of them. "I do have my first appointment in twenty minutes. I need to get down to my office."

"Oh, of course. I can't thank you enough!" Rhonda gushed.

"It was a pleasure meeting you, Miss Hatfield," he said to Kylie, bowing slightly. What was this, Regency England? Then he turned to Rhonda. "And a great pleasure meeting you, Ms. Hatfield."

"Oh! Rhonda!" she giggled, as he took her hand and stroked it with the pad of his thumb. As he bowed, she looked at her daughter like she'd just struck gold. Kylie was surprised she didn't squeal like a kid.

"Rhonda," he said, his mouth traveling over the word like he was enjoying a glass of fine wine. What a Prince Charming. Kylie felt like she'd stumbled into a fairy tale.

"See ya," she said to the man as he stepped away from the hospital bed, thinking, *We'll see what my magic mirror reveals about you, Prince Charming.*

When he finally left, Rhonda wiggled her eyebrows in excitement. Then she grabbed onto Kylie's hand and nearly squeezed the life out of it, with a lot of strength for a woman who'd just been hit by a car. "He's so handsome, isn't he? He's a doctor too!"

"Mom," Kylie sighed. "Calm down. What do you know about him, really? I mean, I heard Ted Bundy was totally charming and handsome."

Her mother wasn't listening. Instead, she stared dreamily to the door he'd just exited. "Yes, but he's a doctor, right in this hospital. An ENT."

"You think doctors can't be serial killers?" Kylie warned. "What about that neurosurgeon in Virginia who was stuffing people into fifty-five-gallon drums?"

"And now you're an expert?" Rhonda practically pouted at her daughter. Ever since the serial killer case, Rhonda seemed to think that her daughter actually liked all things that involved mass-murderers.

Kylie rolled her eyes. "I just want you to be careful."

"Sweetheart," she said, smiling a sad little smile. "I've been careful for twenty-five years. Any more careful, and I'd have been in a coma. I think I'm allowed to be a little reckless for once."

Kylie filled her water glass. Her mother was right. She did deserve to have a little fun. And like Jacob had said, she was a grown woman who could take care of herself. Besides, despite what Jacob thought, it wasn't all the Hatfields who attracted trouble. Usually, it was just Kylie.

It was on the tip of her tongue to mention the New York trip, and her brief run-in with the former love of Rhonda's life. She decided not to spoil her mother's good mood. But she still couldn't stop thinking about what she'd uncovered during her internet search; namely, her father, married, with a whole family she and her mother had known nothing about. And criminal ties? The whole thing was something out of a Lifetime Movie Network flick.

"Mom," she said, sitting down in one of the uncomfortable vinyl chairs. "Do you know if our family ever had any mafia ties?"

She blinked, surprised. "Mafia?" Then she laughed, long and loud, like the mere idea was preposterous. "Well, you know I'm from Georgia. And your father's family moved to

New York from Kansas before he was born. As far as I know, the Mafia isn't very big there."

"But…" Kylie said, thinking. She almost let it spill that she'd been in New York, but what good would it do? Besides, Rhonda didn't know William Hatfield. She only knew Adam Hatfield, and Kylie got the feeling that the two men, though the same person, were like night and day. "Never mind."

She gave her mother a kiss on the forehead and dimmed the lights so that she could rest.

17

That little bitch had stirred up all this shit, then had run back to Hicksville with her tail between her legs. New York had taken a bite of her ass, chewed it up, and spit her out.

She might have been gone, but she sure as hell wasn't forgotten.

The call came in as I was trying to enjoy my lunch, the first meal I'd eaten since learning about William Hatfield's original family. I started with social media, since all twenty-somethings seemed to be addicted to sharing every moment of their day.

The little bitch's Facebook page was set to private, smart girl, but I saw enough. Enough to know that she had her daddy's chin, and probably his drive and curiosity too.

And that wasn't allowed.

That little country mouse and her mom didn't know what kind of trouble they'd unearthed.

I lifted the phone to my ear. "Yes, Nino," I said, my eyes traveling over a picture of Kylie Hatfield, standing in a field with a giant black dog. "What is it now?"

"You said I could call you during the day, boss. Is it okay?"

I gritted my teeth, then found a picture of her with her blonde-haired mother. I clicked over to Rhonda's page, and voila. Her mother wasn't nearly so smart. Her page was entirely public. There were dozens of photos and memes and such. "If it wasn't okay, I wouldn't have answered. Do you have an update?"

"I'm here. I found them." His voice was low and gravelly, as if he'd been up all night. Nino did that. He didn't sleep, especially when there was a job to do, like the adrenaline and excitement of the hunt made it impossible. Of all the men we employed, Nino Capitano loved to do the hits more than anyone else. He was relentless and showed absolutely no mercy, whether his target was an old man or a helpless woman. It was like he actually got pleasure out of ending a person's life.

And he was young too. Not yet thirty. He was fit and muscular and had a way about him that few people wanted to mess with. When people saw him coming, they made way for him.

I toyed with my sandwich. That didn't make him Einstein. I'd *expected* he'd have found them by now. They weren't exactly hiding. "And?"

"And this should be like taking candy from a baby," he said, sounding too confident.

I didn't want swagger. I wanted the job done. "I don't want candy. I want them dead, Nino. And quick. Can you do it, or not?"

"Yeah. Already got some dumb chick here who needed money to fund her drug habit to mow the mother down with her car." He snickered. "All that took was fifty bucks."

Fifty bucks and a blow job, knowing Nino. "And the result?"

He scoffed. "Not much of nothing. Stupid bitch chickened out and laid on the brakes at the last minute."

Fury ran through me. A hit and run? Really? And what was Nino doing, using some stupid crackhead to carry out his dirty work?

"Stop playing around. Put a bullet in their heads. The end."

"I'm on it. Don't you worry."

But I was worried.

Nino didn't fully understand all the implications of this situation. He didn't know how badly William Hatfield had fucked up.

He hadn't officially divorced his first wife, which meant his second marriage wasn't legal. Which meant...

All the money. The power. The carefully built tower of cards.

All of it, could come tumbling down.

"I am worried," I said through gritted teeth. "Paying someone to do your hit for you leaves a witness. And you know how I feel about witnesses."

Silence.

Then, "She was a crack whore."

"Which means nothing aside that she was desperate. And probably not careful. Did she know where the ATM cameras were? Did she use her own car? Know how to remove all fingerprint and DNA evidence? And even crack whores can look at a mug shot."

It was maddening that Nino hadn't thought of these things first. I needed to let the family know that our hit man needed a few lessons of his own.

Which was disappointing. He had such possibilities. And he should have still been hungry to please, unwilling to stop until the job was done to perfection.

Most importantly, he needed to never forget it was me

who'd made him what he was today and put him in the lap of luxury. He'd still have been standing outside the Sudsy Car Wash with a chamois cloth, working for dollar tips if it wasn't for me. He owed me big-time, which was why, although he liked to play macho, he jumped when I told him.

And there was a good chance that one day, that growing ego would take over and he'd go off and do something stupid. Nino may have had a pretty face, a good body, a nice bank account, and all that stuff that made him irresistible to women. But deep down, he was still just a dumb street thug who'd dropped out of high school.

"I'll get it done." He sounded like a petulant child.

"And done quickly. Professionally. I don't want you getting some heroin addict to do something you should be doing yourself. Get it done. Right, this time."

He laughed, but I could hear the nerves behind the sound. "It ain't that easy. You want me to come back to New York, right? I need to bide my time. Can't just walk up to them on the street and gun them down. If I get caught, your ass is on the line too."

I stiffened. "What did we say about that, Nino?"

"Yeah, yeah, yeah. I wouldn't utter a word about you. I know. But don't you think they'll discover the kid's little trip to New York? Discover her little visit with William? The dots won't be too hard to connect from there. This needs to look like an accident."

He was right, but we were running out of time.

"We've done a very good job of covering our tracks. That's the least of my worries. Plus…you won't get caught, will you?"

"I might if you rush me into anything. Just trust me on this, okay? Ideally, they need to be together, so I can end them both at once and be out of town before the police even arrive on the scene. I'm looking for the right moment."

He was just annoying me. "Just do it. And do it right."

"Fine." I could sense his cocky little grin on the end. "And I expect a really good welcome home present after all this is done."

I hung up without answer and shoved my phone across the counter, away from me. My eyes trailed to the laptop screen as I licked chicken salad from my fingers. I scrolled to a picture of the little bitch with her mother, the senior bitch. They had identical smiles and eyes, though the mother was bleached blonde and the younger had dark hair.

They'd pay.

But above all, William would pay too. He needed to learn this lesson, once and for all. He was like Nino—we'd given him everything, and now he wanted to play a deadly little game with the family?

He needed to fall in line and give us respect. We'd been his gravy train for all these years, and this was how he repaid us? No. It didn't work like that.

No one played games with this family and got away with it.

SOME DAYS, Nino couldn't believe that this was his life.

To think, three years ago, he'd been unable to pay rent at his crummy little shithole in Brooklyn. He barely made minimum wage at the car wash, getting dollar tips from rich assholes in Armani suits as he dried their Mercedes and BMWs. He'd been a total loser, licking at their boots, wishing he could be just like them.

Now, his suit cost more than what he used to make in a year. Women threw themselves at him. He had a swanky place in Manhattan, his own car, money to burn.

He'd traveled business class to Asheville and had gotten

blitzed on the free champagne while talking to a leggy blonde hair model who, if the flight had been an hour longer, he probably would've gotten into the mile-high club with. He'd done her in the family restroom at the Asheville airport instead, thinking the whole time that a woman like that wouldn't have even let him shine her shoes three years ago.

Nino had grown up in the projects in Brooklyn. Never expected much out of his life than what his parents had achieved. His father had worked at the same damn car wash until he was gunned down, caught by a gang's stray bullet. His mother had turned to prostitution to keep the family afloat, until he'd dropped out of high school to get a job at the wash. By then, his mother's drug habit had consumed every cent she was making. She OD'd the day after he turned eighteen, leaving him alone in the world, and thinking that he'd be working that shit job for the rest of his life.

And then, one day, he'd been introduced to the family, and his life had changed overnight.

It started with a simple car wash, and a simple compliment. He'd whistled at the sleek black car, then given the swanky Mercedes S-class the tire cleaner for free, and words were exchanged. It spiraled out from there. The next week, he was living in the lap of luxury, eating breakfast in bed with Dom Perignon to wash it down.

It was maybe a week after that that they'd taken him into a basement of a building in Manhattan and asked him if he'd ever fired a gun before. If he'd been willing to kill another person. He was told, in no uncertain terms, if he was willing to give to them, they would continue to give to him, and generously.

Nino had kept out of gangs, because of his mother. She didn't care much about what he did, but all she ever told him was not to get wrapped up in gangs. So, he hadn't. But it turned out he had a knack with a gun. It just came naturally to him. And this was more than a gang. Much more. A gang was a brotherhood, but this was so much more. It was a family.

And he enjoyed it. Sure, the work was nasty, but he overlooked that. He didn't care who the order was for. It was a job, like anything, but one that paid well and had changed his shitty life to something he was proud of. He'd read once that a person could make a good living if they took the jobs that no one else wanted to do. Well, he'd taken on the job that people were afraid to do, he liked it, and he'd made more than a living. The work was damn good.

He pulled up at the address he'd found for Kylie Hatfield's apartment. It was just off the UNC college campus, so there were a lot of college students walking around outside or studying on the steps of the building, a giant Victorian mansion. Some of them were hot pieces of ass, but he couldn't afford to be distracted. It wasn't exactly remote. They'd just provide a lot of problems, if he expected to pull off this hit quickly and cleanly. He didn't need a bunch of witnesses, or even worse, to bump off the wrong girl.

Taking another look at the picture of his target, he committed it to memory, then strained to view the girls across the street. None looked quite like Kylie.

He'd have to get closer.

He stepped out of his rental car, slammed the door, and jogged across the tree-lined street toward them, feeling for the Glock in his jacket pocket. As he got nearer, he became more and more sure. Not one of them was the woman he was looking for. Fucking hell.

A blonde looked up and smiled at him. "You're not from around here," she said.

He silently cursed. He needed to do better blending in.

It had broken his heart to change out of his Armani suit and into a pair of jeans that felt too heavy on his skin. Sure, he'd topped it with his favorite Italian leather jacket and darkened his hair, added some scruff to his chin, but he still stood out among all these uppity college kids who thought a degree was the way to make it.

He gave her a wink and changed his accent to a Boston one. "I'm not. You know Kylie Hatfield?"

She wrinkled her cute nose and shook her head. "Sorry."

"'Salright," he said, heading for the door. Ordinarily, he'd have stopped and chatted the girl up, probably have gotten her to take a ride with him, but he had other things on his mind. He reached the front doors of the place just as a college kid came out. Before the doors could shut, he grabbed the handle, pulled it open, and slipped inside.

In the downstairs foyer, there was a large staircase and a number of mailboxes. It didn't take an Einstein to find Kylie's. K. Hatfield, 2A was written in big black letters. He scanned the downstairs and saw an apartment that said 1A. Looking like he belonged in the place, he strode up the staircase, his eyes focused on the door at the top of the stairs, to the right. That had to be Kylie's apartment.

He'd nearly reached it, intending to listen at it, maybe try the knob to see if it was unlocked when it suddenly flung open, and a man walked out. He used a key to lock both locks before heading toward the stairs.

"How's it going?" the guy said. Hicks were so damn friendly and polite.

"Good, man." He strove to keep the Brooklyn out of his voice, turning it southern this time.

Shit. That had been close. Then Nino did a double take, recognizing the man from her Facebook photos. Her boyfriend, probably. Although his hair was much shorter than in the photos, the guy was big and built.

Nino wasn't worried about that.

What he was worried about was getting his ass caught

before he finished this job. He'd already screwed up, hiring the crackhead to stage an accident. It had been a good idea at the time, but he couldn't screw up again.

He needed to get this done in any way possible.

His two targets lived in separate places, so he doubted he'd find them together like he hoped. His new plan was to get one, have her call the other in a panic, and when the other rushed over to help, kill them both. That would work. For some reason, the family wanted this done quickly. There wasn't time to lose.

He paused at the top of the stairs and looked down. The boyfriend had swiveled his head and was now looking at him curiously, so he quickly made his way down the hall, pretending to go to one of the other apartments farther down the way. Her boyfriend was a suspicious fuck. This could be a problem.

He heard the door to the complex open and thud closed, and went to the landing, peering over. The guy was gone. He thought about listening at the Hatfield girl's door, but the guy had spooked him enough as it was. She probably wasn't in there, anyway. Probably went to visit her poor mom in the hospital.

Shoving his hands into the pocket of his leather jacket, he decided to go and see what he could find out at the old bat's house. He'd scope out the area and see how to make his move.

He pushed out of the apartment complex door, looking for that cute blonde he'd seen before, but she was already gone.

A shame, but it didn't bother him much. There'd be other girls. A lot of other girls. God, he loved this life.

18

Once upon a time, when Kylie was nursing a bullet wound to the shoulder, her mother had taken care of her, giving her all she needed while she was recuperating. Even months after the injury, Rhonda still cooked her dinner and did the things that Kylie was more than able to do herself. Her mother babied her.

So, it was only fair that Kylie babied her mother right back.

Rhonda was released that afternoon, and Kylie brought her home in her VW bug and set her up on the flowered living room couch, then tried her best to make her a nice dinner. Rhonda told her to get lost because Kylie was a big fail when it came to cooking, and Rhonda's injuries only had her a little sore. There were no breaks, no sprains. Rhonda kept reminding Kylie of this as she shooed her from the house. "I'll be fine!" she insisted. "I feel good as new!"

Kylie wasn't sure if that was true, or just the Vicodin talking, but she knew better than to argue with her mother regarding these things. If she tried to take control in her mother's kitchen, it wouldn't end well. That was precisely why Kylie had never acquired kitchen skills—her mother ruled there and never wanted the help, especially from someone as clumsy as Kylie when it came to anything remotely domestic.

When she left her mother's house, Kylie decided that no way in hell was she going to subject Linc to looking at her bag-lady ass for one more minute.

She was on cloud nine now, smiling every time she thought of Linc. She wanted to do something special for him.

Stopping at her apartment complex, she grabbed all the mail she'd been neglecting for too long. After trudging up the stairs, she tried the doorknob, noticing he'd locked both that and the deadbolt. It was something she rarely did, but that was Linc. He was super-concerned about her safety.

Unlocking both, she went inside, went through the mail—it was mostly junk stuff, since she'd had the important things forwarded to Linc's house—then stripped and took a long shower. When she came out, she went through her closet of rejects and pulled out a red dress she rarely wore but knew Linc would appreciate. She put her hair up in a simple twist and looked at herself in the mirror.

She looked happy. In love. But more importantly, she looked to be at peace.

After finding out what an absolute douche her father was, maybe she was. She could put that part of her life to rest.

As she was about to leave, her phone buzzed with a text. Surprisingly, it was from Linc. She jumped to answer it, since he rarely texted, wondering if he couldn't wait to see her as much as she couldn't wait to see him. Instead, her spirits plummeted when she read, *Got another SAR call. Taking Vader and Storm. I'll be home late tonight. Make yourself comfortable.*

Bleh.

No longer in a rush, she collapsed on the couch with her laptop.

She'd promised herself she wouldn't do it, but she couldn't help it. Her fingers were getting itchy again, and she was never able to fight that feeling. Giving in, she opened up her background search website and logged in. Then she typed in: *Jerry Phillips.*

A number of search results came up, too many to go through. She narrowed it down by putting in *Dr.* and *Asheville.* There were fewer results this time, the first photograph a picture of the white-haired man she met, wearing a white doctor's coat and looking as dashing as ever.

Kylie sifted through it all carefully. Yes, he was a widower, married for twenty years until his wife's death two years prior. Breast cancer. According to the news about him, his ENT practice was one of the best in the state, and as a doctor, his patients had given him great reviews. He'd lived in town all his life, except when he'd gone to Duke for medical school and during a stint overseas, working with poor children in Haiti.

Kylie had thought he looked too good to be true. And now, sifting through all his credentials and history, he sounded too good to be true too. But maybe he was. Maybe some people were just amazing people, and they were meant to be taken at face value and not looked, like a gift horse, in the mouth.

Her father certainly hadn't been one of those people. How could he have even thought to get married, when he was already married? How did he even manage that? He hadn't even changed his last name, just started going by William instead of Adam, his actual middle name.

It didn't make sense.

Had the mafia helped cover it all up? The marriage certificate? The birth certificate?

And if so...why?

She typed in her father's name, and then the name of his

second wife, Christina DeRoss, looking for a marriage announcement. One immediately came up, for a marriage that occurred in Las Vegas. It was a long write-up about all the guests attending, names Kylie had never heard about. There was a picture of a much younger looking William Hatfield, who looked exactly like the man in Kylie's little family photo. She checked the date and frowned.

They'd gotten married only a month after Kylie was born.

Holy cow. Talk about moving fast.

Kylie sat back, trying to make sense out of it. Her dad had walked out on her mother four days after she was born. A week later, he'd sent her the Dear Jane, telling her the marriage had been a mistake. If that was true, he must have been planning this while her mother was pregnant with her.

Any way Kylie tried to slice it, that was totally messed up.

Kylie bookmarked the page and then searched for marriage license information. She found that because licenses were held at the state level and not easily searchable, it was entirely possible he could've applied for licenses in both places. That was how he could've gotten away with it.

When she typed in her mother's maiden name and Adam Hatfield, she pulled up only a single line in *The New York Times* wedding announcement section.

Sad.

Typing in the word "bigamy," she learned all sorts of things about it. First, that it was a crime to marry another person when he hadn't yet sought out or received a divorce. Second, that the second marriage to Christina DeRoss wasn't technically legal. And third, that if her father was caught, he could go to prison for a long time.

Her father wasn't just a cheater and a liar and a scumbag. He was also a criminal.

Then why did she feel sorry for him? Was it because he was her dad and she'd care about him no matter what, like she cared about Linc? Some people, it didn't matter what they did. You were just condemned to love them, no matter how awfully they behaved.

When she looked at the clock next, it was because another text came in from Linc. It said: *I'm home from the SAR. Thought you'd be back by now. Hope everything's okay with your mom.*

She couldn't believe how much time had passed. It was almost nine, and the apartment had gone almost pitch-black except for the glow of her electronics. She'd been going down the research rabbit hole for hours. The idea of going back home to Linc sound really good.

Flipping the lid of her laptop closed, she tucked it into her bag. Then she shook out her hair, which was dry by now, straightened her dress, hefted her bag onto her shoulder, and left the apartment.

She remembered to lock the door this time. And because she knew it was what Linc would do, she fastened the deadbolt too.

19

The sun was just about gone as Kylie went downstairs into the foyer. Her downstairs neighbor, Baron Murphy, was already in a partying mood, as the smell of pot was strong and hazing up the common area. It didn't bother her anymore. Nothing did.

One of the ties of her sandals had come loose, so keys in hand, she stooped to tie it. As she did, she looked at the old floor mats. The new superintendent of the place hadn't been keeping it up very well, and the common areas were really suffering.

But that was okay. This wasn't her home anymore. Not really. It felt very temporary, like something she'd finally outgrown.

Even the thought of letting go of this place where she'd spent the past six years didn't bother her. She'd loved this apartment so much when she was an undergrad, but now, saying goodbye didn't seem so scary. She could probably sublet the place to a college kid. It was, after all, supposed to be for UNC students, and she hadn't been in school in a while. And then, maybe, when the lease was up, leave it altogether. That felt right.

She stepped out the door and straight into the October chill. She loved the fall. Warm in the day, chillier at night. She closed the sweater she'd pulled on over her dress more tightly together and headed toward her beloved Jeep.

"Kylie!"

She whirled and looked around. Baron was waving at her, holding a black bag out to her. "You forget something?"

Kylie squinted at what was in his hand and realized she'd left her laptop bag in the foyer when she'd stooped to tie her sandal. So much for being mature and having her shit together.

"Oh my gosh," she said, heading back his way. "Thanks."

Baron may have been a stoner, but he was one of the few people in the building she was friendly with. He was a perennial college student, as she had once been, older than most of the undergrads. The rest of the people there almost seemed like babies to her now. All the more reason to move on, she thought, as she approached him. Baron—unshaven, ungroomed, and bleary-eyed—didn't seem as bothered by the fact as she did.

Wrapping her hand around the bag, Kylie felt the toe of her shoe catch on the broken sidewalk and lost her balance.

Bang!

If she hadn't been so intimately familiar with that sound, Kylie would have thought someone had shot off a firework. But she was intimately familiar with it, and without thinking, she dropped and began to move, making herself as much of a moving target as she could.

"Go!" she screamed at Baron, who yelped as a downstairs window in the building shattered.

Tires squealed as Kylie dove behind the stone sign that named her apartment complex. Peeking out, she tried to see the car, but all she could see was a black blur. A second later, the car was gone.

Heart hammering in her chest, she looked around, expecting to see Baron on the ground. But he was gone. Relief coursed through her that her neighbor had made it into the building safely.

Stunned, Kylie didn't want to wait to see if the shooter came back. She also didn't want to be trapped in the building if he did.

What to do?

Spotting the yellow of her Jeep, she made her decision and ran toward it as fast as she could go. She needed to be with Linc. She'd call Jacob when she got there.

As Kylie drove, everything was a blur as she scanned the road for the black car and checked her rearview multiple times for a tail. She held her breath as she passed the shiny guardrail and didn't seem to let it out until she pulled into Linc's driveway.

As the gravel crunched under her tires, she tried to put everything in perspective. Who would want her dead?

Her father's face flashed in her mind. His panic. His whispered words. He'd told her to leave. Told her she was in danger.

Had that danger followed her here?

She shivered.

What was going on?

LINC WAS surprised that Kylie still hadn't arrived at the house when he got back from the rescue he'd been sent on. It was an average, ordinary case—a hiker went off the trail and got turned around—with a happy ending. The hiker was found only a half hour after the dogs were sent out. He'd fallen off a steep incline and bruised his ankle, was a little shaken, but was able to accompany them off the mountain on his own, refusing medical attention.

When Linc finished up and loaded the dogs into his truck, he thought about what a beautiful night it was. A good night to open all the windows and let the mountain breeze through the house. He was really looking forward to a shower, a beer, and a quiet night on the back porch, listening to the crickets, with Kylie. When he got home, the house was dark, so he got out the beer, texted Kylie to let her know he was home, and settled down to relax. He knew Kylie would be along in a few minutes.

A half hour later, Kylie still hadn't arrived. He pulled out his new phone and sent her a second text: *Is everything okay?*

There was no response, not even an indication that she'd read the message. Maybe she was on her way back.

Pressing his lips together, he picked up the phone and called her.

The call went right to voicemail.

All right. Now he was getting worried. He went to the front porch and nearly tripped over the dogs as he started to pace back and forth.

About fifteen minutes later, when he was on the verge of pulling his hair out, he saw the lights, cutting through the trees at the front of the driveway. A second later, those lights pulled into view. It was her Jeep. He dug his hands deep into his pockets and watched as she came closer.

She opened the door and Vader ran down the steps to her, excitedly licking her bare knees like he hadn't seen her in ages. Linc waited his turn, impatiently, then came in for a kiss. "Hey. I was starting to worry. What took you so long?"

When she came into the porch light, he noticed her face was streaked with tears.

"Kylie," he said, alarmed. "What happened?"

She pressed her lips together, as if she needed to do that to stop herself from crying some more. Then she threw herself into his arms. She was trembling as if she'd touched a live wire.

"Shh," he calmed her, smoothing her hair. "It's okay."

She shook her head. "I don't know," she sobbed. "I really don't know if anything is anymore."

"Wait. Come on inside. Let's talk about it."

He took her hand and led her inside, sitting her down on the sofa. "You want something to drink? Tea? Beer? Wine?"

"Wine," she said quickly. "I need something strong. My nerves are shot."

He jumped up and came back with a glass of her favorite Merlot. He handed it to her, and she took a large gulp. "What was it? Did you nearly get in a car accident?"

"No!" she shouted, then started to cry again. "Oh, my god. It's *much* worse."

Worse? What could be worse than that?

It occurred to him that, because of their little tiff over Faith, he hadn't had a chance to ask her anything about her business trip to New York. Was this a result of that trip? Something had sent Kylie packing sooner than she'd expected to leave. But she'd been fine when he saw her earlier that day.

"All right, well, why don't you start at the begin—"

A knock sounded at the door.

What the hell? The reason Linc liked this place so much was because it was out of the way, and he never got many visitors. Truth be told, he was a bit of a misanthrope. Lately, this place had felt a little like Grand Central Station.

Kylie looked terrified, her fingers digging into his arm.

"What's wr—?"

"Yoo hoo! Linc!"

He groaned. Faith.

Kylie transformed from scared to pissed in an instant. "Is that *her*?"

He was seriously going to kill someone.

He liked Faith. He really did. But he could only take her in small doses, and he'd gotten enough of his fill of her today. What was she doing here now?

"I'll make her leave." Kylie wrapped the sweater more tightly around her, the tears beginning again. He kissed her forehead. "You run upstairs and get into bed. I'll be there in just a minute."

He waited until the bedroom door clicked shut before opening his front door, unable to keep the pissed look off his face. "What do you want?"

She looked at him with wide eyes through the screen. "Bad timing again?"

"You got it," he muttered, turning away to shut the door.

She pushed inside, holding it open. "I know. I know you probably don't want me here," she said. "But I'm desperate."

His jaw worked as he looked at her. What was going on? Faith was constantly on his tail. She'd practically accused him of stalking her, but he got the distinct feeling it was the other way around. And the only reason he could think of her doing so was because…she wanted to get back with him.

"Yeah. But I don't think I can help you," he said, his voice flat. "Look, I told you. You and I are over. And whatever you're coming up here for, I can't help you with it."

"But you can!" she insisted, following him into the kitchen as he pulled open the fridge and grabbed a beer.

He used his keychain opener to pop off the top and took a long swig, his eyes never leaving hers. If she was going to make a pass at him now, with Kylie upstairs, he'd have to set her straight. He swallowed his beer. "Oh, yeah? How so?"

"Because you and Jacob are best friends."

Linc raised an eyebrow, confused as Faith grabbed Kylie's

bottle of Merlot and opened the cabinet. She took down a glass and helped herself as Linc watched, waiting for an explanation. "What?"

Faith did that hair-flip thing. "Don't tell me you've been that blind. You had to notice it, every time we went out together?"

Suddenly, the pieces fell into place. He thought of all the times they'd gone out double dating, and then, this morning, when they'd chatted together so easily, they hadn't even realized Linc was still there. "You and Jacob?"

She nodded. "I'm crazy about him. And I know he listens to you. Respects you."

Linc opened his mouth, but nothing came out.

"Of course, we never cheated on you or anything!" she quickly pointed out. "Jacob was too good of a man for that. But we did have some conversations and...Linc, when I saw him today, none of those feelings had gone away. It was like they were even stronger than ever. I think he felt it too."

"Okay." Now he wished Kylie was down here. "And how do you expect me to help?"

"Well, you guys have a code, don't you? He doesn't want to make a move on your ex-girlfriend, you know, since you and I were almost engaged. He's too loyal to you for that." She drained the glass of wine and smiled. "I was hoping that you could put in a few words where I'm concerned? Give him the all clear?"

Linc couldn't help it. He laughed. And here he'd once thought Jacob was putting the moves on Kylie. But yeah, while they switched between girls in high school, it'd been messy and strange. By college, they'd been keeping a certain respectful distance between themselves and each other's girl-friends. He should've known. All signs were pointing to it. Jacob rarely let just one woman hold his gaze, but this morning, in the coffee shop, he couldn't take his eyes off her. Even in law school, he'd seen it.

He shrugged, relieved. "Yeah. Sure. Of course."

She smiled but still looked uncertain. "You're not upset about it, are you?"

He shook his head. "Hell, no. You guys are good together."

Her smile grew, and she looked like she was going to give him a hug. That was the last thing he needed, so he quickly walked toward the door, holding it open for her.

"Sorry. I don't mean to kick you out, but my girlfriend had a bad day. I have to go talk to her," he said.

"Oh. So, it's serious between you two? You and…Keely?"

"Kylie," he said, looking up the stairs. The door to the bedroom was closed, and if he knew Kylie, she was probably thinking about that voodoo doll again.

"Kylie Hatfield, right?"

Linc raised an eyebrow. "Right."

Faith just stood there. "You're a good person, Linc. An amazing person, in fact. I'm just glad you found someone who makes you happy."

Unsure what to say, he chose silence, and let the open door do the talking for him.

Faith nodded, her eyes sliding toward the steps as she took the hint and left. He watched her as she got into her car and started to drive away.

She was right about one thing. He was happy. Happier than he'd ever been. And it was all because of Kylie.

20

Still feeling dazed, Kylie sat on the edge of the bed, trying to sort out all her thoughts.

Not about the woman downstairs.

Okay, maybe just a little about the woman downstairs. But her thoughts didn't focus there. Linc loved Kylie. Kylie loved Linc. She was the one sitting on his bed. It was her clothes hanging in his closet.

So what if Faith was thinner and prettier and clearly richer than Kylie?

So what if this was the second time she'd come around in as many days?

So what if she was sniffing around, trying to rekindle her relationship with Linc?

So what...

Kylie heard Linc laugh, and her stomach churned.

She crept to the door and tried to listen.

Linc was kind of stingy with his laughter. Few things made him that amused.

Stop it, she told herself. *He already told you, you're the one he wants.*

That didn't help. Maybe it was the nerves. The confrontation with her father. Her mother's accident. The bullet that had nearly hit her. But after the day she'd had, this was the last thing she needed, and she resented that woman for it. She was so on edge, she thought one touch might make her shatter into great big Kylie chunks.

She breathed out a sigh of relief when the screen door slammed shut. Before the car outside even started, Linc's boots were thudding up the stairs.

He was coming to her.

She backed away from the door and perched on the edge of the bed as the door swung open. Linc appeared in the doorway, his eyes seeking her out. He seemed relieved when she simply smiled at him. He couldn't control the actions of others.

"Everything okay?"

He advanced on her, then knelt between her legs, taking her cold hands in his warm ones. For a moment, Kylie wished he'd propose. She would simply say yes.

Yes to the possibility of heartbreak.

Yes to the risk any relationship posed.

Yes to it all.

"She's in love with Jacob and wants me to tell him it's okay for them to hook up."

Kylie blinked. That was unexpected.

"Seriously?"

Linc shrugged. "Supposedly, she's always been. And I think he cares about her too. She wanted me to give Jacob the go-ahead to ask her out, because Jacob's loyal and wouldn't want to step on my toes." He took in Kylie's shocked expression and stroked her palm with his callused fingers. "All right?"

Kylie's nose wrinkled up as she processed this. "And you're…not upset about that?"

"Hell, no. I told you, whatever I had with her is ancient history. Probably shouldn't have happened in the first place. She and I don't fit. You and I do."

Something melted inside of her. "Yes, you and I do."

He pulled her close and kissed the side of her face. "Tell me why you were shaking when you came in. What happened?"

Inhaling deeply, she lifted her chin to meet his gaze. "I need to tell you the truth."

He sat back on his haunches. "About?"

"About the trip. It wasn't a business trip. I went up to New York to find my dad."

Linc scrubbed a hand down his jaw. "Yeah? Wow. Why didn't you tell—"

"I should have. I should have brought you with me. I knew you were okay with me searching him out, but I was nervous about what I might find. I wanted to process it on my own first."

He was quiet for a moment. "Wow. So you went up there on your own. And what did you find?"

"I found him," she said, clenching her teeth at the thought of him sending her out of his office without a second look. "He wasn't hard to find, since his name's on half the real estate up there. He's even worse than I thought he'd be."

"Seriously?"

"He's a billionaire owner of a construction company," she said, still looking at her knees. "D & H Construction. He owns a bunch of properties in the city. He's got it made."

"So? That doesn't sound bad."

Kylie let out a grumble, low in her throat and punched a pillow. "Oh, it's bad. He's a billionaire, and aside from initial money and her house, he never gave another cent to raise me. He wanted to pretend we don't exist."

Linc shook his head. "He gave her a house?"

Kylie waved his question away. "And it gets worse from there. He practically threw me out of his office when I confronted him. He wants nothing to do with me. But the worst part is, he's a bigamist. He's still married to my mother, but he left her four days after I was born and married another woman less than a month later, in Vegas. He has this whole other perfect family, and it was clear I was just an intrusion."

He nodded, taking all of this in. "Holy shit. No wonder you're on edge. What does your mother say?"

"I didn't tell her any of this. I told her I was going up there to find him, and she didn't want me to. She doesn't want to know. I think in her heart, she wants some kind of closure but she's worried that he'll be the big douche that he used to be. And, guess what? She's right."

"Wow. That's messed up."

The burn of emotion returned, and she tried to force it away. Her cheeks felt tight from all of the tears she'd cried in the past twenty-four hours. "When I was up there, I learned that before he started working in construction, he was in tight with some people who later were arrested and tied to the mafia. I wonder if my father picking up and leaving so abruptly might have to do with that somehow."

His face twisted, and she winced, knowing exactly what he was thinking. *Kylie's gone and stepped in it again.*

"The mafia? Are you serious? That's some really dangerous shit, Kylie."

"I'm know. I'm sorry. I just needed to know who he was. But now, I almost wish I hadn't gone up—"

Bang. Bang. Bang.

Kylie jumped to her feet, her heart pounding in her chest before she realized it was just someone knocking on Linc's front door. The dogs went wild and Linc headed to the window.

"Hell, Grand Central Station," he muttered.

"Who is it?" Kylie asked. "Faith?"

"Jacob," he said and headed toward the stairs. "I didn't even hear him drive up. Probably another SAR call."

Kylie watched him head down as Jacob continued to bang on the door. He sounded a lot more urgent than he usually did for a search and rescue call. Linc opened the door and let him in. "What's the deal?"

"Kylie here?" he was asking as she came down the steps. He was holding his hat in both hands and looked agitated, which wasn't usual for Jacob. Jacob was steady, reliable, and not one to get his feathers ruffled. "Oh, hey."

"What's going on?" she asked.

He got straight to the point. "Did someone take a shot at you at your apartment about an hour ago?"

Kylie sucked in a breath and looked at Linc, whose eyes were wide. He spoke first. "Shooting? What do you mean?"

Kylie opened her mouth to explain, but Jacob beat her to it. "Got a call that someone was shooting at Kylie's apartment building. The guy I interviewed said that he thought they were shooting at Kylie."

Kylie's heart began to pound again.

"What the…" Linc's eyes shot to hers, nailing her to where she stood. "Is that why you were crying?"

She nodded slowly. "I—"

"When were you going to tell me about this?"

His interrogation pissed her off. She crossed her arms, indignant. "As soon as your ex-girlfriend left."

Jacob held out his hands. "All right, all right. Calm down. Let's take a step back for a second here." He looked at Kylie. "Did you see who it might have been?"

She shook her head. "No. It was dark, and I was too busy getting out of the way to survey my surroundings. Then, all I wanted was to come…" her throat closed as emotion hit again as she looked at Linc, "to you."

Linc's face softened, and she knew she really would cry if she kept looking at him, so she turned her focus to Jacob in time for his next question.

"You happen to be working any cases that might have gotten you some unwanted attention?"

It was a good assumption, considering Kylie's line of work had made her a target more than once, but Kylie knew he was barking up the wrong tree. All the real baddies she'd had run-ins with as part of her caseload were currently serving time. "No."

"Are you sure?" Linc asked. "I mean, first your mother's hit by a car, and now you—"

"I'm sure. Things are so slow right now that I'm working from home. I hardly have anything going on right now. So, it can't be that," she said as something terrible flickered in the back of her head.

You need to leave. You're not safe. Leave New York now.

Had her father been serious? Not just rushing her out of his sight with a random threat?

Jacob sucked in a breath and let it out as he scribbled some notes into his pad. "Any other idea of who might be trying to shoot at you?"

She already felt foolish enough about her trip to see her father. They'd surely think she was even more foolish to believe that something bad followed her home. She needed to think about it a little more.

Kylie shrugged. "It could have just been some punk trying to scare people," she offered, chewing on her bottom lip.

Jacob and Linc looked at each other, then back at her. She knew exactly what the two best friends were thinking. It was written all over their faces.

They didn't believe her for a second.

K ylie was gnawing on her lip something fierce, something she only did when she'd screwed up. So, it was all over her face. She'd stepped in it. Again.

Linc knew there was something she was hiding from Jacob, and he had a pretty good idea of what. Her apartment wasn't in that bad a section of town. He'd never seen any major crime there. It was mostly a bunch of college students. Rowdy, but not ones to go off firing guns haphazardly. And she'd been honest about the fact that she hadn't had a lot to do workwise, lately. She'd complained about that enough that he knew it wasn't one of her Starr Investigations cases.

Whoever was shooting at her, Linc had a very good idea where that person had come from.

Kylie went upstairs to sleep, since she'd had a crazy day, so Linc and Jacob went out to the back porch to talk. The air was still, and a light drizzle had begun to fall, thrumming softly on the metal roof. Finally, Linc got that beer he'd wanted, and a chance to relax, even though it was nearly eleven. The two of them sat down on the rocking chairs, Storm and Vader at their feet.

Jacob stroked the dogs' ears and took a gulp of his beer, then let out a loud, satisfied, *ahhh*. "Geez. What a day. Your girl is trouble with a capital T."

Linc frowned. Yeah, that was the truth, but he had a strong feeling that this type of trouble wasn't Starr Investigations related. "I don't think this is from one of her cases, though."

"Yeah?"

He'd come out here to relax, but the second he leaned back against the rocker, he knew that wasn't going to happen. Not while Kylie was in danger, again. His body itched with the need to do something, to protect her.

"She just got done telling me she went to New York. She met her long-lost father, and she told me she has reason to believe he's part of the mafia."

"The mob? Jesus." Jacob scratched at his chin. "You think the mob followed her here?"

"She said that when she was a baby, her father left her and got a new family. Maybe he doesn't want anyone to know she exists, and as long as she was down here, he didn't have to worry. But when she came into the picture, he panicked. Maybe he sent someone after her, to get her out of the way."

"You realize what you're saying, right? That someone put a hit on your girl?"

Linc shrugged. "Tell me. You don't believe that shooting was unintentional, do you?"

Jacob shook his head. "No. Not in that neighborhood. And even in the worst neighborhoods, in my experience, people don't take a couple of wild shots for the fun of it and then disappear. But hell…the mafia? Down here?"

Linc set his beer down beside his feet and ran both hands over his sheared scalp. "I don't know. But I know what I'm going to do about it. I'm getting on the next flight to New York and confront this asshole, William Hatfield. If he's responsible for putting Kylie in danger, then I need to know what we're dealing with. I'm going to get to the bottom of this."

Jacob stiffened. "Whoa. No way, man. You can't."

"I can't? The guy abandoned his family and then treated her like shit when she found him. He needs to see what he's done to his daughter, and he should be made to pay. And…if he has anything to do with all this, then maybe I can make him call off the dogs. Keep her safe."

Jacob didn't look convinced. "You going up there and beating the shit out of him won't suddenly make him remorseful after twenty-four years. All you'll likely do is get a hit put on *you*. You go there, and if he really is mafia, you'll probably come home in a body bag, if your body is ever found at all. That what you want? The mafia don't play, and they don't pay. They make other people pay *them*."

Linc dropped his chin to his chest, thinking. Kylie didn't talk about her dad much, but when she did, there was so much hurt there. William Hatfield had done a number on her that he could never undo, no matter how much love Linc showered on her to make up for it. Kylie's heart would always have a hole in it, made by her father. And instead of helping to heal her wounds, this last visit had just ripped it open all the wider.

He hated William Hatfield for it. How could any human being be that shitty to another person, especially one related to him by blood? Linc's father could be an asshole, but he was present, at least. He'd raised him into a man. When Linc thought of Kylie's father, all he thought of was a gutless, spineless piece of scum.

"I don't know. I've got to do something," he murmured, lifting his beer and bringing it to his lips. Before he took a drink, something occurred to him. "You should put a watch on her mom. If they put a hit on Kylie because they want her out of the picture, they'd want Rhonda out too, especially if they're officially married."

Jacob nodded. "All right. Done."

"And while you're at it, man, go talk to Faith Carter."

He raised an eyebrow at the total one-eighty in the conversation. "Why? Is she in trouble too?"

He let out a soft laugh. "No. But she's got it bad for you. And if you don't ask her out, she'll likely go mad. She was just up here about an hour ago, asking me what she had to do to get you to get your act together and make your move."

His eyebrows shot up to his hairline. "You're serious? And you're okay with that?"

"If I wasn't, I wouldn't be telling you. But seriously, if she comes up here one more time to beg me to clear the way for your sorry ass, Kylie's going to think that I've got something going on with her. Not that she doesn't already have her suspicions. You know Kylie. So—really. Just jump Faith and get it over with."

He laughed. "Well, then. Yes, sir. I'll get right on that. She's really got the hots for me?" He was beaming, proud of himself.

"Yeah. Who the fuck knows why?"

"You kidding me? She dated you for a year. She's due for an upgrade."

Linc grinned at him. "You call yourself an upgrade? Just don't screw it up. She might actually have the ability to transform you into a respectable person."

"Me? Nah, that'll never happen."

They finished their beers, and after a while, Linc walked Jacob to his truck. Jacob promised he'd put a watch on Rhonda and keep them posted with any developments. "You're not really going to New York, are you?" Jacob asked.

Linc cocked an eyebrow at him. "Wouldn't you, if your girl had been treated that way by her father? Wouldn't you want to get in his face and tell him what a spineless piece of shit he is?" He shook his head. "Not to mention that he might have put her in danger. I need to do something."

He nodded. "Yeah. I guess. Just...be careful. He made it clear he doesn't want her there. He'll want you there even less."

By then, it was after midnight. The mountain was silent and dark. Peaceful, but Linc's mind was anything but settled. It was whirling with thoughts of just how quickly he could get himself up to New York.

He shook Jacob's hand and after he drove away, climbed the stairs to the bedroom. Kylie was lying in the darkness, on her side, facing away from him. As he walked in, she flopped over. "Can't sleep," she grumbled.

That wasn't a surprise, considering the day she'd had. He walked to her and sat on the edge of the bed. "Want some tea? Warm milk?"

"Alcohol. Lots and lots of it."

He chuckled. "I'm going to fly up to New York tomorrow. I want to talk to this father of yours. But I want you to call Jacob if anything weird happens while I'm gone."

Her eyes widened to full moons as she sat up suddenly. "What? No."

"Listen. This is serious. Someone needs to talk to this guy and get to the bottom of this. If you were shot at, then maybe he knows what's going on."

She shook her head. "It was an accident! We don't even know if it has anything to do with my father! It could've been a college student shooting off stray bullets."

"You don't honestly believe that, do you?"

The doubtful, scared look in her eyes told him everything he needed to know.

"If he's mafia, and you're in trouble, we need to know. Maybe he can put a stop to it."

She gnawed on her lip again, looking like a little school-girl. Her chest was heaving under her thin camisole. She said, "If you're going up there, then I am too."

"Hell no," he said with authority, banging his fist on his thigh. He knew she'd say something like that, and he really didn't need her to trail along in case things got dangerous. "That's not possible. Someone needs to watch the dogs."

"The vet can do that," she insisted. "I want to be with you. You really think it's safe, going up there alone? We'll be safer if we go in a pair, and you know it."

He frowned and shook his head. "Why do you want to go back? You really want to see him again?"

"No. I don't care about him. I care about you. I'd never be able to forgive myself if something happened to you," she said, seeking out his eyes in the darkness.

"All right," he said finally, conceding. "You think we can get up there in the morning? Can you book the flight?"

She'd already begun to scramble out of bed and reach for the laptop. "I'm on it. I'll also book us a room in Manhattan. Maybe I'll have a little more fun, this time, if you're there?"

He smiled at her and kissed her lightly on the lips, tasting her toothpaste. Fun? He wouldn't count on it.

22

William Hatfield had lived enough of his life with his wife to know when she had something up her sleeve.

And now, he was worried. Because her sleeves were looking awfully heavy.

Christina had always had him by the balls, since day one. She never let a single day go by without reminding him of that little fact. He'd been suspicious when she'd capitulated too easily, after he'd told her to drop the subject of the mysterious woman who'd come into his office, and after he'd forgotten about Tyler's game. She'd been saccharine sweet about it, instead of baring her claws and fangs. She never let him get away with shit like that, usually.

She was up to something.

Christina prided herself on being one step ahead of everyone. Knowing Tina, his beautiful rose knew exactly who the young woman who'd visited him was. She probably already knew where his old family lived, where they worked, and what they'd had for breakfast this morning. Probably the whole family did by now.

Maybe he was living on borrowed time because of it.

He told himself there was nothing he could do about it now, except lie and hope that they somehow hadn't figured out the connection. If something happened to Kylie and Rhonda, there was nothing he could do. It was Kylie's own fault for trying to track him down. Rhonda's fault for being foolish and keeping his last name, even after all these years.

But seeing her had made all of his misdeeds front and center, and they had been niggling in the back of his head ever since, driving him insane. He'd done enough to Kylie by leaving her as a baby. He'd consoled himself then by telling himself that Rhonda was a beautiful woman, that when he was out of the picture, she'd have a hundred men wanting to take his place. He told himself that Kylie would have a new father who'd treat her a hell of a lot better than he could. He told himself this was for the best.

But if he let his spoiled, ill-tempered bitch of a wife do her bidding, Kylie and Rhonda could end up dead.

He couldn't just let that happen, could he?

He sat back in the desk chair of his office overlooking Midtown Manhattan, thinking. How could he just let that go? Was there a way he could get his family to back off and let them lie?

No. He'd betrayed them.

Once his family got it in their minds to do something, nothing would stop them. And he'd learned twenty-five years ago that he was powerless when it came to the machine that was her family. He may have been the figurehead of this company, but he didn't run a damn thing. He was just a small cog in the wheel.

He rubbed his bloodshot eyes and dragged a hand down his tired face. He hadn't been able to do his normal workout this morning, too worried about what kind of hell had been unleashed.

Then he picked up his phone and called his wife. He knew she had a lover; maybe more than one. She'd never been faithful to him, even on their honeymoon. Their marriage had always been a sham. She'd told him on the day they said "I do" in Vegas that she hadn't loved him. He hadn't loved her, either. They barely even knew each other, but he'd gone along with it.

He'd had to.

It was a business arrangement. They needed someone to play the squeaky-clean head of their crooked operation, and he'd been tapped. Christina treated him like he was disposable. He knew Tyler wasn't his, and he wasn't sure about any of the others, either. But they played the happy family, keeping up appearances, because if they didn't, the boss wouldn't like it.

That's all this was. The appearance of happiness. Screw the real thing. The only time he was ever close to that was…a damned long time ago. A quarter of a century ago, to be precise.

"Hello, darling," she answered, sounding out of breath. "Just finishing up with my workout."

William didn't buy that at all. He didn't trust a thing she said. Knowing her, she was working out with one of the many young men the family employed to do their dirty work. Christina always had an eye for the boys half her age, and she got what she wanted, which was why she kept her body tight and toned. "That's wonderful. I hope you didn't overexert yourself."

"Me? Never. I'm going downtown to meet with the ladies for a late lunch. I won't be in to see you today."

"That's too bad," he lied. Whenever she came in, it wasn't to visit with him. It was to be her family's spy, keeping him under their thumb.

"Did you call for another reason?" she asked him.

He opened his mouth, trying to think of how to broach the subject. *Have you figured out who that woman who visited my office yesterday is yet?* wouldn't do. Besides, he didn't need to ask. He knew the answer already. Knowing her, she'd already told the boss, and he was setting upon taking care of things. "Um. No, honey. Just missed you and wanted to check to make sure you were all right."

"Oh, I'm fine, sweetheart," she said, so saccharine sweet it made him cringe. "Have a great day, love. See you for dinner?"

"Yeah. See you."

He hung up the phone and buried his face in his hands. What a fucking mess.

It was his own fault. He'd been the ambitious one, wanting to make something more of himself than working as a garbage man. But really, what was so wrong about collecting garbage? It was a good, honest living.

Nothing like the shit he was doing now. His entire life was a lie.

Just then, his intercom crackled. His secretary spoke in a prim, proper voice, with a hint of concern. "Mr. Hatfield. There is someone out here who urgently needs to see you."

Fuck. The last thing he needed was a construction fire to put out. He wheeled himself behind his desk and pressed the intercom button. "No, Valerie. No interruptions. I'm in the middle of something. Have them make an appointment."

"Um…but…" Her voice grew more urgent. "I think you'd better—"

He pressed the intercom again. "No buts. I absolutely—"

He jumped up as the double doors to his office exploded open and a big, muscular man in a t-shirt and cargo pants stormed in.

"What is the meaning of this! How dare you…" William

stopped when he saw who tentatively slipped in behind the intruder.

Kylie.

The momentary pause that seeing his daughter gave him allowed the big man to advance upon him and grab him by the throat, pushing him back against his desk so his ass hit the top of it. He fell backwards and the man grabbed him, twisting him around and shoving his cheek up against his blotter. His arm was wrenched up against his back, immobile, as a voice barked in his ear, "Listen here, you prick…"

Out of breath, William began to choke.

Of all people, Kylie came to his rescue. "Linc. Don't. Let's discuss this like civilized people."

"You want to have a discussion with this asshole? I thought you already tried that," the man said, shoving him harder against the desk. Any harder, and he'd smash his skull. He tried to shake from the steel grasp, but that wasn't possible.

"Linc…" she warned.

He released William slowly, grabbing onto the collar of his jacket and shoving him down into a chair. The guy wasn't from around here, that much was obvious. He crossed his thick arms and leaned against his desk like he owned the place. The hate William expected to see in Kylie's eyes, he saw in this man's. This Linc. Was he her boyfriend? Husband? "You're not getting out of here until you explain yourself to your daughter. Kylie. Lock the door."

"I already did," she said.

"Good. Come here." He motioned her forward, so that she was standing in front of William. Then he kicked his shin. "Look at her." When he didn't do it fast enough, the guy kicked again. Pain screamed up his leg as the younger man practically roared, "Look. At. Her. You bastard."

William slowly lifted his gaze to meet the woman's in

front of him. She was wearing a dress, and was beautiful, just like her mother had been. He felt a dagger pierce his heart at the sight of her as the man, Linc, began to speak.

"This is your daughter. The daughter you threw away twenty-four years ago. Since you left, she's turned into the most amazing woman on this planet, no thanks to you. And I believe that she's owed an explanation."

William hung his head, his eyes drifting down to his knees. "She is. I know."

"And?" Linc prompted.

William looked around. "Look," he whispered. "I can't do this here."

Linc snorted. "The hell you can't. She's waited a long time for this. And—"

"I know, I know. But I can't…" He looked around again and tried to signal to him with his eyes. His office was most likely bugged, and there was no telling who could be spying on him. Valerie had been his secretary for twenty years, and he couldn't even trust her. There were moles everywhere in this organization. There was a good chance that someone already knew these two were in the building. They didn't realize how much danger they were in, just being here. "Not here."

"Then where?" Kylie asked, hands on her hips. She looked at the big man and sighed. "I told you he wouldn't…"

Her expression and disappointed tone of voice was like a knife in William's heart. She didn't trust him in the least. It was easy to think she'd had a grand life without him, but seeing the hurt in her eyes, he knew he'd scarred her.

"Look. It's not me you need to worry about. It's them. You have to believe me. Everything I've ever done is to protect you and your mom. The family business…it's dangerous."

She gave him a doubtful look. "All right. Where do you want to meet?"

"Central Park. Six p.m. By the zoo entrance." He gritted his teeth as he grabbed an ink pen and paper, jotting down: *Not the zoo. Bethesda Fountain in forty-five minutes. Don't tell anyone.* "Please. You've got to get out of here and never come back."

Kylie started to move toward the door, but Linc held back, taking the paper from his hand. He gave William a hard look after he read it. "What reassurance do we have that you'll meet us there?"

"I will. All I can do is promise. You can't stay here. Please. Go."

Kylie studied him for a minute, her eyes so much like Rhonda's it hurt. Then she read the note he'd handed Linc, and her brow furrowed. He silently prayed for her to go with the plan. "Come on, Linc. See you at six," she said to her father, almost like a warning.

She opened the door, and the pair walked through, and disappeared.

William straightened his tie and lapel, then walked to his executive chair and slumped into it. As he did, Valerie appeared in the open doorway. "What was that all about?" she asked, alarmed. "I was about to call the police. I'm sorry, I tried to tell them that—"

He shook his head. "Nonsense. It's fine," he said, but his voice shook slightly as he spoke. He picked up a pen to give her the illusion that it was business as usual, but his hand trembled. "Just a couple of disgruntled people from the union. I took care of it."

She nodded and closed the door behind her, leaving him alone.

Jesus. Kylie was back. In this city. Why had she come back? Didn't she have any idea of what she was getting herself into? He needed to convince her to go away, and never come back. Every minute she stayed in this city made her situation more dangerous.

Damn. She was just as tenacious as he was.

After a minute, he pressed the button for the intercom. "Valerie. Cancel my afternoon appointments. Something came up."

23

"He isn't going to show," Kylie said to Linc as he held her hand while they walked down the busy streets of New York City.

"What do you mean? Of course he's going to," Linc said to her, checking the street signs. "What's more likely is *us* not showing. I have no godforsaken clue where we are."

"Well. It's Central Park. Isn't that the big park in the city? It's right smack in the middle of Uptown, I think. You can't miss it. Or so I've heard."

He squinted and spun around as he took in the unfamiliar surroundings. "Trust me. We can miss it. This city is huge."

He was right. With all the massive skyscrapers around, the streets filled with wall-to-wall people, they'd been turned all around. She had no idea where Uptown and Downtown were anymore. One thing she knew, though. She felt much more adventurous with Linc by her side. Linc, the badass, who'd shown her father who was boss. As much as she didn't want to see her dad hurt, she'd kind of loved seeing Linc wield that authority and those big muscles of his, showing those city slickers who was the man.

"Let's just take a cab," Kylie said. Before he could answer, she walked out to the curb and lifted a hand. A yellow taxi immediately pulled up right to her, and she smiled, proud of herself. She had been in the city one day longer than him, and she was already learning things.

They climbed into the cab and Linc said to the driver, "We've got to get to Central Park. The Bethesda Fountain. Can you help us?"

The driver took them about a mile to the park. When they got out, the driver directed them where they needed to go in order to get to the fountain. They walked through the busy park and found the meeting place with no problem. As Kylie sat on a bench, Linc reached into his pants for his wallet.

"Let me buy you a pretzel," he said, heading off to the vendor before she had a chance to say anything.

He came back with two, handing her one along with a lemonade big enough to share. They sat down, watching the people. Kylie tried to munch on her pretzel, but her stomach was doing somersaults. "I don't think he's going to show," she said again.

"Relax. I think he is. If he doesn't want my fist in his face. Don't think I won't march right back up there and give him hell."

She wrinkled her nose at him. He'd been so sexy, defending her honor like that. For a man normally so quiet and nonconfrontational, it had kind of turned her on. She was glad Linc was such a force and could hold his own in a fight and take care of her, but she wasn't sure that was why her father had agreed to meet with them. "Yes, you can be scary when you want to be. I know I wouldn't mess with you."

"You're the only one I'd let mess with me." He gave her a heart-melting grin.

She smiled back. "But truthfully, Linc? He seemed genuinely terrified, and switching the time and location for our meeting…?" She shook her head. "He's very worried about something. Someone. Not you."

He took a huge bite of his pretzel. "The mafia." He let out a big breath of air. "So, that's your dad, huh?"

She licked a rock of salt off her finger and winced. "Don't remind me."

Not that she needed reminding. For the past few days, he'd been at the center of her mind. She could barely blink without thinking of him.

"You know. I'd barely know you two are related if I saw you on the street. He doesn't look anything like you."

Her mouth twisted. "Good."

Sensing her frustration, Linc put a hand on her knee, and started to run his fingers in slow, calming circles over her skin. It helped a little. Just a little.

Kylie straightened as a rollerblader zoomed by, narrowly missing their toes. "You really think that they could've forced him into a marriage with someone else? For what reason?"

Linc shrugged, ripped off a piece of the pretzel, and popped it in his mouth. "Who knows? With them, it's all about securing power. Business deals that make them stronger. Maybe his marriage was a business deal. We'll find out when he gets here."

"*If* he gets here," she corrected, checking her phone. "It's been forty-five minutes already."

"Well. Give him some time."

"Yeah. I read something somewhere that city-time runs differently than time everywhere else. If you're fifteen minutes late in the city, that's actually early. Thirty minutes late is considered to be on time," she said.

He let out a short laugh. "That's warped. You'd fit right in here."

She shrugged. It was no secret that no matter how hard she tried, she was perpetually late for just about everything.

He stretched out on the bench, looking up and down at the people passing back and forth. "God, I hate the city."

That was a big way in which she and Linc differed. He wanted quiet. The fewer people, the better. Where she'd always loved hectic and busy, he wanted relaxed and laid-back. Even though they were here on such unpleasant business, she found the movement on the streets energizing.

She elbowed him. "What's wrong with this? It's kind of cool. If it weren't for my dad living here, I might like it. Doesn't it exhilarate you?"

He rubbed his temple. "It's giving me a headache." He leaned forward and studied her closely. "You really like this? All this noise and chaos?"

"Yes. I mean, I don't notice the noise and chaos. There's just always something going on. It's thrilling."

He leaned back and looked around. From the expression on his face, he wasn't thrilled. More like annoyed. He jutted his chin in the direction of the path. "Look. There he is."

Kylie looked past her boyfriend's broad frame and saw him, the only man in a suit who was striding with purpose toward them, looking around as if he was afraid of being spotted. He looked so conspicuous in his nervousness, Kylie was surprised he didn't have on a trench coat and dark sunglasses.

"Is it me or does he look like he's going to poop his pants?"

"I guess the mafia does that to a person," Linc said as the man approached.

He held out a hand to shake Linc's, but Linc just stared at it, so he pulled it back and ran it through his hair. God, what an oily weasel, Kylie thought. Did he really think that just by meeting them there, she'd like him? If he did, he had another think coming.

"Look," William said, looking around carefully, his eyes narrowed. He motioned them up. "Let's walk."

They got to their feet and followed him, walking toward the fountain. He held out his hands, balled into fists in front of him, shaking them to make a point. "Kylie, you have to believe that I never wanted to hurt you two."

She almost laughed. "Doesn't matter if you didn't want to. You did. Badly. Not so much me, because I never knew you. But I can only imagine how my mother must've felt as a new mother, having her husband just disappear like that, without a word. That was an awful thing to do."

He nodded and looked at his shiny leather shoes. "Yes. I understand. But I had to."

"But why?"

"Did your mother tell you I took that job in Manhattan for the two of you? I wanted to give you the best life I possibly could, and all the things I wanted for you, I couldn't give you as a garbage man."

"Yes, she told me that. So…what? Did you get involved with the wrong people?"

He looked around again. "Yeah. You could say that."

"If you loved my mother so much, why didn't you get out of it?"

"Because once you're in with these people," Linc said, "there's only one way out."

Every movie Kylie'd ever watched about the mafia flashed before her eyes, and she felt a little sick to her stomach.

"I wanted to," William said, "but I was stuck. My boss, Jackie DeRoss took me in and gave me that life I was thirsting for. He taught me what he knew about the business, until I was indebted to him. He told me that he'd make me one of the most powerful people in the city, if he could trust me. I vowed he could, that I would do anything to protect the family. Then one night, his daughter saw me, and decided she wanted me. And it was made clear to me that what Christina wanted, she got. I had to go along with it, or they'd kill me."

"They told you to leave your wife and kid," Kylie mumbled, more to herself than to him.

He shook his head. "No. They didn't know I was married. They didn't care. You don't understand who these people are. If they want something, they get it. And they wanted me. If I told them I was married, they wouldn't have waited for a divorce. They'd have probably found a way to remedy that situation pretty fast."

Kylie's blood ran cold. "You mean, they would've killed us."

"Right. So, I did the only thing I could think to do. I put distance between us, and when I was afraid that wasn't going to be enough and Rhonda would come looking for me, I bought her that house and mailed her a check, hoping she'd get the hell out of town before it was too late."

"She did. But she always wondered about what happened to you. She never looked for a divorce because she always held out hope you'd come back to her. She loved you so much," Kylie said. "And you just threw her away."

He nodded. "I did it to keep her safe. To keep you both safe. These people aren't ones to show mercy. Christina's father is the kingpin. He's been in jail for murder since 2007, but the rest of the family is very powerful and have been carrying out his wishes just as if he was on the streets right now. It's not safe here."

Kylie ventured a look at Linc. She might have liked the city, but she suddenly felt cold, despite the beauty of the fall leaves all around them. She wanted to go home.

"You know that your second marriage isn't legal. Right? Your marriage to Christina DeRoss isn't even real."

He nodded. "I think they may have found that out. It's only a matter of time before they act on that information. But Christina's not as cautious as they are. If she finds out, she'll kill us all."

Kylie pressed her hands to her stomach. "Then you're not safe, either."

"Yeah, but I made this bed. If I get hurt, so be it. It's my own fault. But if something happens to you or your mother, I'll never forgive myself." He clasped his hands in front of himself and started to wring them. She'd never known those hands when he was young, but they looked old now, weak. "Tell me. Does Rhonda know you're here?"

Kylie shook her head. "She knew I was tracking you down, but she wanted nothing to do with what I found out. She's moved on. It took her a long time, but she realizes she's better off without you."

His frown deepened. "I'm sorry, Kylie. But you really do need to go before they find out who you are. If they do, they'll kill you, and your mother."

Kylie gnawed on her lip as Linc said, "That's why we're here. We think someone's already trying to, and we need to get to the bottom of it. Until we do, Kylie's not safe anywhere."

William stiffened and stopped walking. His eyes narrowed in confusion. "What?"

"Someone took a shot at me last night, outside my apartment in Asheville," Kylie explained. "And someone tried to run down Mom yesterday afternoon."

He pulled nervously on the lapels of his suit jacket, then fumbled with his words, alarmed. "Did you see who did these things?"

Kylie shook her head. "Whoever it was, it seems too odd

to be a coincidence. Is it possible someone could've followed me home after I left your office?"

"Oh, dear," he said, covering his face with his hands and breathing hard. "It's more than possible. Oh, hell. I didn't expect that they would attempt to take care of this so quickly."

He walked to a bench and sat down, murmuring to himself as Kylie silently raised her eyebrows at Linc. He gave her a grave look in return.

"If that's the case, if they really followed you down there," he said softly. "Then you might want to check on your mother. She could be in very serious danger."

24

Kylie pushed on the cab driver's headrest and let out a string of curses she'd been keeping in, ever since she left her father. "Can't this piece of shit go any faster?" she muttered, ignoring the cab driver's eye daggers shooting at her through the rearview mirror.

Linc tightened a hand around her upper arm. "Relax."

They were in a wall-to-wall evening rush-hour traffic jam heading into Jersey, trying to get to Newark International Airport. Forgotten was the idea of a nice night of dinner in the city, with a stay at a fine hotel in the heart of Manhattan. Now, she just wanted to get back to Asheville and check on her mother.

Also, people? She hated people. She hated the city. Right now, she was totally on board with Linc about that. Why were all these people trying to leave the city at the same time?

Linc spoke in soothing, low tones. "Hey. Look. We can only get home as fast as the plane will take us. And our flight's not until seven."

She knew that. Still, she bit on the inside of her cheek,

impatient. She felt like she had to do something. "I don't know. Maybe we can get a sooner flight, if we just get there. Has Jacob called you back yet?"

She already knew the answer to that too. No. Linc had called to give him the heads-up of their meeting with William Hatfield, and Jacob had told him that someone was already on the case, outside her mother's house, watching. He said he'd check in and make sure everything was okay. But that was only five minutes ago, and Linc's phone had been sitting on his lap since then. It hadn't rung or buzzed or flashed with activity since.

"No," he said, checking the screen to appease her. "Don't worry. He will."

She had no doubt Jacob would take care of things down there, because that was just who he was, but nothing was going fast enough for her. She picked up her phone and dialed her mother's cell again. No answer. She let out a big breath of air, and stray tendrils of hair puffed out over her forehead. "I bet she forgot her phone again, wherever she is."

"Maybe she's with that guy. The doctor boyfriend," Linc pointed out. "Do you have his number?"

She was already scrolling through her call history before he'd finished the question. Clicking the call button, after a moment, her heart sank. "Voicemail."

Maybe they were in bed together. Even though a part of her still cringed at the idea, the bigger part of her hoped it was true. Hoped that her mother was busy with the good doctor and would be the rest of the night.

She was still a little weirded out at the thought of her mother dating, but it was a lot cheerier than the grisly game of what-if she'd been playing in her head. What if she'd been kidnapped? What if the gunman shot her in her living room. What if…?

"I just wish she'd answer. I called her cell and her landline. Damn!" She brought her hand down hard on her knee, and the resulting slap was unintentionally painful. She rubbed it.

"It'll be okay," Linc said to her.

She nodded and looked out the window, at the New York City skyline, mostly blocked from view by a maze of highway ramps, smog, and giant trucks, all fighting for purchase as the highway narrowed from six lanes to two. What absolute madness. She didn't hate the city like Linc did, but right now, she just wanted to get the hell away.

"Thanks for coming here for me," she said quietly, leaning against his arm, which he'd draped around her. "I know you hate the city, but it's a lot nicer with you here."

"No problem." He sat up and looked behind him in the stopped traffic. His body was tenser than usual. Was he looking to see if someone was following them?

"Do you really think that there's someone after me?" she asked him after a minute.

"I don't know, but I'm not letting you out of my sight. You got that? Until we know what we're up against, you go where I go. Got it?"

She pressed her lips together. Ordinarily, she hated it when he tried to tell her what to do, but this time, she had to agree it was warranted. And it made her feel safer, even though she doubted Linc would be much of a match for a professional hit man. "Okay."

"Good. Maybe your mother should come up to my house. To stay for a couple of days. It'll be safer there."

Kylie snorted. "Um. It'd be easier to move the mountain to my mother than get my mother to move to the mountain. She's more stubborn than I am. She won't budge."

He rubbed his chin. "Yeah? If you told her what was happening and tried to convince—"

He stopped when Kylie gave him a doubtful shake of the head. "Even then. She won't go. Trust me."

"Damn you Hatfield women. Well, at least Jacob'll have someone stay at her house twenty-four-seven."

That news didn't make Kylie feel much better. She'd been under twenty-four-seven police surveillance once, when a serial killer was on her tail, and the killer had still managed to knock her out and drag her out of the apartment. And that was while there were a lot of college students around. In her mother's quiet neighborhood? It'd be simple.

Before she could respond, Linc's phone buzzed. He lifted it. "Hey, Jacob."

She listened, trying to hear what Jacob was saying on the other end, but could only make out a few words here and there. Linc simply said, "uh-huh," a few times, then said, "Okay, thanks for the update. I'll call you when we land."

"So?" Kylie nearly jumped down his throat, even before he could press the "end call" button.

"He's gotten in touch with her. She's at home. The officer there says she's all right. Everything looks normal."

Kylie's brow furrowed. "Wait. If she's home, why didn't she answer her phone? She had to have heard the landline."

"Yeah, um. It appears," he gave her a look like he wasn't sure how she'd take this information, "she's in her living room with a gentleman. They're talking and laughing, and it seems like they're having a good time."

Kylie stared at him, trying to take this information in. A man? In her mother's house? "You mean that doctor? Doctor Jerry?"

Linc shrugged. "Probably. That's good, right? I know I'm relieved she's okay."

Kylie nodded slowly, trying to imagine her mother entertaining a male guest. A male guest who was interested in her mother. She imagined them sitting on the flowered sofa in the living room, surrounded by all her mother's knickknacks and photographs of Kylie.

She tried to envision her mother offering him tea and her famous key lime pie, like she did to Linc, but for some reason, it didn't compute. It was such a foreign thought, she couldn't even picture it. "Yes," she said absently.

An hour later, they arrived at the airport, and even after all that time, Kylie hadn't been able to shake the weird thoughts and feelings she was having regarding her mother. She should've been happy that she was safe, but instead, she kept thinking of her mom, being wooed by this strange man.

A strange man who came out of nowhere?

Was he involved in all this?

Kylie shook her head. The PI business was making her paranoid.

What if they kept dating? She couldn't marry him. She was already married. But what if they started living together? How would it feel to come to the home she grew up in to see this strange man living there? Or what if she moved in with him and sold the house she grew up in? What if other people lived in *her* house?

A stab of pain hit her square in the chest.

"Are you okay?" Linc asked her as she slid out of the cab.

She realized she was clenching her teeth and willed herself to stop. Her mother was laughing. Happy. That was all that mattered, right?

A second later, though, she found herself clenching her teeth again. She needed to get a grip, she told herself. Her mother finding a boyfriend wasn't the end of the world.

It only felt like it.

"YOU'RE VERY KIND. I probably could've made it on my own,"

Rhonda said as she patted Dr. Jerry on the hand. They sat across the dining table from one another, enjoying a nice meal. "But it wouldn't have been very pretty."

He laughed. "Anything I can do to help."

The truth was, that was a lie. She wouldn't have even bothered to make the trip on her own, since she was bruised and feeling rather achy all over when she woke up. The Vicodin had also made her woozy, so she'd planned a day of taking it easy on the couch.

But then, Jerry had called her bright and early that morning, asking if he could be of service in any way. He sounded so like a knight in shining armor, she couldn't resist. Suddenly, she had a lot more energy and couldn't wait to see the dashing doctor again.

When Kylie had brought her home the day before, she'd viewed the contents of her fridge to see if she had enough, since the supermarket was where she'd been headed when she'd been mowed down. Kylie had determined that she would be fine, for at least the next few days. But Kylie's idea of a full fridge differed drastically from Rhonda's, and Rhonda simply couldn't refuse such a kind offer. So, she'd said, "I could use a ride to the supermarket, as I have a few odds and ends to pick up."

To which he'd replied, "My pleasure. I'll pick you up at say, noon?"

He'd arrived just when he said he would, driving a luxury BMW the likes of which Rhonda had never been a passenger in. By the time he arrived, she'd changed clothes a dozen times and found that putting on makeup with a sprained wrist and a bunch of aches wasn't exactly easy. But she'd managed and was well-rewarded. When he arrived, he came to the door with a bouquet of irises.

She nearly swooned, and it had nothing to do with the Vicodin or her banged-up knee.

They'd had such a lovely time, chatting over coffee at the little café inside Harris Teeter. Then he'd helped her with her entire trip, taking her through the store and to the Publix so that she was able to get everything on her list. He'd insisted she use one of those mobile scooters, and he'd pushed the cart, patiently reading over her list with her and reaching up to the high shelves to get things that were out of Rhonda's reach.

When he helped her inside, she thought it only right that she invite him to dinner. Lasagna, of course, since it was her specialty, and she'd wanted to impress him.

He accepted, delighted.

So now, they'd spent a full eight hours together, and the night was growing long. She remembered vaguely, when she was a kid, all those awkward moments she'd had with boys at the end of a date, anticipating that first kiss. As night started to fall, all of those worries came back to her. The last time she'd dated was approximately a million years ago. What did people do nowadays, at the end of dates? A kiss? A hand-shake? Did they even date anymore? Maybe they just hopped into bed together and then watched movies later.

Oh, she didn't even want to think about sleeping with a man. It'd been so long. Too long. She probably wouldn't even know what to do.

Kylie would probably know all the answers to the ques-tions buzzing around inside Rhonda's head. She wished she'd talked to her about these things, but she'd done very well for a long time, pretending she was a saint. How awkward would it be, asking her own daughter for sex tips?

No, she would just navigate this uncharted territory on her own. As bumpy as the ride might be. Perhaps Jerry was in the same boat. He'd lost his wife of twenty years to breast cancer two years earlier. He might not have been as rusty as

Rhonda was, but maybe he had the same worries and reservations she had.

Luckily, Jerry made for easy company, so she didn't have time to dwell on all those dating worries. He was an easy conversationalist, a born storyteller, making her laugh in a way that Adam had so long before. The hours seemed to just slip by.

When dinner was over, gentleman that Jerry was, he offered to clear and do the dishes. "Please. You're recuperating. Let me take care of these," he said as the phone began to ring. Again. For some reason, it'd been ringing off the hook today, but it was probably some of her old friends, who'd heard through the grapevine about her accident and wanted to gossip. She normally loved gossip, but now, she wasn't interested. "Want me to get that?"

"No, it's nothing important, I'm sure. Just let it go to voicemail." She limped out to the kitchen and sat at the center island to guide him as to where to put the pots and pans when they were washed and dried. "Are you sure I can't help?"

"No. This is the least I can do after that amazing meal. Please."

As she watched him work at the sink, wearing her pink rubber gloves, she had to admit, he pulled them off well. And maybe it was that she was older, or that he had a kind, self-deprecating sense of humor, but whatever it was, she wasn't as nervous as she could have been, considering she hadn't felt this way about a man in decades. "I have to say, you're very good at that."

"At what? Washing dishes?" He gave her a sexy wink.

She winked back. "I didn't know men...my ex...Kylie's father didn't set foot in the kitchen." Now why did she have to bring him up? She wanted to throttle herself.

"Ah. Well, I feel like the kitchen is the heart of the house. Not all men are afraid of this room."

She felt a little silly. "Well. I don't know. You see…I haven't been on a date in…" she trailed off. "I don't know. Is this even a date?"

He laughed. "I guess that's what they call it. I haven't, either. So I guess we're alike in that way."

She laughed too, relieved.

When he opened his mouth to speak next, she thought he would compliment the meal again, as he'd been raving about her lasagna nonstop for the past hour. Instead, he said something that completely mystified her. "Did you know there's a police car outside your house?"

She slipped off the stool and limped over to the window. The sun was setting, but sure enough, there was a car across the street, and a young officer's form was visible in the driver's seat. "Hmm," she said, losing interest. "Maybe it's for one of my neighbors. I'm not exactly on anyone's most wanted list."

"I don't know about that," he said with another of those sexy winks, making her stomach flutter in a way it hadn't since she was a teen.

She limped over to the refrigerator and pulled out a pie. This one was store-bought since she hadn't had time to make one of her specialties, but it would have to do. Jerry seemed the easygoing type, who wouldn't mind at all, and that was what she liked about him. Actually, she liked so many things about him, it was starting to scare her. She hadn't even liked this many things about Adam—she could distinctly remember thinking he was kind of crass and not her type the first time she'd met him.

But Jerry? If she'd have written a list of things she wanted in a man, it'd have looked something like…well, him.

She tried to tamp down the excitement inside her in

order to at least make it through the date without fawning like a starry-eyed teenager. She knew she'd been scaring Kylie by how quickly she'd succumbed to his charm, and she had to at least fight the good fight, for Kylie's sake.

As she was attempting to cross to the dining room, Jerry whipped off the pink gloves and tsked at her. "Allow me, Rhonda. You really should be resting in your condition."

In her condition? She hadn't felt this good in years.

She smiled and sat, then instructed him where in the breakfront she kept the teacups, saucers, and dessert plates. He laid everything out in just the way she would have, then cut her a slice. He was so very neat, methodical. Adam had always been a bit of a slob, and from her limited knowledge of men, she'd always assumed most men were. This was a surprising and welcome change.

As he was placing the plate in front of her, the phone began to ring again.

She groaned. "As you can tell, I have very persistent friends," she said with a smile. "I'm sure they heard about my accident and they're all just offering to help me out."

"That's good that you have such thoughtful friends. You sure you don't want me to get it?" he said, pouring her some tea. "I don't mind."

She sighed. They'd been having such a nice conversation that she didn't want anyone else to intrude. "All right. But I don't feel like talking to them. Just tell them I'm resting and I'll call them back tomorrow."

"Sure," he said, standing and walking into the kitchen, where the phone was attached to the wall. As soon as he disappeared, the doorbell rang. He called out, "Busy lady, you are! Why don't I get that instead?"

Rhonda struggled to her feet. "I swear, I can't remember a time when I've been this popular!" she exclaimed as she limped to the phone. Jerry had gone to the foyer to open the door, so she lifted the phone from the receiver. "Hello?"

"Mom?"

It was Kylie. She sounded far away, and she could hear the tension in her voice. "Kylie, what's the problem? Was that you who's been calling?"

"Yes," she said, the word clipped. "I needed to talk to you. Listen. I'm just getting on the plane from New York."

"New York? You mean…did you go to…don't tell me you went to track him down. You're just asking for trouble!"

"Rhonda," Jerry called from the foyer. She looked up.

The rest of her daughter's words were lost as Rhonda craned her neck to look into the foyer and spotted a policeman standing in the doorway.

She blinked.

Well, here comes trouble, she thought.

"What does he want?" she mouthed.

"This officer needs to speak to you," Jerry said.

She realized her daughter had spoken at the same time, when Kylie suddenly paused and said, "Did you get all that?"

"Actually, no. Kylie, hon. There's a police officer at my door. Can I call you back?"

Her daughter let out an exasperated sigh. "That's what I was just saying, Mom. Linc called Jacob to have a patrol officer put there. He's there to check on you and make sure everything's okay."

She let the words sink in, trying to make sense of them. "I don't understand. Everything's just fine. Why do I need police surveillance, Kylie? What's going on?"

"I can't explain right now. Just make sure you stay put and listen to the officer. He's there to protect you. I'll be over as soon as I can, and I'll fill you in on everything. Okay?"

"Yes, honey, but protect me from what? You didn't run into any trouble in New York, did you? Are you all right?"

"I'm fine. Sorry, Mom. I've got to go. Just…be safe."

Safe…from what? Or whom?

Rhonda opened her mouth to ask that question, but Kylie had already ended the call. She looked down the hallway, to the burly young officer silhouetted in the doorway. "Can you tell me, young man, just what are you keeping me safe from?"

He shrugged. "I don't know, ma'am. I'm just under orders to keep an eye on you. I'll be across the street, and I won't be going anywhere all night. If you need anything, you just let me know."

"Thank you," she said before the officer retreated down the driveway, and she and Jerry watched him leave. When she started to close the door, she gave the doctor a confused look.

"Well, my dear," he said, smiling warmly at her. "Hit by a car, now under police surveillance. Never a dull moment with you, is there?"

She didn't know what to say. Maybe Kylie's knack for getting into trouble was rubbing off on her, because this was more excitement than she'd seen in all of Kylie's twenty-four years.

Now, she wasn't worried at all about that goodnight kiss. She had other things on her mind.

She locked the door tight and turned to face the man she was inexplicitly attracted to. "Let's finish up dessert so you can be on your way. I think you're right. I think I may just need to have a little rest."

25

William had to take an extra-long lunch to meet with his daughter in Central Park. That alone was suspicious—he didn't take long lunches, or any lunches, for that matter. Funny, for a company with his name on it, he had surprisingly little power within these walls. When he came in through the lobby, he made sure to do it with his head up, returning any friendly hellos.

He needed to act normal.

All it would take was for one of them to let slip to the family that he'd been gone longer than usual, and heads would roll.

Namely, his.

When he got within sight of the double doors to his office, he started to breathe easier. He'd made it. Everything would be fine.

He told himself that until he pushed open the door to his office and saw Dennis DeRoss sitting in his chair, elbows on the desk, hands tented under his chin. "Hello, Billy," Dennis said, his voice full of menace.

William's blood went cold.

Dennis DeRoss wouldn't have ordinarily been a frightening person. He was small, short, and ugly, like his father, Jackie. He had a hooknose, slightly off-center, and his hairline had receded so much in the past few years that it was clear he was way past his prime. Even when he was younger, William had always thought he looked like a dark, slinky weasel. But it wasn't his business partner and brother-in-law's appearance that had William's bones shaking in his skin.

It was his family.

The family he'd been forced to marry into so many years ago.

He may have been welcomed into the family, but he still wasn't one of them. He was a second-class citizen in their book. He'd been that way from the moment they cleaned him up and put him forever in their debt.

As Dennis glared at him, demanding an explanation without saying a word, William thought back to the first time he'd met him, when he was on his garbage route in Brooklyn. He'd just been taking care of business when he'd seen Dennis, dressed sharply in a suit and tie, leaving one of the businesses they serviced. He'd stood out in that crappy neighborhood, in his fancy outfit and new BMW, and all William could think was how if he had that kind of life, he'd have it made.

Their route was almost over, so he'd taken a few minutes to talk to him, and at the end of the conversation, Dennis had given him his card. "Call me," he'd said. "Our business is always looking for good, trustworthy men like you."

He'd called the second he got off work, praying that this was his ticket out of his shitty life.

It was the first of many mistakes he wished he'd never made. The day after that, his life changed, and kept changing, until he was virtually unrecognizable from that stupid kid who used to collect people's trash.

What he wouldn't give, he thought, to talk to that stupid kid and shake some sense into him. Sure, they'd been poor, but his life back then hadn't been so shitty after all.

He gathered his courage and shot the bastard a smile. "Hey, Dennis. You caught me coming back from lunch."

"Did I?" His voice was a low rumble.

Those two words said it all. He didn't believe William one bit. In fact, just Dennis being here was a bad thing. His partner was a silent one, and usually conducted all of his business from his sprawling home in Connecticut, away from the city. He only came to Midtown when he had skulls to crush.

After his conversation with Kylie, he knew his skull was definitely on the line.

"Yeah. It's been a crazy day. Had to take a walk and clear my head a little," he said with a weak laugh.

"Oh yeah? Problems with the company?"

If only that was all he had to worry about. No, the company ran like clockwork. He barely needed to do a thing, as he was just the de facto leader, a stooge. In fact, his knowledge of construction was entirely inconsequential in this position.

"Yeah," he lied, advancing toward his desk, "but nothing I can't handle. Why are you here? Problems?"

He waited for Dennis to vacate his chair, but he didn't. "You can say that," Dennis said, pushing away from the desk. Instead of standing up, though, he lifted his feet onto the shiny surface, crossing them at the ankle, and laced his hands behind his head, making himself comfortable.

Classic Dennis. The man loved his shoes and did everything possible to show them off. When they'd first met, he'd told William he didn't wear anything but custom Italian leather that ran north of ten-thousand dollars. "Shoes make the man," he'd said.

He'd tried to get William into it, but William preferred to spend money on suits instead. William looked at those shoes, resting so easily on his blotter, and swallowed as Dennis said the name that made his entire body tense like a steel rod.

"Jackie's not happy."

Jackie DeRoss, his father-in-law.

He'd been in prison on a murder charge for over a decade, but that didn't stop him from managing things outside his cell walls. William assumed someone must've bought off the warden or guards, because he managed quite well from Rikers Island, doling out his orders to his underlings and keeping the family strong.

He made Marlon Brando look like a sweet old grandpa.

William cleared his throat. "That's a shame. And what is he not happy about?"

Dennis laughed. "I think you know. My father doesn't have a lot of rules, Billy. The first and only rule is that family comes first. That's it. You got it?"

He nodded. "Of course."

Dennis's face transformed into a blank mask that was more horrifying than any scowl. "No, I don't think you do. Because if you knew that, you wouldn't have been playing games with us all these years."

William tried to draw breath into his lungs, but it was like his entire body was frozen. "I have been loyal to your family for decades. I've never done a thing against you or your father."

"Don't give me that shit, Billy. You have a wife that ain't my sister. And a daughter too. We know all about them. We know where you were just now. We know everything."

Panic was like a hand at William's throat. "That was my

old life. I swear, I tried to tell you. But then she left me, and I didn't think—"

"Bullshit, Billy. You really thought you could get away with that? We know you married her before you married Christina. And I can tell you right now, Jackie's not happy you kept your first marriage a secret all this time. You know how big he is on trust."

He gritted his teeth. "I can explain."

"No, you can't. There is no explanation needed, Billy. You fucked us. And bad things happen when family members play games. It's...deadly. You should know that by now."

He did know that. That's why every time he saw one of the family's trusted associates—and there were a lot of them —gunned down or throttled or hog-tied and dumped in the Hudson River, he grew more and more fearful over what would happen if Kylie or Rhonda ever resurfaced in his life.

Now, it had happened, just as he'd imagined it would.

And it was time to pay for his misdeeds. They all would.

Rhonda and Kylie too.

He couldn't save himself. But maybe, he could save them. Maybe God would be merciful to him if he made the attempt to help them.

William forced himself to stay calm, fiddling with the Rolex on his wrist to keep his hands from shaking. "All right. So, what are you going to do?"

Dennis shook his head. "I could've had you killed already, but Jackie wants to see you one more time. You're the head of this company, and if we lost you now under suspicious circumstances, it could look bad to all our investors. So, you're lucky. You'll get a few more days," he said, shaking his head. "We've already sent our best fixer over to take care of your first family."

William's legs almost gave out beneath him. Their best

fixer. Nino Capitano. The man was as ruthless as they came. "Already?"

"Went down to visit with them last night. We're expecting to get an update in a few. Your little girl threw us for a loop when she flew back up here, but it won't be long until she's back where she belongs, and Nino can take care of her. I expect your first wife is already dead."

A lump grew in William's throat, and he swallowed painfully as Dennis dropped his legs to the floor and stood up. He nodded at William, then went to stand in front of him and straightened his tie. He patted his cheek twice.

"Jesus, man. You're the head of a billion-dollar company and you look like shit. You should get some rest," he said, grinning sardonically at him.

Then he walked out the door, and before it closed behind him, William heard Dennis say to Valerie, "Cancel all Billy's appointments for today. The man looks like he's on the verge of a heart attack. He needs a break."

The second the door clicked closed, William wiped his sweaty hands on the front of the trousers and dove for the phone. His fingers trembled as he dialed. "Listen to me," he said the second the call was answered. "Kylie and Rhonda need to be put in protective custody right now. Do you understand me? They're in trouble. The family's sent someone to take care of—"

The phone went dead in his hand.

Seconds later, the door burst open, and two large men rushed in.

William dropped the phone and backed against the wall.

It had been over two decades. But his day of reckoning had finally come.

Nino Capitano inspected his handiwork and frowned.

His fingers itched to take that next step. To spill blood. But no. He'd have to wait for the signal.

He'd thought people in Manhattan were idiots, but these morons in downtown Hickville brought stupidity to a whole new level.

Manhattanites were dumb, but they were suspicious, at least. These people were the fatal combination of dumb and trusting.

And everything was working out just as he'd hoped. Maybe he'd be on a red-eye back to New York tonight, if things continued to go his way.

Tilting the blinds, he looked out and made sure that the coast was clear. It was. This was easier than taking candy from a baby and had gone even better than he'd expected. The street had been practically empty when he'd come upon the police officer waiting in his car.

Pop. Pop.

Damn, he loved his silencer.

Now, that oblivious officer was in the trunk of his cruiser, feeling no pain.

It'd only taken a minute to strip the man from his uniform, badge, and gun. Another minute to don it in the back of his rental.

And no one noticed.

When he emerged from the car and walked over to the police vehicle, no one seemed to care that the uniform was at least three sizes too small for him. He couldn't button the shirt, but the tie covered that. The pants? Well, that was another story. He'd ended up wearing his suit pants with it. By that point, he figured it wouldn't make much of a difference. This whole town was damn oblivious.

"How're you doing, officer?" a man on a bicycle had said to him as he'd sat in the driver's side of the police car, cleaning the blood off his hands.

He'd waved. "Fine," he said, then muttered under his breath, "*moron.*"

He'd tightened his belt and checked out the officer's weapon. They actually issued this kind of worthless piece of shit to police in this city? It was unwieldy and felt like a brick in his hand. Tossing the gun onto the passenger's seat, he'd filled his holster with his own gun, his baby, his Glock 9mm. He never went anywhere without it.

Then he'd stepped out of the car and went across the street, to his victim, to "introduce" himself.

The old bat and her man were just as clueless as everyone else in the city. They looked at the badge on Nino's chest and didn't even bother to ask for ID. If they had, they'd have noticed that Nino, at six and a half feet and packing muscle, bore little resemblance to the tall but much less bulky Officer Reardon, whose uniform Nino now wore. He'd introduced himself, told them he'd be across the street, and then went back to his car to wait. He'd wanted to lull them into a false sense of security.

An hour later, he returned, asking the target if she wouldn't mind him using the restroom.

She'd been so easy, it'd almost been a shame. She and the old man she was shacking up with were sitting at the dining room table, eating pie. After he washed his hands in a powder room that smelled like lavender, he sneaked up behind the man, and knocked him from his chair with a crack to the back of the skull.

He went out like a light as the woman screamed and backed herself up against a wall. He gagged and tied them both up, back-to-back, and dragged them out to the middle of the living room.

Then he snapped a picture with his phone. He liked taking pictures of his handiwork. He had quite the collection. He thought of texting it to his boss, but his boss was hands-off about those things. Just wanted it done, didn't want to get involved with the nitty-gritty details.

Nino dialed the number for his boss and waited until someone picked up. "Done. What do you want me to do with them?"

"You've got them both?"

"Half. The daughter's still on her flight back. I'll get her later tonight."

"Who do you have?"

"The old broad. And…" He reached into the old man's jacket pocket and pulled out his identification. He squinted at it. He needed glasses but didn't like to wear them. "Some guy named Jerry Phillips. A doctor."

"Dead?"

He threw the wallet down on the old man, who moaned in pain. "Naw. I thought you might enjoy hearing them die."

He waited for a few seconds, listening to his boss breathing. "Actually, I think I'd like to participate in this one. Look the bitch in the eye as the life drains out." In the background, he listened to what sounded like fingers typing on a keyboard. "Hold tight. I've got a flight booked. I want to see this myself."

Nino raised an eyebrow at that. Whoever this bitch was, she must've done something really bad to piss his boss off so much. "You sure? I can end it pretty quick. Nothing to worry yourself over."

"Yeah. I'm sure. Give me the address."

He did.

"All right. Stay there and keep guard. The young one coming over?"

"Yep. Soon. I had the old bat leave a message on her daughter's phone. She should be getting it when she lands, which is right about now."

"Perfect. I want to see her, too, before you end it. You got it?"

"Aye, aye," he said, grinning. "Whatever you say, boss."

When the call ended, he looked at his two prisoners. The man was still out, slumped in a fetal position with his chin to his chest, but the blonde woman was awake and alert, staring at him with wide eyes, and whimpering into her gag.

He brought the gun to her cheek and smiled at her. "Don't worry, baby," he hissed out. "It'll all be over soon."

He straightened, went to the fridge, and opened it. She had some artsy fartsy craft beer in there that he'd never heard of. But he was game. He grabbed a bottle, cracked it open, and took a swig. As he closed the refrigerator door, he caught sight of a picture of a family in the hospital with a newborn. The woman was a thinner, prettier version of the hag currently tied up on the living room rug. The man?

Well, he knew that man. It was William Hatfield,

Christina DeRoss's husband. He'd met him a couple of times at events but had never been formally introduced.

He laughed. Talk about a moron.

The guy might have his own company, but really, the company had him. He had no balls, whatsoever, and was just their little yes-man. Nico might have owed all he was to the family, but at least he got respect for it. The gun did that for him.

Taking his beer, he went to the living room and kicked the man to see if he was awake yet. He didn't move. Shrugging, he turned on the television, grabbed the remote, and kicked up his feet to watch a little Mets baseball. The Mets were winning, ten to nothing. It was a good night.

JACOB LEANED back in his office chair and rubbed his bloodshot eyes. There was a time, not long ago, that he had no problem staying up late into the night, but maybe he was getting older. He'd only been out until one last night, shooting the shit with Linc, and now he was beat. It had been a busy day.

In addition to all the little annoying shit he had to tackle on a daily basis, there was also the matter of Kylie. He could've probably assigned an officer from his force full-time to the little troublemaker, and the guy never would've run out of things to do. Now, it looked like she'd gone to New York, picked up some enemies from the mob, and they were out to kill her.

The girl couldn't possibly be any more of a trouble-magnet if she tried.

Which reminded him. He hadn't heard from Joe Reardon in an hour and twenty minutes. Hadn't he told him to report in every hour on the hour? He checked his watch. It was after nine, and no report.

Dammit. Just another thing to worry about.

He leaned back in his seat, stretching out his tight muscles. He probably should've found someone other than Joe to take the post, since Joe was a rookie and wasn't the most with-it guy on the force. But all the rest of his men were in the middle of other things, so he'd reluctantly given the job to Joe, telling him explicitly, at least thrice, that he needed to keep him posted every chance he got.

Dammit. It would be nice if the rookies on his force actually did what they were told now and again. He had too many irons in the fire to be babysitting them all the time.

He finished up some paperwork for a case he was ready to close, and picked up his phone, calling in to Joe. There was no answer. The guy probably forgot to charge his phone, again. He picked up the police radio. "Headquarters to—"

He stopped when he realized his phone was ringing. It was Joe's number. He lifted it up and said, "Hey. Everything okay there?"

"Yeah. All good."

"What happened to you radioing in every hour? Remember that? My orders?"

"Oh. Will do. Everything's slow here, though. Lady's with a guy. Lost track of time."

Something seemed off. Joe might have just been disguising the fact that he was sleeping on the job. Jacob tapped his fingers on his desk, thinking. "Well, next time, don't."

"Yeah. Got it."

Was it him, or did Joe Reardon not seem like himself today? "You okay?"

"Yeah. All under control. The subject is fine. She's turning in to bed right now."

He nodded. "All right. Still, keep me posted."

As he ended the call, something was niggling at the back of his brain. In his ten years on the force, he'd never felt so out of sorts before, like something was wrong, but he couldn't put his finger on what, exactly, was out of place.

Kylie and Linc should've been coming in from New York soon. During his phone call, Linc had sounded anxious, so maybe he'd go and pay them a visit to see what, exactly, they'd turned up and what kind of threat they were facing. If they'd invited the mob down here, he needed to know about it before they wreaked havoc in town, or else he'd never hear the end of it from the commissioner.

He had everything under control.

Or so he thought.

And then he looked up, through his open office door, which provided a perfect view of the front desk, and saw Faith Carter walk in, like a gorgeous mirage.

The truth was, the first time Linc introduced them, he'd been whipped. Faith, with her waist-length blonde hair that she wore in these long, loopy curls. She was taller than most other girls, statuesque, like a goddess. As formidable as she was, she had these big blue swimming-pool eyes, framed in long lashes that always made him melt. It was like she'd walked right out of his dreams and into his life.

And she had been dating his best friend.

That was the kicker. The worst part about it was that Linc didn't even seem to notice that he had perfection on his arm. She wasn't just beautiful—she was witty, smart. She put them both in their place a number of times. He'd had a killer of a time whenever they'd double date, because all he wanted to do was talk to Faith. But she was off-limits. When he'd say goodbye to them, he'd bring his date home, and maybe he'd score, maybe he wouldn't...but every time, he was pretending the woman he was with was Faith.

She looked around uncertainly, fluffing her hair in that maddening way she sometimes did, and Jacob felt his temperature rising. All those thoughts about work and the mob and Joe Reardon not being able to follow directions dissolved, and he was left with one overwhelming thought: Faith sure looked pretty right now. She was wearing a pink blouse which complemented her sun-kissed skin. She was even more beautiful than he remembered.

He swallowed and found his mouth dry as a desert.

He watched as Faith, not noticing him, leaned over the front desk and said, "Could I please speak with Detective Dean?"

Then her eyes lifted and caught sight of him. A smile dawned on her face, and it spread heat all over his body. He loved her smile.

And she wanted him. Maybe that was the reason everything seemed so off. Ever since Linc had told him last night about Faith having a true interest in him, he'd been able to think of little else. He'd thought about tracking her down and talking to her, but the thought made him seize up. After all, he did so much better with women when he didn't care. On the rare chance that he did like a woman? He usually ended up doing something shit-stupid and ruining all his chances. He was almost thirty-one now. He felt like he was running out of opportunities.

She waved.

He stood up, wiped his sweaty hands on his thighs, and crossed his arms, trying to keep cool. He missed the first time he tried to lean against the doorjamb but caught himself just in time. Trying again, he said, "Well, look who it is."

"Hi, Jacob," she said, smiling a little. Of course she'd noticed his little flub. "You're here late. I went to your apartment and your neighbor said you were still working."

He motioned her toward him. "Always. Come on in."

When she came around the front desk, he saw that she was wearing a short black skirt that bared her phenomenal legs. If his level of want indicated how badly he was going to crash and burn, then he was going to fuck this up beyond recognition. Definitely.

She was still smiling at him as she swept past him and into the office. She smelled sweet, like ripe peaches. When she came inside, he closed the door tight and turned around in time to see that little skirt riding up on her as she sat in the chair across from his desk.

Lord help me, he thought.

He took a deep breath as he went to sit down himself. "Look," he said gruffly. "I know why you're here."

She raised a perfectly manicured eyebrow. "You do?"

"Yeah. Linc told me."

That cute little nose of hers wrinkled. "Linc told you what?"

Did she really want him to say it aloud? He had a sinking feeling that Linc might've just been putting one over on him, but that was far from Linc's style. So he started out, as vaguely as possible, hoping she'd catch his drift. "That you... you know..."

She shook her head, looking genuinely confused. "I don't know."

All right. Now he was starting to feel stupid. "You didn't talk to Linc the other night?"

She smiled. "Oh, no. I did. But I'm not here because of that."

He straightened his posture. "You aren't?"

"Yeah. We can talk about that later, but I'm kind of in a rush."

He nearly choked. "A...rush?"

"And I don't really have a lot of time to explain, so..." She reached into her purse and pulled out her wallet, which she opened and pushed over to him.

He ran his tongue over the front of his teeth as he took in the FBI badge. He coughed some more. "Well. I'll be damned. You? Are FBI?"

She nodded.

"Well." He scrubbed a hand down his jaw. "Fuck me. Is that what you were doing over in Virginia all these years?"

She nodded. "Yep. I was at Quantico getting my badge."

"Holy shit. And you went up to New York? What are you doing here, then?"

She crossed and uncrossed those amazing legs, and he did his best to ignore it. "I'm working on a case. A case involving Kylie Hatfield, Linc's girlfriend."

He stared at her, still trying to wrap his brain around the disappointment that she wasn't here for him. She was a Fed, here for a case. "Kylie?"

"Yes."

It suddenly occurred to him. "Does this have anything to do with the mob?"

"Yep. I'm working with her father, William Hatfield, to bring down a branch of the Colombo family tree in New York."

His eyes widened. "You mean…the Colombos…one of the five families? That Colombo family?"

"Yep."

"Shit. How's Kylie involved in this? Spell it out."

"From what I can tell, Kylie's from William Hatfield's first marriage, when he was known as Adam Hatfield. Then he went and sloughed off Kylie and his first wife, and took up with the Colombos, setting up a nice clean front from under which they could carry out their dirty work. D & H Construction. He's the de facto owner of the company, but it's really all dirty, dirty business, built on racketeering, extortion, fraud, tax evasion, murder...you name it."

Jacob leaned back and scratched his head. He knew Kylie was trouble, but he didn't figure for quite this much. "Well, shit." He crossed his arms over his chest. "So, what can I do to help you out, Agent Carter?"

"You can loan me the manpower I need to help bring them down," she said. "There's rumblings up in New York that they're on to William, and if they're on to him, they'll find out about his first family. I get the feeling that all of this is going to come to a head pretty soon."

"Pretty soon?" He leaned forward. "Hell, I've got news for you. It's already coming to a head right now. Kylie went up there a couple days ago and stirred up a shit storm. Someone tried to run over the mama, and then someone fired a bullet at Kylie last night."

It was Faith's turn to be surprised. "Did she see the perpetrator?"

He shook his head. "Kylie and Linc are traveling right now. I'm not worried about her. She's safe with Linc. I've got a man watching the mother's house right now."

"You do?" Faith grinned. "That's what I like about you. You're proactive. Can you get him on the horn with me? I want to talk to him."

He nodded and dialed the officer's number. "Why?" he asked, handing his cell phone over to her.

"Because these guys are professionals. Trust me. I've seen them operate. If I were you, I'd put more than one officer on watch," she said, listening to the phone. She ended the call and frowned. "Went right to voicemail."

"Son of a bitch." He lifted the radio and tried to get Joe's attention that way. Again, no answer. Then he called for any available cars in the area to get over there. As he put down the transmitter, he rose to his feet. "You think they're in danger."

It wasn't a question.

She was on her feet too. "When the mob starts to move, they move fast."

"All right. Let's go," he said, holstering his gun and putting on his hat. "I'll drive."

27

As the plane taxied toward the gate, Kylie already had her phone out, checking for messages. The last she heard was that Jacob was putting an officer in front of her mother's house, but she was still nervous about the whole thing. She'd seen how frightened her father had been, and it hadn't helped that the guy in the seat across the aisle from her had been watching *The Godfather* on his laptop.

She had a message from her mother, but it didn't make any sense. In it, someone was talking, but she couldn't hear it. It was just like her mother to have her phone on speaker and not be close enough to the receiver. Sighing, she turned to Linc. "Any news?"

He'd been listening to his voicemail messages. He brought the phone down from his ear and said, "The last message I got from Jacob was about a half hour ago. He said the situation was stable."

Stable or not, she didn't feel like she'd be able to rest until she talked to her mother. She rang her mother on both her cell and her landline, but they both went right to voicemail.

"She's probably sleeping," Linc noted, observing the wrinkle of worry over the bridge of her nose.

That was a good assumption, since her mother usually called it a night at around nine, and here it was, nearly ten. But ever since Kylie had found out that she was sharing the sofa in the living room with her "gentleman friend," she'd wondered what else that might lead to. After all, her mother had transformed into a giggly teenager around the good doctor. What else about her would change? Would her mother invite him to stay? Make out with him for hours? Invite him to spend the night?

Why did the thought of her mother having a sex life suddenly make her feel sicker than the possibility of a mobster lurking outside?

She needed to get herself some perspective.

"I know," she said, her lips twisting as she checked her phone display again. "But I should really just go and check on her. I couldn't make out a word in the message she left me."

He lifted his phone to his ear. "I'm checking in with Jacob." He met her gaze. "Eh. It went right to his voicemail too. I'm sure everything's fine."

"Still…" she said, peeking over the seat. The plane had stopped taxiing. People were standing in the aisle, grabbing their luggage from the overhead compartments. The doors to the plane had opened and the fastened seatbelt sign had dinged off. Why was nobody moving?

She was three seconds from shouting for people to move when Linc held out a hand. "Relax. We'll go check on her. Don't get worked up."

Kylie smiled and put a hand over his. If she didn't have him, she'd probably have gone insane by now.

It took another ten minutes to disembark, and then a few more minutes to get to his truck, which they'd parked in the long-term lot. Luckily, they'd just brought carry-ons, so they didn't have to wait for luggage. By ten-fifteen, they were cruising away from the airport, headed for her mother's home.

The street Kylie grew up on was considered urban, so it could be busy at times, but it was usually quiet. When they pulled up the tree-lined street, they saw the cop car, parked at the curb. As they pulled past it, Kylie rolled down the passenger's side window and squinted to look inside. "There's no one in there," she muttered, swiveling her head to look up at the little row home. "You think he's inside the house, with her?"

"It's possible," Linc said, moving ahead to parallel park as Kylie took inventory of the house. The lights were off, except for a dim glow in the living room. That wasn't unusual. Sometimes her mother fell asleep watching television. If she had, then it made sense why she wouldn't answer the phone, since it was in the kitchen, and not always easy to hear.

But then, where was the police officer?

A tendril of fear snaked its way up her spine. Something was off.

Before Linc could even throw the car into park, Kylie opened the door and jumped out onto the curb. She started to run across the street, but Linc held her back. "Careful," he said. "Let me check it out first."

"If she's in trouble, every minute counts," she said, trying to rip her arm away from him, but he held her firm.

"If she's in trouble, barreling in there without thinking will only get you more trouble," he growled at her as they made it to the stairs. "Stay here."

Well, he was right. As usual. She was being rash again and going off half-cocked. As usual. Glowering, she crossed her arms and watched as he climbed the stairs and peeked into the window. "Do you see anything?" she whispered.

He shook his head, opened the front screen door slowly

and silently, and tried the knob. He turned back to her. "It's locked."

That made sense. She reached into her bag and held up her keyring. "I have the spare."

He motioned to her to toss it to him, but she climbed the steps and placed it in his palm.

"If you go in there, I'm going with you," she whispered.

"Fine." He twisted the key in the lock and pushed open the door.

They walked into the mostly dark home, and Kylie ran an eye over the living room, bathed in a blue light from the television. The couch was empty, her mother's favorite afghan lying in a rumpled mess on the cushions. No sign of her mother.

"Maybe she went up to bed and forgot to turn off the television," Kylie whispered.

"Uh. Kylie," Linc started. He pointed upstairs. "Listen."

She did and was mortified to hear muffled noises, like the creaking of a mattress.

Oh, my god. Her worst fears were about to be realized. Her mother and Jerry were getting it on. On their first date, no less. Her mother was going to get a lecture.

She blushed furiously, wondering whether they should just back out and call it a night, when she froze as her eyes fell on the television.

Everything seemed normal, except the television was tuned to a sports channel.

Her mother never watched sports. And she might have liked Jerry, but Kylie didn't think her mother could like anyone enough to withstand watching sports with them. She detested them so much that Kylie had always been sure that her father must have been a sports nut, and she'd decided to hate them out of pure spite.

Then her eyes trailed to something on the floor. It was

the photograph of her with her mother and father. The one that her mom had stuck to the freezer door. What was it doing over here?

She opened her mouth to say something to Linc, when out of the corner of her eye, something flashed.

She looked past Linc in time to see a figure in the shadows, leveling the barrel of a gun in their direction.

"Linc!" she screamed, grabbing him. He instinctively dove forward, his arm going around her waist and throwing her behind the couch.

Stunned, she rolled over just in time to see Linc tackling the shooter to the ground with a great, guttural "oof!"

She yelped as a gun went off with a silenced *pop*, taking a chunk of plaster out of the wall. "Linc!" she shouted, the sound of their scuffling barely audible over the pounding of her heart.

She had to do something.

Inching to where the two of them were fighting in the hallway, she was relieved to see Linc gaining the upper hand, wrestling the gun out of the assailant's hands. She rushed forward, trying to help, when the gun went off again.

Pop.

The sound didn't jive with the mist of blood that peppered the wall behind the men.

"Linc!"

Rushing forward, Kylie dropped to her knees just as the man slumped to the floor. Within seconds, he started to shake uncontrollably, a trickle of blood spilling from his mouth. His eyes were wide, like two full moons.

Linc grabbed his shirt, shaking him hard. "Who the fuck are you, you bastard? Who are you working for?"

Kylie knelt in front of him. "And what did you do with my mother?" she demanded.

The man didn't answer. A moment later, his eyes lost focus, and his body went slack on a long exhale.

Kylie scrambled away. "Is he dead?" she asked, her heart in her throat as she remembered the noises she'd heard upstairs.

Without waiting for an answer, she raced for the staircase, taking the steps two at a time.

28

L inc fell back against the staircase, breathing hard.

The man—whoever he was—was dead. He'd shot him, protecting himself and Kylie, but that didn't make it any easier to watch him bleed out in his arms. His hands shook as he realized they were covered in the man's blood. He closed his eyes to stop thoughts of Syria from invading.

"Linc!" Kylie called from the second floor.

Grateful for the distraction, he jumped up and ran up the stairs, pushing open a door to a small bedroom. Rhonda and Jerry were on top of the bed, tied back-to-back, as Kylie worked furiously to loosen the gag in her mother's mouth. Her mother's eyes were like golf balls, and mascara ran down her cheeks. Linc rushed to help, coming to Jerry's aid. He was knocked out, but alive.

As soon as Kylie freed the gag, Rhonda began to sob. "Kylie, thank god. I was so sure that you were dead."

"Mom! Are you okay?" Kylie asked, crushing her mother in her arms.

"I think so," she said, stunned, looking around. "I don't know what happened, or who that man was. He was wearing a police uniform, and…where's Jerry?" She twisted out of her daughter's arms, looking wildly around. When her eyes fell on Jerry, she immediately began to panic again. "Is he dead? Please, god, no."

Linc shook his head. He freed the rope around them and laid Jerry down flat on the bed, with his bleeding head on one of the pillows. He had bruises on his face, and a bloody gash on his forehead, which had probably knocked him out.

As he was checking him, Jerry began to stir, and his eyes flickered open. "Dr. Phillips," Linc said, gently luring him back to consciousness. "Can you hear me?"

Jerry slowly opened his eyes more widely, then brought a hand to his forehead. "There must've been something in that drink," he said groggily.

Rhonda burst into relieved laughter and wiped at her tears. "Where is that man? That police officer. He came in and wanted to use the restroom, and then he hit Jerry over the head while his back was turned."

Kylie grabbed her mother's hands. "It's okay, Mom. You're safe now. I'll tell you everything, but I think right now we need to call the police. The real police."

"Yeah." Jerry sat up, rubbing his head. "Well, you sure know how to show a man a good time."

Rhonda let out a laugh that was half humor, half sob. "It's been very nice knowing you, Jerry. I—"

She grew quiet when Jerry kissed her.

Kylie's eyes grew wide.

Taking her arm, Linc pulled her from the room, lifting his phone from his pocket to call for help just as a commotion sounded downstairs. Someone was calling his name. It sounded like Jacob.

Sure enough, Jacob and Faith were there, stooping over the body of the dead man. Faith shook her head. "This is him. Their fixer."

Before Linc could ask how Faith could possibly know something like that, Jacob looked up. "What happened? Anyone hurt?"

Linc forced himself to look at the dead man. "This guy must've been impersonating an officer and got inside. Tied up Kylie's mom and her friend and roughed them up pretty bad."

"But they're okay?" Jacob lifted his radio and called for an ambulance. His eyes went over the dead man, who was dressed in a uniform, but it was clearly ill-fitting. Shit. "Where's Joe?"

"Joe?"

"The officer I put on the case. Shit." He backed out the door, then flew down the porch stairs, across the street, toward the patrol car. Linc followed him as he opened the door and reached down, popping the trunk.

Linc slowed to a stop when he saw the huddled form, the pale face of the officer. He looked like a young guy, probably no more than twenty, a rookie. He was completely still. "Dammit to hell," Jacob said, reaching in to feel the guy's neck. "Joe. You hear me?"

"He got a pulse?" Linc asked.

"Barely. He took a bullet to the back of his head." He lifted his radio and called it in.

Linc turned around just as Faith joined them. "You find him?" she asked.

He tried to bar her view from the grisly sight, but Jacob said, "Let her see. She's FBI."

Linc did a double take. "What?"

She frowned at the body. "Surprise! I've been following William Hatfield for a long time. He's been my informant, helping me by providing me with information to put the Colombo crime syndicate out of commission for good. That dead man inside is Nino Capitano, one of their fixers. He's been wanted for a long time."

He stared at her. So, she'd known about Kylie all along. When she'd come up to his house to see him, she hadn't really been there for him after all. She'd been there to get more information on Kylie. "Then you know Kylie has nothing to do with it, right?"

"Oh, I know," she said with a wink. "I know everything. I know that William got dragged into the family and has been looking for a way out. So, like they say in the mafia, I made him an offer he couldn't refuse. A reduced sentence in exchange for inside info on the Colombo family."

Linc's world tilted on end. Sure, Faith had always been interested in crime, but he'd thought she'd become a litigator, not a federal agent. "Holy shit," he breathed. "You're serious."

She nodded.

He looked at Jacob. "And you knew about this?"

"Nope. Just found out about a half hour ago."

In the distance, sirens screamed. Linc jogged back into the house. Jerry and Rhonda were up now and starting to walk down the stairs. Rhonda had stopped crying, but she still looked dazed. "How are you doing?" he asked her.

"Fine," she said in a faraway voice, looking at the man on her floor.

"Mom," Kylie said, rubbing her back. "Why don't you come with us tonight?"

"Right," Linc added. "You can stay as long as you want up at my house."

Her eyes were still fastened on the dead body. She inhaled sharply and nodded. "I don't know if I ever want to come back here."

"That's all right," Kylie said, giving Linc a worried look. "You can stay with us as long as you want."

"Yeah. Come on, let's get you in the truck." He looked at Jerry. "You going to be all right? The ambulance is here."

Jerry nodded. "I'm fine. It was just a little smack." He smiled past Linc, focusing on Rhonda. "I think for our next date, though, we might try doing something a little less exciting?"

She smiled, her face practically melting in admiration. "You're on."

Kylie linked her arm through her mother's, escorting her to the screen door. "Let's go."

Linc went outside and helped the two Hatfield ladies into his truck. Kylie shivered from the passenger seat, so he turned on the ignition and pumped in a little heat. "You guys okay?"

They nodded.

He looked over as the officer was being loaded onto a stretcher, and saw Faith talking on her phone. He held up a finger to Kylie. "We'll be out of here in a second."

He jogged over to Faith. "So, you know more than anyone else. What the hell is going on, and more importantly, is it over?"

She dug her hands into her pockets. "Like I said, his name is Nino Capitano. The Columbo family usually calls him when they want their dirty work done."

This didn't sit well with Linc. "But he's a nobody. Who's calling the shots? Who ordered the hit?"

She shrugged. "That's what we're working to find out. The main boss for the family's in prison, so we need to pinpoint who ordered this."

He clenched his fists and looked back at his girlfriend and her mother in the truck, whose faces looked so pale and stricken. They couldn't take much more of this. "Well, can you find it out a little faster? Doesn't William know?"

She scowled. "We're doing everything we can, Linc. We

think it's got to be Jackie's son, who's partners with William Hatfield. If so, we have eyes on him, so he can't so much as blink without us knowing about it. Once they find out Nino's dead, they'll make another move. That's assured. They won't stop. And now we have people in place, and we'll catch them."

"All right. But if I take the women up to my home, will they be safe?"

She didn't meet his eyes but nodded. "I think so. We'll send extra protection."

"I don't want what you think. I need you to know it, Faith."

She sighed. "What do you want me to tell you, Linc? Nino's dead. They're scrambling now. We're putting tabs on the other big players in the family so we know where they are at all times. So yes, they should be safe. For tonight, at least."

"Would they risk coming here after this?"

She met his eyes this time. "I don't know. If they were smart, they'd pull back and circle the wagon, stay out of sight. But…"

"They're not smart?"

Faith snorted. "They're very smart, but their arrogance can take over and…" She shrugged.

Jacob finished with the officer and wandered over to them, his voice grave. "Shit. He's really bad. I'm going to head over to the hospital to meet his wife." He looked at Faith. "You need a ride somewhere?"

She shook her head. "I'll call myself an Uber."

"Jacob," Linc said pointedly. "I'm taking the women up to the house with me for tonight. But I need you to make sure you get your best men watching Kylie and Rhonda around the clock. You hear me?"

His best friend looked exhausted. "Yeah. I'm on it."

Linc and Faith watched Jacob as he turned around, heading toward his truck. Suddenly, Faith called, "Jacob!"

He turned, and she ran up to him, wrapped her arms around him, hugging him tight.

Linc turned away. That was probably something they didn't want an audience for.

He went back to the truck, climbed inside, and shut the door, just realizing country music filled the cabin. Kylie hugged herself in the passenger's seat. "Well?" she asked as he turned down the radio. "Who was that guy?"

"One of their hit men," Linc grumbled.

"Hit men?" Rhonda blurted. Linc looked into the rearview mirror and knew, from the mystified expression on her face, that Rhonda didn't know a single thing her ex was up to. "Kylie, what is going on?"

"Dad's been involved in some pretty bad things. I'll tell you everything I found out when we get back to the house," Kylie said to her, then looked at Linc. "So, you're saying that whoever ordered the hit is still after us?"

He threw the stick into drive and the truck lurched ahead. She needed to know. If she didn't, she was liable to go off half-cocked again, and get herself killed.

He nodded. "Yeah. That's what I'm saying."

29

The plane landed shortly after midnight, and as it taxied to the gate, I checked my messages.

And promptly went insane.

There was a frantic message from someone named Valerie. She was so hysterical that I could barely make out a word she was saying, blithering something about William and the office and an arrest. I had to play it a second time, and that's when I remembered Valerie was William's secretary, and she was saying the offices of D & H Construction had just been raided by the Feds. William had just been arrested, and all of the company files had been confiscated pending FBI review.

This was not good.

"William Hatfield." I said the name like a curse. He'd always been such a pussy. I should've known he'd screw all of us, sooner or later.

You didn't play games unless you were prepared to lose.

And William Hatfield was about to lose. Badly.

But would he really care?

That was the question.

He tossed away his first family, then was a robotic participant with his second. The real family. The family that needed to be protected.

And the first family could destroy it all.

William Hatfield had been chosen for his personality, not his smarts. The family needed a figurehead and the money-hungry bastard had been perfect for the role.

Malleable and ambitious.

Teachable and adaptable.

Personable and persuasive.

Hell, he'd persuaded me, and I wasn't one to be easily swayed.

The entire family had agreed that he'd make a good match. After all, he had no one to turn to. He was alone in this world.

Or so we'd thought.

Fire blazed through my blood.

Now, the entire house of cards could tumble down, all because of a woman and her girl.

They were the legitimate heirs to William Hatfield's entire fortune. The fortune we'd put in his name for safekeeping. With a smart attorney, they could take half of everything.

Which wouldn't do.

It wasn't smart to go after them so soon, but the family had agreed that time couldn't be wasted. If I had been smart, I would've just let Nino take care of it all.

But the heart wants what the heart wants. And my heart wanted vengeance.

Rhonda Hatfield.

Kylie Hatfield.

Then William would fall soon afterward. But not until he looked at the pictures of his dead first family. Not until he watched the live feed of their funerals.

Not until I thought he'd paid enough.

How would I do it? I'd been considering that. The bastard couldn't simple disappear, and his death couldn't come under any suspicion.

Poison. Like the witch handing an apple to that gullible girl, I could feed him bite after bite of death, then watch him succumb to his illness.

Employees would watch their boss wither away. Stockholders would wholeheartedly agree that he needed to be replaced. William Hatfield would watch his name be systematically removed from every board, every agenda.

Until he simply disappeared.

Ding.

The sound of the seatbelt warning turning off brought me back to the present, and I forced myself to be patient as the doors opened, and I stepped in line to exit the plane.

In the first bathroom I came to, I pulled off the brunette wig and traded it for one with auburn highlights. I switched glasses, too, then changed my jacket and made a few other adjustments.

Presto-chango. My new cover was executed in less than a minute.

Security cameras could be such a nuisance.

Looking fifteen years younger than when I strode into the bathroom, I made my way to the rental car counter with my fresh identification.

The luxury car was nice, but I quickly became irritated when the representative of the company dragged his feet, wanting me to do an inspection of the vehicle before I drove it off the lot.

"Look," I said to him, handing him a hundred-dollar bill. "If we can dispense with all the formalities, the car is fine. I'm in a bit of a rush?"

"Yes. Of course, whatever you need," the idiot blithered, practically salivating at the sight of the cash.

That was one thing Nino had learned very well from me. Money talked. With money, you could do absolutely anything. Which was why I taught Nino to always travel with a wallet full of hundred-dollar bills. They got respect and attention more than anything else. It was amazing how they even allowed us to bypass security with our weapons in our carry-ons.

When I slipped into the driver's seat of the sleek black S-Class Mercedes, I punched the address Nino had given me into the GPS on my phone.

As I drove, I thought of William. He'd constantly let me down, since Day One, but I'd always given him the benefit of the doubt. I'd picked him up out of the slums and changed his life around, much like I had Nino and dozens of other men. I always looked out for him, took a special interest in him, helped him become what he dreamed of being. And how did he repay me?

By screwing us all.

And I wasn't going to let this betrayal go unpunished. Jackie wouldn't either.

I could almost imagine how relieved William had been to be arrested. He was going to prison instead of a grave. Or so he thought. I bet he thought that he'd be safe from us in there. What he didn't know was that I'd put a price on his head so high that our men in the prison walls would kill each other to be the one to rip him to shreds. They'd destroy him in the most painful way possible, until there was nothing left of him.

He deserved the worst, and I would make certain he got it.

As I reached my destination, I glanced at the seat, at the carry-on where I'd kept my gun. As I put on my blinker to turn onto Rhonda Hatfield's street, I frowned at the police cars blocking the road. I exhaled and powered down the window as a police officer neared the car. "What's the problem here?"

"Sorry. Only residents allowed through. Otherwise, if you go down to the next block and—"

"What happened?"

"Domestic disturbance," he said. "You're in no danger. If you'd like—"

Making up my mind, I motioned to the blockade. "I'm not a resident, but my elderly grandmother lives on the street. She called me. Can I make sure she's okay?" Glancing at the GPS, I spotted a house number at the end of the street and gave it to him.

The dumb prick nodded. "Oh. Of course. Back up, and I'll let you through."

I did, and the officer moved aside the cones for a makeshift blockade and waved me through.

The neighborhood was what nice people would've called quaint, but what I considered a slum. That was all Rhonda Hatfield was good for, clearly. She'd lived in a slum with William in Brooklyn, and she lived in one now. I drove along the road slowly, inching by at a snail's pace, watching out for the police cars and ambulances.

I ground my teeth so hard, they ached in my skull.

What exactly had Nino done?

I'd made it exceedingly clear that he needed to wait for me. He'd always had a bit of a happy trigger finger. Had he gotten overexcited and offed them too soon?

I sighed. Well. At least the job was done. The family would punish Nino later. He needed to follow directions.

I pressed on the brake and slowed to a complete stop when I spotted a stretcher being wheeled toward the house.

The medics didn't appear to be in a hurry, and I thought I could see a folded black body bag laying on top.

Was it for Rhonda?

The boyfriend who'd been in the wrong place at the wrong time?

The daughter?

The door to the house opened, and a man and two women walked out. A blonde and a brunette.

They were familiar. I'd seen them both in pictures.

Rhonda and Kylie Hatfield.

My gloved hands tightened on the steering wheel.

A young man escorted the women to a big truck, then walked over to talk to a group of law enforcement officers standing at the back of a patrol car.

What was going on?

And where was Nino?

I turned my attention to the women sitting in the truck. The very fact that they were alive scraped at my nerves. Rage gripped me by the throat, and I forced myself to breath slowly in and out.

A car door slammed, pulling me to the present. The lights to the truck turned on, making me squint. They were leaving. And so was I.

Putting the car into drive, I waited until the gas guzzling behemoth was nearly to the end of the street before pulling back onto the road. At this hour, I wasn't worried about losing them. The family was always prepared, and we each not only relied on protection, we'd learned to be our own protector from a young age.

I knew how to shoot.

I took a defensive driving course every year.

My defensive fighting skills were honed each and every week.

I was ready.

I wasn't going home without the blood I'd come to see spilled. If I had to do it on my own, then so be it. I would.

Happily.

Turning on the radio, I found a jazz station in the midst of all the country ones and settled back in the luxurious seat as I followed from more than two-hundred yards away.

The trip up the mountain was tricky, and I found myself falling back farther as I navigated the sharp turns. For a panicked moment, I thought I'd lost them. But then I noticed dust settling back onto a gravel road.

Peering hard through the trees, I spotted the red lights of the truck. The mailbox said Coulter.

Perfect.

As I searched for a place to hide the rental, I inhaled a deep, soothing breath.

Since Nino had clearly not finished the job, I'd do it myself.

The game was over.

30

K ylie listened to her mother's sniffles and sobs from the back seat of Linc's pickup as he drove toward the house in the mountains. The only thing that kept her from freaking out was that she was trying to stay calm for her mother, who looked about two seconds away from flipping out entirely.

"How do we know that they won't find us up here?" her mother asked.

Linc looked in the rearview mirror. "I spoke to the FBI. Nino was sent from New York to carry out the hit. Right now, they're probably scrambling to figure out what to do, so we should be safe."

"But we won't be for long," Rhonda said, connecting the dots. "Someone will come for us, eventually."

Kylie swallowed. Her mother was right. "But the FBI is looking into it?" she asked Linc. When he nodded, she replayed the scene in her head. "I didn't see the FBI there."

"Faith. She's FBI."

Her eyes widened. "Your ex is a Fed?"

Linc nodded.

Great, so not only was she beautiful and wonderful, she was fearless and badass too. There were more pressing matters to think of, but for some reason, that stuck in Kylie's mind. Cursing herself, she forced it from her squirrely brain and back to the problem at hand. "Well, what did she say?"

"She said that she's been working with William Hatfield to bring down the Colombo family in New York for a long time. He's their informant."

"The...Colombo family? Are they mafia?"

He nodded. "They're one of the most powerful. Part of the Five Families."

Behind them, Rhonda blew out a shaky breath. "This is so hard to believe. I can't believe that *my* Adam would do this."

Kylie turned around and reached between the seats for her mother's hand. She figured that now was as good a time as any to spill the whole story. "I know. It's absolutely crazy. Adam was a better man than William, I think. He started going by William when he began working for the DeRoss family, who are somehow involved with the mafia. Apparently, I stirred some things up when I went poking around New York a couple days ago."

Rhonda's eyes narrowed. In the headlights of oncoming traffic, she looked older than her years, with the mascara caking in her wrinkles. "He joined the mafia? Surely your father wasn't that suicidal?"

Kylie sighed. "Maybe he didn't realize what he was getting into when he was getting into it. He wanted a better life for us and thought this was how he could do it. But by the time he was so involved, they wouldn't let him go." She squeezed her mother's cold hand. "That's why he left so suddenly. They forced him into marrying the mob boss's daughter so that he could act as the figurehead for one of their shady companies."

Rhonda blinked, stunned. "So, he just up and disappeared and married someone else?"

"He said he had to. And he couldn't acknowledge us, or they'd have had you killed."

Rhonda was silent for a moment. "And you spoke to him? To Adam?"

Kylie nodded. "Linc and I both did. At first, he just tossed me out because he knew the mob would be after me. But then he spilled the whole thing."

"And from what I hear," Linc said, "he's been working as an informant with the Feds, even before Kylie went up to see him. He's been trying to find a way out. I guess the whole dirty business was starting to wear on him."

They pulled up into the driveway. The house was dark and silent, the dogs in the yard barking their greeting.

When Kylie slipped out of the truck, her mother just sat there, unmoving. "I just can't believe that he would do something so asinine."

Kylie shrugged and offered her a hand to help her out of the back of the truck. "Well, if it's any consolation to you, he didn't leave because he didn't love you. He was forced to."

She didn't meet her eyes, but simply took her daughter's hand. "I told you. It's of no consequence what he did, or why he did it, to me. It was a lifetime ago. He's long since stopped mattering in my life."

Kylie walked her to the door, knowing that was a lie. Linc had opened the front door and was already tending to the dogs. She opened the screen door and walked her inside. "All right. You want something to drink? Some tea?"

She looked around the house. At first Kylie thought she was scrutinizing it, but that wasn't her mother. Her mother was simply dazed and in shock. Kylie wasn't even sure she'd heard her question until, at least thirty seconds later, she heaved a sigh. "Honestly, sweetheart, I'm just bushed."

She knew the feeling. She was running on pure adrenaline now. Like if she stopped, just for a little bit, to think about what they'd gone through, she'd break down in tears, crawl under the bed, and never want to come out.

Because holy god. They had a mafia hit man after them. One of the most powerful crime syndicates in the country wanted them dead.

She quickly batted that thought away. *Keep busy,* she told herself.

"Okay. I'll get the guest room set up for you, if you want to go and freshen yourself up in the bathroom." She reached into the linen closet and handed her a towel, then pointed up the stairs. "It's the first door you come to. Do you want something to sleep in?"

She nodded.

Kylie grabbed fresh sheets and followed her mom up the stairs. She went into the bedroom she shared with Linc and opened her closet to search through her pajamas.

Crap.

All her warm, comfy ones were at her apartment because she'd only used her sexy ones when staying with Linc. She couldn't let her mom see those.

Biting her lip, she looked at the yoga pants and shorts, which would be about two sizes too small for her mom. Sighing, she closed the closet and headed to Linc's armoire. A pair of his boxers and a t-shirt would have to do for now.

Digging through the drawer, intent on finding one he didn't wear too often, her hand closed around a box. A satin box. THAT kind of box.

Her heart began to pound even as curiosity hammered at her soul.

Just a peek.

"No, Kylie," she muttered to herself. "No!"

It was the strangest thing, the thought of what was in that box didn't cause her to break out in a cold sweat. She felt…

Joy?

Happiness?

Hope?

Sure, there was still fear there too. Maybe that fear would never go away.

But wasn't that a good thing too? Didn't that fear make you try harder, like pre-game jitters prepared a player for the championship game?

A door slammed downstairs, and Kylie rushed to pull out a t-shirt and boxers, then quietly closed the armoire doors. She handed them to her mom and hurried to the guest room to dress the bed.

She was smiling.

She tried to make her mouth turn serious, but by the time she was fluffing the pillows, the smile was back.

Which was ridiculous.

She was supposed to be afraid. Not just of relationships, but because they were being freaking hunted by members of a mafia. Her mother had been hurt. Her life had been in perilous danger. Heck, Kylie'd just witnessed a man's death. Watched the man she loved pull the trigger. Knew that very act would probably make him have horrible nightmares that night, the PTSD being tripped so abruptly.

And yep…still smiling.

ABOUT TEN MINUTES LATER, her mother came out. It was strange to see Rhonda not dressed up with a full face of makeup since she always made the effort when guests were around. Kylie went to her mother, wrapped her in a tight hug.

When Rhonda winced, Kylie pulled away. "Oh! I'm sorry. Are you okay?"

She nodded and rubbed at her wrists, where she'd been tied up. She didn't have marks there, thank goodness, because Kylie didn't think she needed any more reminders of what was hunting them. "That bad man didn't hurt me much, but I could use one of my pain pills. My shoulder is starting to act up from the car accident. I left them in my purse downstairs."

"Oh, sure! I'll be right back."

Kylie ran down the stairs, returning with a glass of water and her mother's little knock-off Coach purse. Rhonda dug in and pulled out a little white pill and drank it down. "These things make me a little loopy."

Kylie smiled. She wouldn't mind taking something to make her mind go a little loopy too.

Her mother surveyed the room, grabbed one of the pillows, and sat down on the edge of the bed, cradling the pillow on her lap. "That awful man really hurt poor Jerry, though. I need to call him."

Kylie's heart squeezed. "You like him?"

A warm and mysterious look flitted over Rhonda's expression, so personal that Kylie looked away. "How can I not? I mean, what's not to like? Don't you?"

Kylie nodded quietly, her heart in her throat. More than anything in this world, she wanted her mother to be happy.

Her mother put a hand on her daughter's. "But don't worry. I *like* him. I'm not a kid anymore. I'm not going to run off and elope. I enjoy his company, but we barely know each other. At this point, I simply know that I want to risk learning more about him. That's all."

Kylie let out a small laugh. "Right. Well, I'm glad he makes you happy. You deserve to be happy."

"I am happy, sweetheart. You made me happy." She tried

holding back a yawn but couldn't. "Anyway, we'll see where it leads. Either way, I'm fine."

Kylie was glad to hear it. And glad that for, even a fraction of time, there was a world outside the horror that was stalking them. She gave her mother a kiss on the cheek, said good night, and turned out the light.

When she went downstairs, something different struck her right away.

It was fall, and the mountain got the most heavenly night breezes. Linc loved opening every window wide and letting it into the house, letting it rustle the curtains and whistle through the air. There hadn't been a night that Kylie could remember where the doors and windows had been closed. It felt claustrophobic.

She found him, sitting on the couch with his feet up on the coffee table, a couple of empty beer bottles already by his side. Storm was on the couch, her head on Linc's knee. He absently stroked his hand through her fur.

Vader was there too. He jumped up and excitedly bounded to her side. Kylie stroked the pup's ears, and he glued himself to her as she tried to get around him and make her way to Linc.

Linc took a swig and looked up at her. "Where's your mom?"

"In bed. She was exhausted."

He nodded and stared at the fireplace, though he hadn't started a fire. He didn't have to say a word. He was worried.

"You look tired," she said to him. "You should go to sleep too."

"Nah."

She knew what that answer meant. He'd stay up all night, keeping watch, because he always erred on the side of caution. But he didn't need to. They were safe up here. The hit man was dead. There might have been a price on their heads, but they were a long way from New York.

She inched around the coffee table, indicating to Storm that she'd like to sit, but Storm didn't get the picture until Linc gave her a little nudge and said, "Go on girl. Let Kylie sit."

The dog hopped off the couch and joined Vader on their beds near the fireplace. Kylie slipped beside Linc on the couch and curled up next to him. He took in a breath, and the muscles of his chest tremored under his tight t-shirt. He'd been rattled.

He may have seen a lot in Syria, but it seemed like every time he got into a tense situation, those things snowballed inside him. The therapy was helping, but it wasn't a magic cure-all. Tonight had probably undone all the progress he'd made in weeks of therapy.

Because of her.

"Are you okay?" she asked, stroking the stubble on his cheek before pressing her lips to his jaw.

He nodded and wrapped an arm around her, holding her tight. "Yeah. Just…stay here with me for a minute. Okay?"

She didn't want to move. It was stuffy in the house, with the windows closed, and Kylie was known to be spastic. Whenever she was someplace, she was always thinking about being somewhere else. But right then, as she rested her head on his shoulder, there was really nowhere else she'd rather be. She stayed there, listening as his heartbeat slowed a little.

"Are *you* okay?" he asked her after a while.

"Yeah. This is nice."

She felt more than heard his chuckle. "Could be nicer. Your mom's upstairs. It's not like we can get it on."

She shoved his arm, laughing too. "It doesn't matter. I'm so tired I'd probably fall asleep in the middle of it anyway."

He snorted. "With me? Never. Give me a little credit."

She smiled and kissed him again, just as both dogs bolted from their beds. Linc sat up, placing his bottle on the coffee table, and craned his neck to look into the darkness outside the window.

Kylie followed his line of vision, at first noticing nothing but black upon black.

Then, a bright orange glow began to spread through the darkness, flames lapping at the sky. Kylie stood up to look closer. It appeared to be coming from the direction of the pasture, and…

"That's the barn," Linc murmured as the dogs began to bark.

Even as she stared, he burst into action. Giving herself a mental shake, Kylie ran for the window to get a better look. Stepping into his boots, he raced for the door and threw it open. Then he ran back and shoved a shotgun in her hands.

"It's loaded and ready to shoot. Keep your finger off the trigger unless you mean business." He gave her a hard, bruising kiss. "Lock the door, and whatever you do, don't open it for anyone. And stay away from the windows."

Before she could argue, he'd grabbed another gun and went slamming out the door. She rushed up to it, thinking there had to be something more she could do than just wait there.

But what could she do?

She looked at the heavy gun in her hands and remembered her mother, who'd just taken a powerful painkiller.

Kylie needed to protect her mom.

Twisting the lock, she peeked out the window to see the flames grow higher. Even from the distance, she could hear the fire crackle as it ate through the old barn wood. Soon, the light from outside grew as bright as a second sun.

31

I t was easier said than done.

Keep the doors locked. Stay away from the windows? While the man she loved was in danger? How did Linc expect Kylie to do that?

The answer…he couldn't

He knew Kylie. She was just too curious for her own good.

Still, she resisted. She backed away from the windows as the fire began to consume the entire barn, lighting it up from the inside like a glowing fireball, clutching hold of a gun she didn't know how to shoot.

Note to self: take lessons on gun safety, dammit.

This had to be just a coincidence, right? The house was on top of a mountain. There were lightning rods atop the roof of the farmhouse and a weathervane on the barn that often conducted bolts of lightning. Maybe a stray bolt had hit the barn?

Kylie was kidding herself, she knew.

On the ride up here, the sky had been calm and cloudless.

As she backed to the staircase, her fear grew as her

thoughts continued to race. Maybe Faith was wrong. Maybe the hit man had brought an accomplice, and that person was outside right now.

With Linc.

As much as she hated to think it, that sounded more likely.

What should she do?

She needed to think it through and not go off half-cocked like she usually did. It wasn't just her life at stake right now. She had Linc to think about. She had her mother.

Rhonda!

Making a decision, she grabbed the railing and flew up the stairs. Running to the end of the hallway, she threw open the door to the guest room. And realized two things. One, she could protect her mother better, and two, she'd have a perfect vantage point to see the barn. And Linc, hopefully.

The glow from the fire made the room almost as bright as day. She rushed to the window and looked out, shading her eyes against the glare. Where was he?

The barn door was open, but there was no sign of Linc or any of the animals. A sob caught in Kylie's throat, but she forced it down. This was no time to panic.

"Mom!" she shouted sharply, shaking her mother to rouse her.

Rhonda didn't move. She just let out a little snore. Her eyes didn't even flicker.

The pain pill had knocked her out.

"Mom!" she tried again, shaking her harder. Downstairs, the dogs were going crazy, scratching at the windows and leaping at the door. Storm would take down anyone who wasn't Linc coming inside, and Vader would most likely help her. Kylie found some comfort in that.

After almost a full minute of shaking her mother, Rhonda began to move, trying to open her eyes. "Kylie? What—?"

"Mom, listen to me. The barn's on fire. I need you to get up." Her own phone was in Linc's bedroom, so she rummaged through her mother's purse. She punched in 911. After telling the dispatcher about the fire and giving the address, she said, "We need police backup too. Contact Jacob Dean. We're involved in a case he's working. Please tell him that he needs to get to the farm right away. Tell him that I think there is an accomplice. He'll know what I mean."

She had no time to repeat the entire story.

"I'm handing you off to my mother, Rhonda Hatfield. She was a victim of an attempted murder a few hours ago." She thrust the phone at her mother. "Stay on the line with the dispatcher. Let her know what's going on."

"But…" Rhonda pushed her hair from her face, struggling to sit up. "What is going on?"

Kylie jumped when Storm nudged against her legs, almost knocking her off-balance. The smart dog had come upstairs and was now resting her front paws on the window ledge, barking and growling at the barn.

"Good girl." She hugged the dog tight. "You stay and protect Mom, okay. Stay. Protect." She'd heard Linc call out those commands and hoped the dog would listen to them coming from her beta mouth.

Rhonda was finally sitting up in bed, looking more fully awake. She hugged the phone to her ear. "Oh my goodness," she said breathlessly, craning her neck to look out the window. "What are you—"

But Kylie was already halfway down the stairs, Vader at her heels. Twisting the lock for the deadbolt, she yanked open the door and rushed outside, making sure to keep the business end of the gun pointed down.

The heat of the fire was surprisingly hot, even from this distance. It made her eyes tear up and her skin prickle. She gasped. The barn was nearly completely consumed.

When she ran across the porch and down the stairs, she saw Linc out in the pasture. He was leading the llamas and other animals away from the blaze. She heaved a sigh of relief. The animals were precious to him. She had to help.

She needed to protect him. She needed to—

Behind her, Vader let out a sharp yelp of pain.

Kylie whirled, just as she heard the unmistakable sound of a gun being cocked.

A figure slowly emerged from the shadows and into the blazing light of the fire.

Kylie knew this person. Knew her.

It was the woman she'd seen in her father's office. The plastic platinum blonde with the spiky hair. Christina DeRoss. His wife.

For an older woman, she was dressed like a college girl, with thigh-high boots and a small sweater dress that barely covered her ass. Her model-perfect, pert little features were painted with so much makeup, Kylie was surprised the heat from the fire hadn't melted her. She looked magazine-cover perfect.

The only thing ugly about her was her smile. She was smiling, but not in a kind way. Her lips stretched wide like a hideous gash as she held the gun in front of her with both hands, leveled right at Kylie. From the way she was handling the weapon, Kylie knew she wasn't a stranger to using it.

Unlike herself.

She would get lessons asap…if she lived to see another day.

"Don't move, bitch," Christina DeRoss seethed. "And drop the gun."

Loath to let it go, Kylie had no choice but to lean it against the porch railing. There was no way she'd have time to bring it to level, sight Christina, and pull the trigger.

Bringing her hands to shoulder height, she looked at the woman. "Christina, I—"

"Was it you?"

Kylie swallowed, trying to think of what she could possibly mean.

Her lack of answer only seemed to infuriate Christina more. The smile slipped into a scowl. "Answer me! Was. It. You?"

"Me, what? I don't understand," Kylie said, her voice quivering as she tried to gauge where, behind her, Linc had gone off to.

"You know what I mean. Nino." The gun never wavered in her hands as she kept it trained on her target. "Is he dead?"

Kylie's thoughts raced and landed on a lie. "No...just injured. Th-they're taking him to the hospital. They said he'd be fine." She shut her mouth before she blathered herself into an early grave.

Christina's eyes narrowed. "Why did you go to New York?"

Kylie knew better to lie about this. Christina surely already knew everything. "I've wondered about my father my whole life, so...I wanted to find him. Ask him why he'd abandoned us."

Christina sneered. "And get your hands on his wealth, I'm sure. Were you hoping to guilt your rich daddy into a Porsche or maybe a Lambo?" The woman's eyes ran down to Kylie's feet and back. "Although a redneck truck seems more your style."

Kylie bristled at the insult.

Who was this plastic bitch to judge her? To judge anyone, in fact?

But when you were staring down the black hole of a gun wasn't the time to argue. Unlike Kylie, this woman looked like she knew how to utilize a weapon pretty well.

Christina took a step closer. "If your pathetic father was half a man, maybe you wouldn't be looking at the end of my gun right now."

Kylie shivered, even in the heat of the fire. Where was Vader?

"Your father was a piece of shit," she continued, taking another step closer in her high-heeled boots. "He betrayed us, again and again. Starting with you and your whore mother." She scoffed. "I've been with him for over twenty-four years, yet you two are his legitimate family?" Her face transformed into a mask of hatred. "His heirs? I don't think so."

Behind the woman, the shadows changed, and Kylie held her breath as Linc appeared from the darkness. She forced herself not to look at him. She needed to keep this crazy woman talking.

"I was four days old when he left us for you," Kylie said. "I've spent my entire life wondering what was so bad about me that he felt the need to just leave us, without a word. That's all I ever wanted…an answer."

The woman repositioned her gun, one of those sickening smiles slitting across her face. "I have an answer for you. For you and your whore mother. I—"

The screen door flew open so hard it slapped against the house with a sound almost as loud as a bullet leaving a gun.

Kylie jumped, and Christina whirled just as Rhonda came rushing out the door, a cast iron skillet in her hand.

Kylie was frozen to the spot, but only for a moment. She leapt at the woman's back just as Storm flew from the open doorway. The dog knocked Christina off balance, and the gun roared, the bullet fatally wounding the wooden red chicken hanging over the door.

The next few seconds appeared to be in slow motion. Christina was falling under the dog's heavy weight. Linc came rushing up as the gun roared off another blast. Kylie screamed as he was blown backwards, almost like he'd run into a wall of glass.

It was Kylie's mother who saved them all from another bullet. Bringing the cast iron skillet down as hard as she could, she slammed the heavy pan down on the hand holding the gun. The crunching of broken bones was followed by Christina's bloodcurdling scream. That scream was cut short when Storm's wide jaws clamped down on her throat.

Rhonda pried the gun from the woman's mangled hand, holding it with two fingers, as if it was contaminated. She stood that way, as if uncertain what to do.

Adrenaline pulsed through Kylie's system as she took in the scene. Linc was moving, blood blooming on his shoulder. Christina was neutralized, but were there more bad guys lurking in the dark? Had this terrible woman brought backup with her? Were they all still in danger?

Feeling more like a target than she'd ever felt, Kylie grabbed the shotgun from where it rested on the porch railing and turned, scouting the area. She had to protect her family.

Eyes moving from shadow to shadow, she held the gun at the ready as she headed toward where Linc was now sitting, leaning up against the house. There was so much blood, but he was awake. He gritted his teeth and looked down at himself. "Shit," he said. "Another fucking shoulder wound."

She gushed out a relieved sigh. She'd survived one of those. So would he.

Ripping her sweatshirt over her head, she pressed it to the wound, her eyes still scanning the area for any other immediate danger. "It could've been a lot worse."

He winced as he tried to move. "Could've been a lot better too. Like me *not* getting shot." His eyes trailed over to the inferno. "And shit…my barn. My grandfather built that barn. We've got to make sure—"

"Shhh," she soothed. He was getting too worked up, not focusing on the fact he'd saved her, again. Well, him and her mother and Storm. Where was Vader? "I'll help you rebuild it."

When the wails of the sirens reached her ears, Kylie felt like she might burst into hysterical sobs. Then, she really did cry as Vader came limping across the porch. He looked okay, if a little unsteady.

Kylie patted her thigh. "Here, boy. Good boy."

But the big dog didn't pay her any attention. He limped over to where Christina lay, Storm still at her throat.

Then he lifted his leg and peed directly on her chest.

Yes. Good boy, indeed.

32

This was insane.

Linc had been in bed for the past week, except for the occasional bathroom break. Under Kylie's very bossy direction, he hadn't so much as been able to go downstairs and make himself his own food. All he'd been doing was staring at the ceiling since he was released from the hospital five days ago.

He'd told her he was fine, but she insisted otherwise.

It brought new meaning to the phrase "stir-crazy."

And she was constantly starting every conversation with the same thing: "When I had my bullet to the shoulder…" As if he hadn't sustained a bullet first, on the field in Syria. And as if her injury now made her an expert on all parts of his life.

This was all completely unnecessary.

But if he was admitting it, kind of nice too. He liked when she'd bring him breakfast in bed, insist on feeding him his waffles, since Eggos were the only thing she really could make. He liked that she was babying him. Mostly because he felt her love for him in everything she did. She'd been so worried for him that she'd barely left his side all week.

That was nice, considering Kylie had always been kind of like a wild animal—impossible to tame, constantly flitting from thing to thing, seeking out what made her happy.

That she'd stayed put with him all this time?

Maybe she'd finally found it.

So, there was no question in his mind that this was the day. He'd get out of bed and not look back. He wanted to make it special, though, and at least be freshly showered and shaved before he made the attempt. So, while she was downstairs, getting his lunch, he dragged himself into the shower, got himself changed, and was waiting for her on the edge of the bed when she brought up the tray.

She stopped in the doorway, holding on to his soup and grilled cheese. "You shouldn't have! I could've helped you."

"I'm fine, sweetheart. It's time I get out of my bed for good."

Her lips twisted as she set the tray down on the bed next to him. "When I—"

He put a finger on her lips. "I know. But you're you. And I'm me. Face it, we're not the same."

Her lower lip jutted out in a pout.

Standing, Linc's heart started to pound as he reached into his pocket.

"Kylie," he began, his voice so thick with emotion that he had to clear his throat. "I love you, and I know that you love me."

Her eyes grew wide, her hands flying to her mouth. "Linc…"

He bulldozed on. "Kylie Hatfield, I think you know what's in my heart, and I think you know what's been on my mind. And if you'll stay in one place long enough for me to ask, I have a question for you." Turning his hand over, he held out the key to his house. "Move in with me."

She looked…disappointed.

The hammering in his chest picked up speed as she just stood there, looking at his palm.

"Kylie?"

This was a mistake. It was too early, he knew. It wasn't like she hadn't given him every hint in the world that she wasn't ready for something so committed.

He closed his palm, ready to make a joke and pretend he was just kidding, when she looked up at him. Confusion and something else she couldn't name was written across her face. She began to move, but not toward the door like he first feared.

She went straight to his armoire.

Then began tossing his things on the floor.

A second later, she turned, the satin box in her hand. "What about this?"

He swallowed. She knew?

"I—"

Before he could say more, she stalked back to him. "Is this a ring?"

So, she didn't know? She hadn't looked?

He only nodded, not knowing what she was thinking. Tears filled her eyes, and she did the last thing he'd expected. Kylie Hatfield sank to one knee, holding the box out to him.

"Will you please give me this ring in addition to that key?"

Linc Coulter felt like his entire body had turned to concrete. He couldn't move. Couldn't think. At least until one of those tears trailed down Kylie's cheek.

That brought him out of his paralysis.

"Are you sure?"

Love was like a living thing in her eyes. "Very sure."

Sinking to one knee in front of her, he took the box from

her hand. Kylie stayed there, still on one knee too. Which was actually perfect. Two people on the same level.

"Kylie, I know we've only known each other a few months, but—"

"Yes."

He smiled, relief and love flooding his chest, but he wasn't done yet. "You drive me crazy, in the very best possible ways. You've pushed me to the brink of insanity and then yanked me back, a better man."

Kylie looked like she was about to burst. Into tears. Into laughter. What he didn't spot in all that sea of emotion was fear.

He still wasn't done.

"I love you, and there is no one else but you I want to do life with. Will you—?"

"Yes."

"Will you let me finish?"

She laughed, more tears breaking free from the movement. "Yes."

He laughed and opened the box. For the first time, her gaze left his as her eyes dropped to the ring. "Oh…" It was the only sound she was able to make. It was enough.

She loved it. He knew from the moment he'd seen it in the store window that he'd never find another ring more perfect for this precious woman, or one that would match how they'd been brought together.

The two-carat stone was topped with three smaller diamonds, and when you looked at it just right, it resembled a dog's paw.

For the first time in a long time, she was speechless, her lip trembling from a hurricane of emotion he could tell she could barely suppress.

"Kylie Hatfield, will you marry me?"

She was already lunging at him as she shouted, "Yes!"

He couldn't stop the wince of pain as she plowed him onto the floor, forgetting his injury. "Oh!" she said, loosening her grip.

He adjusted her arms around him and hugged her close, kissing her until neither of them were able to breathe. Still lying on the floor, he took the ring from the case and slipped it onto her finger.

"It's beautiful," she whispered. "It's just what I would've picked out if I'd had a million rings to choose from. It's absolutely perfect."

He kissed her again. "I just happened to spot it in a window not long ago, and even though I knew it was too early, I went ahead and bought it because I couldn't let it get away."

She laughed. "A week ago, I would have thought it would be too early too. I was actually terrified of being in a committed relationship because I was so scared I'd somehow inherited my father's inability to commit, but…"

"But?" Linc prompted.

"As crazy as it all went down, finding my dad was wonderful because I realized that he really did try to do what he felt was best. It kind of released that fear in me." She softly kissed his shoulder. "And the fact that you once again proved that you'd do anything for me, well, I just couldn't see the sense in not embracing the love that was right in front of me."

They laid on the rug, just holding each other for a long time, talking about a wedding and how she wanted her mom to give her away.

They didn't stop talking until the dogs started barking and the sound of a vehicle on gravel made Kylie shoot up.

"Oh…I forgot. Jacob is coming. I was going to tell you that before…" she waved her left hand around, the diamonds sparkling, "this."

Leaving the cold sandwich and soup on the tray, they headed downstairs and reached the front porch just as the first car door slammed shut.

"I'm nervous," Kylie said, running her fingers through her hair.

Linc wrapped his good arm around her shoulder. "You look perfect, and everything will be all right. Promise."

She smiled. "Thank you." The smile faded as her father slipped out of the vehicle.

He was surrounded by Jacob and Faith, and he looked stoic as he climbed the stairs to join them.

William…Adam…had insisted upon seeing his daughter one last time, and the FBI had agreed to it.

It was because of William Hatfield that she'd become the target of the mafia. But William Hatfield had received a reduced sentence because of his cooperation in the case, and the members of the DeRoss family had all been taken into custody. The Colombo family was weakening by the day, and it was all because of her father.

He and Rhonda had met earlier and had agreed to an amicable divorce, and now he was on his way to New York to face his sentence. The entire family's assets had been frozen, so it looked like no one would be an heir to his fortune.

Which was fine.

Kylie had everything she needed right here. She petted Vader when his cold nose nudged her hand. Poor guy had gotten a concussion but was doing much better.

"Hi," William Hatfield said, and Kylie wondered if this would be the last time she ever saw him.

She'd overheard Jacob telling Link that her father was probably still in danger. Though the Feds would keep him in protective custody until all the trials were finished, he'd eventually have to serve his time in prison, and there, he'd be a target to his enemies.

"Hi," Kylie managed in return.

"I'm sorry," he said. "For leaving you and for putting you through all this. I never wanted this for you or your mother."

She smiled through her sadness and nodded. "I know. You tried to protect us."

William scratched at his jaw. "I did but did it poorly. I should have added more to that letter. I should have asked her to change her name back to her maiden name. I should have tried harder, but as the years went by and you two appeared to be safe, it became easier and less painful to forget that my previous life ever really happened."

"One minute," Faith said from behind them.

It was time for him to go.

Kylie had two options. She could kick her father in the nuts and push him off the porch. Or…she could do the one thing she'd longed for all this time.

Heart pounding in her ears, Kylie took a step forward and wrapped her arms around her father's waist. She closed her eyes when his arms went around her for a hug that was twenty-four years in the making.

She breathed him in, wanting all her senses engaged so she could remember this moment for all of eternity.

Her, wrapped in her daddy's arms.

They stayed that way, wrapped together until Faith cleared her throat. "Time to go."

William pressed his lips to her cheek. "I love you," he said before stepping away.

Tears blurred her vision as she watched Faith escort her father back to her car.

"What's this?"

Her attention turned to Jacob, who was staring at her

finger. She smiled, wiping at her cheeks. "What's it look like, Detective?"

Jacob looked from her to Linc and then back again. "It looks like my asshole best friend just put a ring on it."

She lifted her hand and wrapped her arm around Linc's waist. "He sure did."

Linc laughed and kissed her temple. "I thought you were going to beat me to it."

She grinned, happiness filling her every cell.

Jacob shook his best friend's hand. "It's about damn time."

Linc clapped his friend on the shoulder. "Is that what you're going to say in your speech? Huh, best man?"

Jacob looked surprised. "So, you're not doing the quiet thing...you, her, a justice of the peace? I'm shocked."

"Hell, no," Linc told him.

This was going to be the biggest party Asheville had ever seen. He wanted the entire world to know Kylie Hatfield was his.

33

Greg came back to the office of Starr Investigations three days later. His assignment for Impact in Raleigh went even longer than he'd expected.

"So, what'd I miss?" he asked as he walked in, pulling off his ratty blazer and hanging it on the back of his chair. "Pretty quiet, huh?"

She just laughed, almost sadistically.

He stared at her. "What?"

"Oh, we had a little bit of excitement," she said with a casual shrug. "Nothing work-related. Just personal."

He let out a groan. "Meh. I don't care about that."

"Did you hear about the Colombo family that was cracked apart?"

"Ye-es," he said slowly, suspiciously. "Wait. I thought you were on vacation. Don't tell me you had something to do with that?"

By some miracle, the FBI had managed to keep Kylie and Rhonda's names from the news. So far, they'd only been listed as "victims."

Kylie hated that word.

She smiled innocently and held up her thumb and fore-finger a centimeter apart. "Maybe a little."

He dragged his hands over his face. He suddenly looked like he'd aged ten years. "What? Spill it, short stuff."

So, she spilled. Everything about her whole mafia connection, the reunion with her dad, the hit that had been put on her and her mom, the exciting standoff at the farm-house. He listened, his mouth partially open, then quietly pushed away from his desk. "I need a drink, but I guess I need to settle for coffee."

She stood up and ran to the Keurig before he could get his hands on it. "Please, allow me."

She made him a cup, doing her best to flaunt her rock. She wiggled her fingers as she got the cup and put it under the dispenser, hoping he'd notice. She planted it right in his face as she set the coffee down.

For a private investigator, he seemed blind to what was right in front of him.

"So, other than you getting roped into the mafia," he scratched his temple, "and I have no clue how a little girl from Asheville managed that one. Of course, we're talking about Kylie Hatfield here, the girl with an unnatural gift for attracting all sorts of trouble. But aside from all that, anything else happen?"

The guy was oblivious.

She waved her hand around some more. "Well, yes. Something else happened."

"Yeah?" he muttered, taking a sip. "What?"

She put her hand on top of his coffee and pointed to the ring with her other hand.

"Ah. So, congratulations are in order, huh?"

She nodded. "Yes. Great big fat congratulations."

"Ah. Well, it's about time."

She admired her ring, turning it to catch the light. "He

didn't drag his feet. It was me, never sitting still. I made it really difficult for him to propose."

He squinted at her. "You? Difficult? I don't believe it."

She smacked his shoulder. "Doesn't this mean you need to take me out to lunch? To celebrate?"

He wheeled away from his desk and crossed his arms. "I'm thinking about it." Then his tone turned serious. "So, you met your dad, huh?"

The smile slid from her face. "He was a little bit of a disappointment, to say the least. But I guess I didn't expect very much to begin with. I've got closure now. Things are good. Really good. My mother's going to give me away at the wedding. I'm happy."

He stood up and rubbed her shoulder in a very fatherly way. Really, he'd been more of a dad to her in the past months than her father ever had. "I'm glad. And you're right. It's slow around here. Let's blow this joint. Lunch is on me."

She clapped her hands excitedly. "Let me just check on my mom. She's dating someone now."

Kylie thought she'd done a good job of hiding her phone conversations from her boss, but apparently not, because he grumbled, "Should I make reservations for two hours from now?"

Rolling her eyes at him, she picked up her cell phone and dialed her mom. Her mother had gone back to the house a couple of days after the incident at the farmhouse. She'd been smiling a great deal, even more than usual, and Kylie attributed it to one person: Dr. Jerry Phillips.

He was in her life constantly now, always making sure she was okay, taking her out on little dates, and generally being a knight in shining armor. Apparently, their rough start had done nothing to drive him away. And Kylie was gradually coming to accept it. She liked Jerry a lot, but what she *loved* was seeing her mother's eyes glow in a way they never had before. He was good for her.

Her mother answered on the second ring. "Hello!" Rhonda Hatfield sounded positively spirited. Well, she always had spirit, but now, she sounded like a firework getting ready to go off.

"Hi, Mom. How are you?"

"Oh, fine. How is my daughter and her lovely fiancé?"

"We're great," Kylie said. "But I want to know how you are. I didn't have a chance to find out yesterday because you were too busy running off."

"Oh, yes. I know! I have a busy social calendar now. Everything's fine."

"You still good about the divorce?"

"I'm fine. You were right. It was good to see Adam… William…again. To get that closure. I guess I always wondered, deep down, if I'd done something wrong. It's good to not have that in my head anymore."

Kylie smiled. "Yeah. It was good. I'm trying to decide if I should write him in prison."

"Yeah. Well. Only if you want. You don't owe him a thing." She lowered her voice. "Honey, I've got to go. Jerry's coming over. He's taking me to see a movie. When was the last time I went to the movies?"

Kylie grinned. Her mother had always considered movies to be a waste of money. When Kylie was a child, she used to scrimp to take the two of them, and they'd never go to the snack stand. They'd always have to sneak candy in. But it made Kylie happy to think Rhonda was having fun. "Cool. Enjoy."

Kylie hung up, still smiling, about to tell Greg that she was ready for their lunch date. She bit her tongue when she heard his gruff voice and realized he must've gotten a call while she was talking to her mother. He sounded a little on edge. He scribbled a few notes on a pad. "Yeah. Yeah. Right away." When he hung up, he looked at her as he punched his pen down on his desk.

Kylie frowned. "Are you cancelling our lunch date?"

He shrugged. "Unfortunately."

She stuck out her lower lip. "Okay. Raincheck. Where are you off to now?"

The corner of his mouth quirked up in a smile as he lifted a sheet of paper and pointed his pen at it. "Not me, short stuff. You. This has your name all over it. Your name, and the name of that ever so dreamy fiancé of yours."

She raised an eyebrow. "For what…?"

"Pack your bags, sweetheart. There's a SAR volunteer down in Georgia who went missing during a search yesterday, and her team hasn't had any luck finding her."

Kylie's eyes widened. "Georgia? Why Georgia? Don't you think that's a little out of our—"

"That was the missing woman's husband. He's convinced there's more to it than meets the eye. Possible foul play, and it could get pretty ugly."

Kylie's ears pricked up. "Ugly?"

"Annnnd he asked for you and Linc specifically," he said, spinning in his chair. "I figured it sounded like it was right up your alley. So, are you game?"

Kylie straightened in her chair. She felt like a famous detective, being requested by name based on her "body of work." Just call her Sherlock, or Hercule Poirot. She was moving up in the world. Getting married, advancing her career, becoming a real adult instead of just playing at it.

And the possibility of foul play? Hell, yes. That was all she needed to hear. Those mere words sent a shiver of excitement down her spine. As much as her husband-to-be wanted to play it safe, and she respected that, she also loved that he respected *her*. She lived for all kinds of play, but the foul kind? It happened to be her favorite.

"Yeah," she said, jumping up and grabbing her phone to call her fiancé and fill him in. "I'm game."

The End
To be continued...

Find all of the Kylie Hatfield books on Amazon.

ACKNOWLEDGMENTS

How does one properly thank everyone involved in taking a dream and making it a reality? Here goes.

In addition to our families, whose unending support provided the foundation for us to find the time and energy to put these thoughts on paper, we want to thank the editors who polished our words and made them shine.

Many thanks to our publisher for risking taking on two newbies and giving us the confidence to become bona fide authors.

More than anyone, we want to thank you, our readers, for clicking on a couple of nobodies and sharing your most important asset, your time, with this book. We hope with all our hearts we made it worthwhile.

Much love,

Mary & Bella

ABOUT THE AUTHOR

Mary Stone lives among the majestic Blue Ridge Mountains of East Tennessee with her two dogs, four cats, a couple of energetic boys, and a very patient husband.

As a young girl, she would go to bed every night, wondering what type of creature might be lurking underneath. It wasn't until she was older that she learned that the creatures she needed to most fear were human.

Today, she creates vivid stories with courageous, strong heroines and dastardly villains. She invites you to enter her world of serial killers, FBI agents but never damsels in distress. Her female characters can handle themselves, going toe-to-toe with any male character, protagonist or antagonist.

Discover more about Mary Stone on her website.
www.authormarystone.com

Bella Cross spent the past fifteen years teaching bored teenagers all about the Dewey Decimal System while inhaling the dust from the library books she loves so much. With each book she read, a little voice in her head would say, "You can do that too." So, she did.

A thousand heart palpitations later, she is thrilled to release her first novel with the support of her husband, twin girls, and the gigantic Newfoundland she rescued warming her feet.

Made in the USA
Las Vegas, NV
27 March 2022

46401122R00174